LF Meleyal

Everyday Wendy

D1458468

Published by New Generation Publishing in 2022

First Edition

ISBN

        Paperback   978-1-80369-296-8
        Ebook   978-1-80369-297-5

www.newgeneration-publishing.com

 New Generation Publishing

The **Book**Challenge

WHAT'S YOUR STORY?

This book was published through
The Book Challenge Competition part of
The London Borough of Barking and Dagenham Pen to
Print Creative Writing Programme.

Pen to Print is funded by Arts Council, England
as a National Portfolio Organisation.

WHAT'S YOUR STORY?

Connect with Pen to Print
Email: pentoprint@lbbd.gov.uk
Web: pentoprint.org

Supported using public funding by
**ARTS COUNCIL
ENGLAND**

**Barking &
Dagenham**

For Andrea who loved yellow.
Forever in my heart.

Unlocking the achievement of your goals is not to focus on the goals but on the steps towards them. Celebrate each and every step along the way and you will grow to understand the importance of the journey to success.

Sanskrit Proverb

Welcome!

I am thrilled you have taken the bold step to join Everyday Grace. You are about to embark on a glorious adventure and discover the wonderful, powerful and sacred essence of your potential self.

The course will address three aspects of personal growth:

- *Spiritual development through which you will learn about yourself, the person you wish to be and how to navigate and improve your connection with your environment.*

- *Emotional development, how you react and how to stay strong and embrace the opportunities presented by change and uncertainty.*

- *Mental development to keep you mentally strong and improve your capacity for learning.*

Lessons will be regularly emailed for the duration of your subscription. Each will include coursework which is not compulsory but many Everyday Grace students find great benefit in discussing their learning with other students*. Our social media pages will facilitate contemplation, reflection, learning and personal growth. You might even make new friends as committed to self-development as you have shown yourself to be by purchasing this course!

About me

I have been a student of Eastern philosophies and spirituality for many years. I do not claim to be a wise woman, goddess, sage, guru or spiritual teacher but more someone who, through sharing my own learning, can impart encouragement, give new frameworks through which you might engage with the world afresh and offer support to enable your heart to embrace change. I am based in the UK and live with my three cats - Luna, Eve and Lillith.

I look forward to working with you and hope your change journey brings great joy.

Namaste.

Melody Skyhorse.

Students wishing to improve social communication skills may be interested in taking our 'Be a Great Communicator' course (*additional course fees apply).

CLEARING

Change What Is Not Working

The only thing of permanence is change itself. Only by
ceasing to be afraid of being, can we come into being.
Everyday Grace

Clearing a space and bidding farewell to what no longer
serves me is, apparently, virtually the same as clearing a
little bit of my soul but I wonder if I should've started with
a bathroom shelf. I've sat looking at the wardrobe so long,
the dip in the bed has become far too comfy. The wide-open
mirrored doors are supposed to begin a fun adventure. But
they don't. They're portals to silly aspiration, what-was-I-
thinking madness and Mrs sensible. It's all there. Hanging
while I sit on the bed, dappled by the winter sun on the duvet
noticing the layer of dust on top of the framed photo of me
and Andy. I'm failing miserably at my first 'Everyday
Grace' task.

Melody Skyhorse promised the course would teach me
how to put myself first, discern my true nature and clear out
old habits. It would be fun and life-changing she promised.
On the course website there's a picture of a woman with her
arms outstretched to the sky, bathing in a waterfall. I'm not
sure if it's her. It looks a bit chilly. I've a sneaking suspicion
Melody Skyhorse's idea of fun and mine may be a bit
different but I was fed up and needed something to change.
I had no idea where else I might start so for only thirty
pounds the course seemed like a good deal.

We get emailed lessons so as soon as I get my first I jump
right in. New year new start. It's about clearing cluttered
spaces and lightening my cosmic load. I'm not sure what a
cosmic load is but the contents of my wardrobe need a lift.
According to the lesson, getting rid of wardrobe errors and
giving thanks to what I love will make me feel refreshed and
re-energised. I have a plan because my course PDF says
becoming a better person is making deliberate choices. You

can't just hope, you have to do stuff.

Melody Skyhorse is quite pushy that we write down our thoughts and feelings in a 'self-development for aware women' course journal. She sells them online but I bought a lovely faux leather Moleskin at Waterstones. I didn't bother decorating mine with inspirational quotes. I keep it in my bedside drawer. We're supposed to 'write to the universe'. I imagine the universe is a woman so I write to her. I try to write in it at night while Andy's brushing his teeth but it can be difficult reflecting while he gargles. I'm guessing Melody Skyhorse probably has a thing for Patchouli but I'll always associate my self-development with the smell of spearmint. Andy could look at my journal whenever he wanted but I know he won't. When I told him I was feeling a bit fed up, he never wobbled about it being about him, or us, because we are solid. He didn't go into that man-space of believing my needing to take stock was something to do with the menopause or getting old. I know he loves me and wants me to love myself more. He said Melody Skyhorse's course sounded less intensive than Botox and not as scary as a skydive and we left it at that. He bought me a lovely posh pen to go with my journal.

I've set up a charity shop box and bags for the bin. The clothes I'm going to keep and re-hang will be put on the bed until I can 're-dress/redress' the hanging rail. We're not supposed to just chuck the stuff back in but ponder on what balance we're achieving when we allocate a space. In theory, it seems straightforward but without having moved a single thing I can see the stretch lycra velvet trousers, hanging over the rail taunting me from the open doors. 'Start with me' they sneer in that velvety way and I almost give up on the whole thing.

Velvet trousers are too posh for work but with a nice blouse and a necklace, right for a semi-formal gathering. I can't remember when I last wore them. Melody Skyhorse says we all carry a lot of psychic baggage which can pin us down. She says we need to carefully consider how we let it happen to enable us to unblock ourselves and gain enduring success. I've been looking at the wardrobe for so long but I'm still properly blocked. Enduring success is starting to feel like a pipe dream. I force myself out of the duvet and stride to the wardrobe. I've never liked the feel of velvet which makes me think of furry teeth and drinking out of cups made of Styrofoam or eating with biodegradable wooden forks. I've no idea what possessed me to buy them but according to the lesson small steps make big changes happen and I feel liberated that I won't ever again let velvet be a part of my life. I pull the trousers off the rail and throw them into the charity shop box.

As I yank them they catch on a hanger and pull down The Dress. My mother-of-the-bride dress. It is the most expensive and ugliest item in my clothes collection. The anaemic pink skirt lurks under autopsy grey chiffon. The waterfall draped top part does, to be fair, hang beautifully and makes my neck look long and elegant, but the lack of a sleeve can only be the design of a man because no-one of bride mother age wants bingo wings flapping about untethered at a wedding. The tiny pearls littering the lace top look like teenagers' spots.

'Mum it's lovely. It will complement the sugared lilac of the bridesmaids perfectly but not be too over the top'.

I'm not sure which top my daughter, Pippa, had in mind when she demanded I buy it but it was sure to be a fairly high reach because everything Pippa does must be high end and expensive. I allowed myself to be persuaded to buy something she thought suitable - Pippa is very clear about the positive relationship between suitability and cost. I loathed it when I bought it and still do. Melody Skyhorse says we need to change what isn't working for us and the dress definitely fits into that category. I'll never wear it again. I have a spiteful little moment imagining telling Pippa I've thrown it away but she would say I shouldn't even think about re-wearing it anyway. Instantly I feel like not a very nice person because I had a thought about being mean to my own daughter.

Melody Skyhorse's idea is that every choice we make is a little opportunity for change. She calls students her Graces which is nice. For this task, I'm supposed to tap into my wisdom and feel the vibrations of each item of clothing to decide if it still serves me. I'm not sure what this means and none of my clothes vibrate with anything other than the odd moth but it's such a buzz dumping the corpse frock in the box I grab armfuls of clothes from the rail and throw them on the floor for sorting. The tepid clothes sit there in a pile and I start to feel wibbly.

I have so many shirts! They're fine as shirts go but how many white shirts does any woman need? Ditto the black skirts. Blazers, sensible shoes, a couple of evening gowns, two winter coats. The charity shop pile is the largest but there are no memories clambering out of it. Melody Skyhorse cautions about being our own worst enemy and says we over-focus on what's wrong instead of what makes us happy. I know what she means. All I see is white shirt, dark skirt sensible which drags the fun out of it and leaves me feeling a bit sad because the pile is not just clothes, it's me – bland, which is not a happy thought.

The keep pile is tiny. It's a little bit daring though. It holds a promise of something or someone. There's one top, a scarf with a hint of purple and a drip of red and a beautiful pair of unworn Capri blue linen trousers. They were bought in a moment of impulsive holiday preparation but I had second thoughts they were too vivid and didn't even pack them in my suitcase. They still have the price tag but I don't throw them in the charity pile, because they look like happy trousers. They haven't served me yet but I'm going to give them another chance.

One pair of shoes should be taken back to the Dogs Trust shop because I doubt I'll ever wear them but they are so much the woman I'd like to be. I knew the girl behind the counter was unaware of the significance of the barely marked blood-red sole when she priced them up at four pounds, but I was. I read magazines. The Louboutin black patent leather heels are needle-thin and ankle-breaking high. I saw the pique of the other woman who had them in her sights, but I grabbed them before she did and handed over my coins without even trying them on. They almost rattle with vibrations. I've never worn them but I can't throw them away. They're my aspirational shoes. They'll stay like a promissory note. A memo to self. Confident, graceful women wear red-soled patent leather shoes though I'm not sure Melody Skyhorse would.

Once the wardrobe rail is stripped there are a lot of hanger vacancies and I wonder what I'll wear to work so I decide some things can still be allowed to serve me and I hang onto a few work outfits. As I re-hang them I say out loud that I'm committed to change and they won't be staying for long. Melody Skyhorse calls it talking to the universe and assures it will listen but I feel a bit daft talking to a blouse.

At first, I nicely fold each donation, but the boring clothes suddenly get a seductive vibration, trying to remind me of how sensibly useful they could be and I don't want to fall for that. Melody Skyhorse would call it 'identifying with stuck energy' and I've no intention of being stymied by a Marks and Sparks skirt. The Dogs Trust can be bogged down with the ironing. It's the least they can do.

Move Out of Your Own Way

Fear of success can lead to counterproductive effort. Make way for you!

Everyday Grace

I'm supposed to write in my journal how I'd introduce myself to the universe? I don't know what to say. Doesn't she already know what there is to be known about every single thing and from the beginning of time? So, I start with 'hello Universe, this is me' and take it from there.

People always introduce me using my full name.

'This is David, this is Helena and this is Wendy Wooldridge' they will say. I'm not sure why I'm always 'Wendy Woodridge' rather than just 'Wendy' but I am. I'm almost 58 years old. Andy is my rock and has been since we married at eighteen, and that is pretty much all I need to say about Andy. We have two adult children. Pippa is self-assured. Matthew is gay. He thinks we don't know. Everyone knows.

I have an ordinary lovely life and I'm grateful for it but for a while I've felt pinned and tethered to some choices I don't remember making. I wonder who I might be if I wasn't pinned.

People like me don't embark on adventures or go on journeys of self-discovery. That's the realm of millionaire businessmen with more money than they know what to do with and young yodellers who audition for fame in gladiatorial talent competitions. Sometimes there's a word on the tip of your tongue and it dangles almost there but you can't catch it or you think you might have seen someone in a crowd but the more you look, the more the crowd turns into a mush of anonymous faces. It's a bit like that. Something just a bit out of reach. Andy sometimes asks me what is wrong and I truthfully say nothing is wrong because it isn't really. I'm not a dissatisfied person as a rule but I've a nibbling doubt-ache like when you go on holiday and can't remember if you locked the front door.

A few weeks ago, I heard John Lennon on the radio. I can't remember the song title but one of the lyrics is 'It's time to spread our wings and fly' and when I heard it I had to stop and catch a breath because I felt it was some kind of message from the universe. I'm not a 'message from the universe' kind of woman. I don't even like avocado.

Angela my oldest friend, suggests I'm having a mid-life crisis and a jowl lift via Botox might help. Pippa thinks I am having panic attacks and suggests an urgent need for anti-depressants. They both mean well but I know what I need won't be helped by a pharmacy. It was time to listen to what Melody Skyhorse calls 'inner urgings'. Mine told me it was time to deal with debris and clear a path.

It's all very well deciding on a different future. Shedding the old and embracing the new is exciting - if a little bit scary too - but the carpet still needs a vacuum and the days of ironing free clothing are still stuck in 1960's promise of bri-nylon. As a nod to the new me and what Melody Skyhorse calls 'self-actualisation' I've decided to stop ironing sheets and duvet covers which on reflection is a job created by lunatics. I iron Andy's boxer shorts. Where did that decision come from? When the first pair of underpants arrived out of the wash basket and in front of an iron, how did I become the woman who decided they needed to be crease-free? I hope Pippa doesn't notice as the shame of wrinkled bedding might lead her to cardiac arrest. If I tried to explain about self-actualisation it would be enough for her to decide I'd joined a cult. I've no map. I don't know how to find my way to somewhere else, especially as I've no clear idea where somewhere else is but carrying on in the same old way is not an option. Ironed underpants are not a failure. They, and sock matching, were me doing my best and that should be good enough for anyone. When I look back at my life I don't understand if I made choices as such, rather than let things happen but the choices I made led to Andy and Pippa and Matthew which I won't feel bad about. I can't change the past but there's merit in honestly assessing it. Learning from my own history seems to have the potential to be the best kind of learning of all.

Melody Skyhorse says that people who take control over their lives are brave warriors who should yell to the universe with proud, loud lion breath. I pack my lunch into my eco-friendly, re-usable sandwich bags which is a start on the warrior path but I pass on lion breath yelling so the neighbours don't report me to our cul-de-sac Residents' Association for noise nuisance.

When I was a teenager I used to pore over the personality quizzes in my weekly girls magazine. Years later I found out they were written by work experience interns and not psychologists. I always come out on the optimistic, cheerful part of any spectrum of personality types. I've been thinking about it a lot. Until recently I've never seen any reason to feel differently about myself. People seem to like me as I am.

'Wendy Wooldridge lights up my day' they say, or 'it's hard to be down around Wendy Wooldridge - she's always so chipper!'

I like seeing the rainbow rather than the rain. When you mull it though, being referred to as chipper is like being referred to a 'quite pretty' or 'fairly intelligent' - as if something is lacking. It seems, on reflection, to be potentially a bit of an insult. There's more to me than that, but they never say I'm clever, or wise, or strong and being chipper is not enough anymore. I don't want to change completely because I'm OK. I open windows to let trapped bees out but I want to sort out a bit more about who I am. Even writing that out loud makes me anxious.

Melody Skyhorse says that to create a more harmonious relationship with ourselves we must be clear about what goals to aim for. She sent a worksheet. For the task I was supposed to choose my top three values out of a list of twenty-five. They all seemed like top values to live by and I couldn't narrow it down to three so that wasn't much help. I once saw an old gravestone which said, '*Jayne were not fair of face but were a good mothe*r'. It made me sad for Jayne. I don't want my epitaph to be 'she was chipper'. I won't be throwing the baby out with the bathwater but will be heading towards some decent effort at positive tweaks. I've started a list of things to stop and things to start. Obviously, tea towel ironing will also be a thing of my past and pluck will be my new watchword, hopefully.

I can't help thinking about those quiz interns though and wonder if I'm allowing myself to be Melody Skyhorse's guinea pig. Is she actually Mel Jones of Woking writing twaddle for a bit of pin money? I hope not.

I'm not ready to embrace full-on warrior woman just yet. I'll tweak a little and try to 'go with the flow' which I think means not resisting making changes and riding out the wibbles.

I bet no one ever calls Melody Skyhorse chipper. I bet she doesn't wear lycra velvet either.

Try

*Effort leads to knowledge - of self, of the world, of others.
Better for things to go wrong than to live without the
abundant possibilities of discovery.*

Everyday Grace

I wear the purple scarf to work and absolutely no one notices. Do people have to notice me being a bit different or is it only important if I do?

A few days ago, I went next door and asked, politely but firmly, that Kieran and Donna stopped promising they would sort the rats out and get it done or I'd need to insist they got rid of their chicken coop. I'd been working my way up to it for days. I'm fond of Cluck Rogers and Attila the Hen. We all have to move with the times. I've liked the free eggs too. I don't even mind rats - they're doing their thing, being rats, and if they stuck to their own business I could allow us to get along, but now they are running amok digging up my tulip bulbs and pooing on the patio. It's as much a surprise to me as it is to Donna that I tell them to sort it out.

'What do you want me to do?' She asks.

'I haven't a sodding clue Donna' I say. 'Just get it sorted'.

From the look on Donna's face, you'd imagine I'd asked her to ritually sacrifice her children. Andy's usually the one sorting neighbour stuff about hedges and parking and the like so me going round was a surprise for us both.

I expected at least the women in my team to see the new me, but a scarf is maybe a bit subtle and I wonder if I should swear more. I never swear at work of course.

When I was at school I thought I might like to be a food technologist or an archaeologist. In history, we did a project on Tutankhamun and his tomb in Egypt. The teacher made it so alive, I could almost taste the musty air as the tomb was opened but it was found by someone called Howard which struck me as a posh name. We didn't have a single Howard in our school so I understood from early on I needed to be more realistic. Food technology interested me after a science lesson about dehydrated space food. I imagined spacemen passing Jupiter eating my dehydrated version of Mam's hotpot out of sucky bags.

I was good at languages. My teacher, Looney Langer, said I had a natural flair for German and Russian but during lessons he used to stand with the bin on his head like a hat so his idea of flair was not to be trusted. Job wise, there didn't seem any potential in languages.

I loathed typing because I could never type without looking at the keys which would drive Mrs Stimpson into an absolute rage of knuckle slapping with a ruler, which was allowed back then, so office work was not a draw. University was not even on the horizon. I'd heard and read about university but I didn't personally know anyone who had ever been. University was for people who punted on rivers. We only had drains where I lived.

When I was fifteen I got a job cleaning holiday camp chalets in summer season weekends for money in the hand. The money was good for a teenager, but it was the hardest work I've ever done.

Some holidaymakers are lovely and would strip the beds and have a bit of a tidy round before they left. Others could be filthy. I once found a bottle of pee in a fridge and a slice of bacon under a mattress. It makes you question humanity. Our supervisor would run her fingers along the top of doors and if we had missed any dust, she would dock our wages. Do people on holiday care about dust on door edges?

When Clean Right offered me a proper job my mam and dad were pleased.

So, as it turned out, I became a professional cleaner and eventually an area manager of a team of cleaners - or 'cleaning operatives' as they're called to make them feel a bit better about the job.

As any of the millions of annual visitors to Yorkshire will tell you, the area is breathtakingly beautiful with everything from candy floss to blue flag beaches, Neolithic monuments and awe-inspiring gannets. They might also say it's an area well served by public conveniences and it's been my job to ensure they're kept in a suitably pristine condition.

People take toilets for granted but, as I tell my team, they are crucial to all of us and we certainly know if they're not there when we need them. Not everyone can hang on, especially kids, people with disabilities and older people so it's down to us to make sure they're clean and safe. Lately, we've all had training on the needs of non-binary people for gender-neutral toilets too so we are at the vanguard of making toilets properly convenient for everyone. I tell them to remember how important our work is and especially for people's holidays which is why, since the council cut budgets, we have to focus mostly on the seaside toilets. We don't get the complaints from people using the country facilities if there's no toilet roll or soap in the dispenser because hikers are obviously a bit more able to cope.

I don't clean toilets myself anymore, though I'll get stuck in if needed. My team know I've worked my way up through the ranks so I hope I'm a bit of an inspiration. They wear our uniforms of green polo shirt with the embroidered Clean Right logo. Most uniforms tend to smell of disinfectant. I wear my white-shirt, dark-skirt combo along with my Estée Lauder perfume, which marks me out as a manager.

I have to check all the cleaning is done to the quality spec agreed with the council or they dock pay to my company. It's not that different to my first Saturday job but with more than two quid per room at stake. So I've to visit all the toilets along the coast which can be lovely in high season. There's one right next to a seafront cafe with an outdoor seating area. There's a fountain dedicated to Princess Diana the kids can paddle in when it's warm enough. Jamila covers the Diana patch. I send her a text alert that I'm doing my rounds so she has enough time to make sure the loos are up to snuff. I suggest we meet up for a cuppa when I get there. Her toilets are always immaculate and well stocked with loo roll. She leaves a little bowl of potpourri by the sinks which technically doesn't meet health and safety requirements but I let it pass because some arguments are not worth the breath they take. When we meet for tea I always buy her a shortbread. She calls them butter biscuits.

When I arrive she's already sat outside the cafe wearing her thick fleece and matching hijab. There's a cool breeze blowing off the sea and I notice her look at my scarf as I wrap it more tightly around my neck.

'Bloody hell this wind is a bit chilly eh Jamila?' I say.

I've never sworn in front of Jamila.

'Wendy Wooldridge!' she says back and we both laugh.

I know it's not the job of everyone's dreams, or of mine, but as Melody Skyhorse might agree, we have to do our best with what we get and it's a job worth doing well. I'm a better person for having done it. It doesn't matter what busyness is calling, nothing calls louder than a blocked, flooding public toilet on a hot August bank holiday. I can sort it in a moment. I'm good at managing and motivating people. Some of the other managers think I'm a bit soft but my team know better; 'firm but fair' they say about me and it's true. I could use a map to navigate around a whole county long before we had sat navs. It pays reasonably well which helped put both Pippa and Matthew through university but of course, Pippa always refers to me as an 'Area Manager with the Council' because 'toilet cleaner' is an embarrassment to her. She never imagines I could've used my earnings to put me through university too though, to be fair, I never thought about it myself until recently.

I don't see myself as having much of an ego so it's a bit of a mystery to me why I find myself a bit awry with life. Angela had obviously given more thought to my alleged need for mid-life botox because she emailed me a link to a clinic in Poland offering top to toe lift and tuck surgery for just 20 thousand UK pounds. They throw in a four-star hotel in Warsaw for aftercare.

'We should book a consultation!!!!!!!!!!!!!!' she wrote.

I've never been much of a fan of the exclamation mark.

Angela is my best friend. It's funny how we still use the language of school when we're in middle age. The two of us acquired the label when we were teenagers and it stuck. I'm not sure we ever really were or that we are now but you fall into going along with life sometimes.

I met her in the dining hall of my new secondary school. A look around showed the newbies by their shoes. Most of the older girls had wedgies on. Angela, who'd spotted my uniform policy lace-ups, sat next to me and we got talking. She wore eyeliner which also wasn't allowed. I remember being impressed.

'It isn't fair they didn't give me my first choice of school. Wilbington is a far superior school in my opinion' she told me. She said 'far superior' in a grown-up posh kind of telephone voice my dad sometimes used. Her family recently moved into a street near ours and we agreed to walk home together later. She never turned up to meet me after the last lesson and I waited for ages because I didn't want to let my first new school friend down. This has formed the pattern of our relationship ever since. I can't explain how we've stayed friends all these years because she hasn't changed. We got into a habit of being together and as other school friendships faded over the years of new jobs and growing families, somehow ours didn't. She's still the girl I met at school and, to be honest, not always likeable but it's hard to decide to turn your back on someone because, even now, I don't want to let her down.

Angela got the hump when I said I wasn't interested in Polish plastic surgery She said I was a misery guts, effectively stopping her from having it though I'm not sure how. She seems irritated a lot recently. I wonder if it might be hormone-related but I'd never voice it out loud because Angela is on HRT and convinced it keeps her looking 25. It doesn't.

One of Melody Skyhorse's mantras is that we must allow ourselves the opportunity to be revealed to ourselves and that 'experiences equate to greater self-knowledge'. We have to do stuff to learn. I spotted the evening class being advertised a few days ago.

Andy's watching some real-life police car chasing thing on the telly with cops who are all called Wilko or Dobbo or Jonno when I pass my laptop over,

'What do you think? I fancy trying something different'.

He mutes the sound on the telly and looks at the open page. Only if you noticed the ever-so-slight raise of his eyebrow would you know he's a bit surprised. He isn't one for making a big show of things.

To be honest, I'm not sure the evening class will lead to greater self-knowledge, but I've always wanted to be able to do it.

'Well then sign up love if you want - why not?'

He puts the sound back on as Dobbo and Jonno search a couple of youths with trousers hung down so low their bums are on show and I type our credit card details into the booking page.

As soon as I click to confirm payment I have doubts and wonder if one of the other options might be more suitable. I'm mildly interested in pottery but I don't like drinking out of thick-rimmed cups. The chap who found the haul of Viking jewellery with his metal detector is running a class on local history which looks interesting. I guess he's cashing in on his celebrity. My laptop pings and there it is, my confirmation email. I've booked myself in. What on earth will I wear to a hula hoop class? I've barely anything left in my wardrobe.

CURVEBALLS

The Privilege of Joy and Pain

Both the most difficult and joyful of experiences can be our greatest teacher if we gratefully welcome the gifts they bring.

Everyday Grace

'Like having your boob slammed in a car door' is probably not the response most mammogram nurses expect after they've scooped your breast up into the vice-like grip of the machine and asked, 'is that OK?' I'm not sure Melody Skyhorse would deem this was a strong woman response either. I don't imagine nurses expect an answer at all which might explain her frown. I guess they don't see the woman or the breast as such. They see the portion of flesh they need to corral into the gravity denying space. I wonder why we can't just bend over and droop our boobs into a drawer-like machine and whether the sideways-on, nipples pointing north-east design was thought up by a man. My average, but still quite perky, sized mounds are refusing to be corralled. The chilly spring air is making my nipples stick out which seems ridiculously inappropriate and is not helping me relax into it. I wonder if the increasingly brusque nurse thinks I'm trying to sabotage the whole thing as she kneads my skin into submission, though I do the best I can. The machine nips especially firmly as if it's getting its own back. On the upside, this is my second mammogram in less than four years. The first resulted in a letter two weeks later confirming all appeared normal along with a pink bordered, chatty leaflet advising on the importance of regular self-examination. On the downside, I'm here so soon after the first because of sometime recently arrived Eric. I'm sure it will be fine. With hindsight, I should've taken more notice of the leaflet.

Andy noticed the lump before I did. We were painting the kitchen ceiling. Surely by middle age we must have earned the right to pay others to do the decorating for us but Andy said it was daft to pay people to do things we can do ourselves. He also said he thought it would be fun and he was wrong about that on many levels. I know over-loading paint onto the roller doesn't get the job done quicker but I was impatient. Lemon silk emulsion dribbled off the roller and onto my t-shirt like a great fat seagull poo. It's exactly the right amount of paint for me to have a full-on sense of humour failure and yell at Andy about what an idiot he is to imagine decorating our kitchen was a good way to spend a Sunday.

Just as I throw my ruined t-shirt at Andy's annoyingly smiley face he pulls me into his arms and tells me how beautiful I am covered in paint poo. He does that a lot. He isn't a drama out of a crisis type of person and it often drives me mad but he has this way of making sure we always end up on the right side of a hug. It's one of the reasons I love him to bits but sometimes want to thump him. That's when he noticed it. He felt it against his chest and knew it was a bump out of place, a stranger-bump that didn't belong on me. Once it'd been noticed neither of us could stop noticing it. We take a photograph of it with Andy's phone but I tell him to delete it so it doesn't end up on the dark web or Facebook. I don't know why I hadn't felt it sooner. It's like the great wall of China right there on my boob. Hard and present and shaped like a small Chantenay carrot. Eric, we call it. We agree no one could be scared by an Eric. Neither of us sleep well that night and Eric is still there in the morning. I book an appointment with the GP the same day.

It's funny how words can have different meanings at different times. I hadn't expected an emergency referral to take two weeks so we had quite a wait to see someone. I'm glad I didn't break my arm. A breast lump felt fairly urgent to me but to be fair, it didn't seem to get any bigger and I watched it carefully.

A woman of my age knows breast lumps are never a good thing, but I'm fairly sure it can't be anything serious.

Andy and I both smoked when we were teenagers but stopped as soon as we got together. We only did it to be cool and once we became a couple, we had nothing we needed to prove to anyone else. I've heard red wine can cause dodgy lumps but I'm not sure what 'excessive quantities' means when it comes to wine. It must mean rolling around in a gutter rather than a half bottle once in a blue moon surely? I don't think Eric can be anything too terrible. I tell Andy I'm sure it will be fine and he says the same trying to persuade ourselves, as much as each other.

When I did eventually get a call to go to the hospital it was, all things considered, a peculiar day.

The scuffed mint green walled clinic is a conveyor belt of efficiency. Unfortunately, efficiency seemed to leave little room for simple kindness or understanding of how hard it is to be there. I try hard to transform my feelings into peace in my heart and to imagine the space as calm as an un-splashed pond but even Melody Skyhorse would feel challenged in a cancer clinic I think. First, they scan me. Next, the radiologist sticks needles in places no needles should be stuck - and lied when she recited the medics mantra 'this won't hurt' as she took a biopsy. It did. Junior doctors observed by trainees, none of whom introduced themselves, use latex'd fingers to ferret around in my embarrassingly stubbly armpit with more interest than I ever knew an armpit warranted. After all the prodding and poking I join the queue of crumpled women hugging themselves into their coats, waiting to see the doctor. The air smells of fear. Some of us are alone. I don't know why I didn't ask Andy to come other than he still had the tile grouting to do. We'd lost momentum on the decorating front since Eric but it needed to be finished. We'd done a good job of persuading each other there was no need for dramatics.

It's quiet in the over-warm waiting room. Like at the hairdressers the nurse hands me a celebrity gossip magazine. All I can think about are the vast number of bogie finger germs on its curled pages but it seems a bit ungrateful to refuse it so I leave it on my lap for a while to avoid any embarrassment before casually placing it back on the coffee table. As I'm sat there my phone pings with a text message that says to check my online lottery account and contact their security team. As soon as you see the word security you imagine you've been hacked so it felt like another worry I could do without. I try to find a signal and log in as a nurse with blue hair, the same colour as her uniform, calls my name. Eventually, cursing my geriatric phone I manage to get a signal and open my account. As I sit in yet another waiting area I read the message through several times just as I'm called into a room where my efforts to achieve the peace of a calm pond are well and truly splashed.

Dr Mhoya has a frosty air about her and an asymmetrical face with startlingly high arched eyebrows. She reminds me of a Picasso portrait. The results from the needle biopsy will, she expects, confirm her initial diagnosis based on the scans. The irregular shape of Eric, she tells me, though of course, she doesn't call it Eric but 'a mass', indicates to her it's likely to be a tumour. Tumour is such a horrible word. As she talks I'm completely distracted by the news that my lottery account hasn't been hacked. They'd noted, the message said, I'd won but not yet tried to claim what it referred to as 'a significant prize'. There'd been only one jackpot winner and I was fairly sure the numbers were mine. I'd won seventy-eight thousand pounds.

Wearing a fake-looking best attempt at an empathy face she said, 'I can see this has come as a shock'. I'm guessing she hasn't heard patients laugh at that before.

I must admit it's much easier to consider the lottery win as a gift than Eric, my new lodger. According to Melody Skyhorse all experiences, both good and bad, offer the opportunity to change how we experience life by thinking about the blessings in any situation. The course lesson on 'gifts and blessings' suggests if the gifts are proving to be elusive we must look harder. I wonder if it isn't referring to cancer because all I can feel about cancer is that it's a great big ugly bastard of a thing with no manners, no grace and absolutely no bloody blessings. Maybe I'm not looking hard enough. Sat in my car after I left the clinic, switching between deep breathing and hyperventilation, as much as I try to focus my gratitude won't come. I'm not feeling forgiveness, tolerance or acceptance. All I feel is anger. Raw, horrible, brutal rage that makes me want to sink my teeth into the steering wheel. I'll need to give the gifts and blessings lesson a little more time. I'm out of warrior woman patience, wisdom or fortitude and could easily thump the smug trendy glasses man who taps on my window to ask me if I'm leaving the parking place he has his eye on. He certainly feels my lions breath.

I don't understand why breast cancer is a two-week 'emergency' but a lottery win requires a 'critical' visit within hours. I hadn't expected the lottery people to visit in any case and it seems a bit over the top but the security team explain they have to check our identity before handing the win over. Andy and I are both reeling from the clinic news, moving between terrified and not believing it. We could've done without them visiting but they won't be put off.

Jenny and Abdul, the lottery validators, visit within hours of my call to their security team. I offer them coffee but wonder if I should've put on a few sandwiches as well because they seem keen on small talk and ask us if we've thought about how we might spend the money. It feels like a trick question.

I've told Andy I won't be doing any more decorating but I don't tell them about that. I want them to get on with it really but trying to enter into the spirit I say I might fancy a new laptop and judging by their nodding heads that meets expectations.

'I might have a few golf lessons' Andy says. It just goes to show, people can surprise you all the time. Andy is interested in golf - who knew?

Jenny and Abdul are helpful and smiley. They fill the room like policemen. I notice Jenny wears the white-shirt, dark-skirt combo too and I consider telling her about the livening potential of scarves but I don't want to offend.

As the owner of the account, I have to show my photo ID. I look like a criminal on my driving licence and I hope they don't think I am one. We fill in lots of forms. I'd no idea there was so much to it. They tell us about private bank accounts but I say it won't be necessary because we have an account already. Jenny gives Abdul a look. It isn't a proper eye roll but there's a hint of conspiratorial knowing exchanged. I think she thinks me and Andy are idiots. It's all a bit confusing.

'We usually find it's better to set up a private account for sums such as this'. Abdul begins and like a well-rehearsed double act, Jenny chips in.

'The banks we work with are used to working with celebrities and seriously wealthy people so discretion is assured'.

Abdul jumps back in.

'It gives you a chance to plan through what happens next and puts you in the driving seat. They also give good advice on investments and charitable giving'.

I am, of course, pleased to have won such a huge amount of money but am a little bit offended by Abdul's airy expectation we should give some of it away. Although in all honesty I don't really feel it I try to sound like a carefree - but caring - woman of the world when I respond.

'Thank you so much Abdul but you don't need to worry about us. We have our favourite charities and won't let the win go to our head!'

I feel as if I've said something offensive because the air in the room between the four of us crackles. Abdul suddenly laughs. He has a nice deep bass throaty chuckle.

'Can I just ask, how much is it you think you've won?'

I don't want to actually say the words 'seventy-eight thousand pounds' out loud because I'm worried I've read the results checker wrong; this is a terrible mistake and they are wasting their time. Andy sees I'm discombobulated and he only knows what I've told him. He didn't double check. I can see he's feeling a wobble of uncertainty so he repeats what I told him as a question.

'It's seventy-eight thousand pounds - or thereabouts - isn't it?'

I see another look pass between Jenny and Abdul before they both start laughing together.

'Will you tell them or shall I?' Jenny says.

It turns out I hadn't read the results checker properly.

When Abdul said we'd won a little under eight million pounds I went deaf. In films when bad or good news is given people shriek or drop cups which shatter everywhere or they pass out or some such. I went deaf. It was as if I was under water. I could see OK. Not long after Andy and I got together we were out in town on a date. A drunk woman came and slapped his face. She slurred an apology about mistaken identity and stumbled away but in our living room, I could see Andy wore exactly the same expression as after that slap. Abdul was as smiley as sunshine. I could see Jenny's mouth working as she reached to lay a hand on my arm. I couldn't hear a word. It was nice of her to make us a fresh cuppa because I'm sure that isn't in her job description. She adds sugar without asking if we take it so it's obvious she's prepared for all sorts of reactions. Once the coffee is finished we get back to the business in hand. Unexpectedly getting a windfall is a lot more complicated than I could've imagined.

There's an undercurrent of unsaid concern when I confirm, twice, our new private account should be joint but they are too nice and smiley to ask me whether I trust Andy. They can't know I trust him with every fibre of my being but he knows which is all that matters. After checking they've handed back our passports, council tax bill and driving licences that, apparently, is that. 'Congratulations on your lottery win' Abdul says, shaking mine and Andy's hands. He has a firm grip. I can see Andy feels as embarrassed and awkward as I am to be hand-shaking in our conservatory at teatime. The money will be in our new account within a few hours.

'The bank will send a car for you first thing tomorrow so you can meet their specialist advisors'.

Abdul actually says 'send a car' which I've only ever heard before when booking a taxi and in films.

'We'll need to ring in sick Andy' I say. We never skive off work.

'Good idea' says Jenny. 'Consider very carefully what you tell people about your win'.

Abdul jumps in with his advice. 'The press are focused on the chap from Burnley and his immense EuroMillions win but a £7.8 million win is enough to get the local paper interested you don't want to be inundated with freeloaders'.

'Give yourself the rest of the evening to enjoy your news!' Jenny says, pulling a bottle of champagne out of her bag and handing it to us.

'Winning this kind of money is life-changing. We have specialist counsellors available to help you cope. If you'd like to talk with them, do contact either of us and we'll set it up'.

I don't want to spoil her day so I don't tell Jenny about the cancer but it's funny that the breast care clinic offered me exactly the same services this morning.

Wisdom of Strong Women

Your inner Goddess is your ultimate true guide. Learn to listen to her.

Everyday Grace

Weeks ago, before Eric and the lottery win, when Matthew first told us he was going to come over for a visit for my birthday we planned a birthday buffet. We decided not to cancel it.

'They have to know love'. Andy says we should tell them about the cancer and the lottery win while we're all together. I know he's right but how to do it is the question. Do you have a big rabbit out of the hat moment, like one of those 'ta dah' gender reveal parties with pink glitter - 'Its breast cancer!' or slip it into conversation over a beef and horseradish sandwich? 'By the way, did I mention we are millionaires?' Andy says he thinks we'll know the moment when it comes and I should just try to enjoy us all being together. Once everyone has arrived and discussion of the merits of the kitchen decorating have been exhausted I do my best and start the ball rolling with general chit chat to work up to it.

Angela, mirroring Pippa, is not especially supportive when I tell her I've signed up at the community centre.

'A hula hoop class? Why there needs to be classes for something any idiot could do I'll never know.'

She's on a roll of telling me how weird I'm getting in what she calls my 'old age'. I don't remind her she's four months older than me.

'It'll be fun Angela. Maybe you'd enjoy it too' I say.

'Fun? You need to get a grip if that is your idea of fun girlfriend. For goodness sake'.

She's taken on the use of 'girlfriend' from American TV sitcoms. I think you need an American accent to carry it off.

With a Yorkshire inflection it sounds a bit silly.

I've some way to go on getting to grips with Everyday Grace lesson five and becoming confidently assertive, though I'm working on it. I mindfully note the needling for the next half an hour but I don't rise to it. I've other things to think about. Focusing on my breath makes me a bit light-headed. I hope Melody Skyhorse would approve of my efforts to follow the 'Life Choices' lesson plan and choose how I experience Angela. All things considered, it's a bit of an effort to be calm, empathic, kind *and* grateful. It's a demanding lesson.

I don't explain the concept of 'mindful noting' or my online chum Melody Skyhorse to Angela because she'd go off like a rocket about that. Instead, and maybe not very warrior woman, as she's helping me lay the buffet out I take a calming breath and tell her I can't make our next planned lunch.

'Ooh it's 'active wear' now is it?' She says when I tell her I need stuff for my hoop class.

I don't even know what active wear is. It's a bit of a mean-spirited fib because I'd planned no such thing and intended to go to the class in a pair of leggings and a baggy tee-shirt.

'Maybe we can go and see the film with that actor you fancy?' I suggest and she says she'll 'try' to get to it to inject a bit of a 'oh please do come' drama. I let it fly over my head because I know she'll want to go.

'Help yourselves then' I say to everyone once lunch is on the table.

'Plenty of beige food Mum. Been to the freezer shop? I haven't seen creamed mushroom vol au vents for years.'

There is a great deal of theatrical eye-rolling towards Matthew. She's far too self-involved to notice he's embarrassed by her critique of the buffet. His body stiffens up when he doesn't

know what to do and, smiling in my direction, he loads his plate with sausages on sticks.

'Is the hummus homemade? Rose may have it with carrot sticks if it is'.

Of course it isn't. Its shop bought. Pippa can be tense about things. My cute little granddaughter, rubbing a sugar-laden millionaire shortbread I'm certain she isn't allowed to have into the carpet, appears not to care about missing out on the inadequate dips.

The Le Creuset kitchen set is on the floor next to the sofa. Apart from the orange skillet which prompts enough oohing and aahing to satisfy Pippa, the other boxes of the set are unopened. I act appropriately grateful but most people, perhaps even Pippa, might suggest pans are a bit of a naff birthday present and there's an 'elephant in the room' vibe at present giving time. Melody Skyhorse calls it 'contracted energy' which, as I understand it, means in most situations we each are expected to behave in particular ways or the atmosphere in a room goes off-kilter. This month's lesson on dodgy energy suggests I should witness and have a sense of curiosity about what I feel without making negative judgements. I'm supposed to reject bad atmospheres and instead express positive energy such as love, joy and being appreciative to the universe and people in it. It seems like a heck of a responsibility. She makes it sound lovely but I'm not sure filo wrapped prawn parcels are contributing to a positively vibrating environment and I do feel negative about the pans. Pippa's energy is a part of who she is and I do accept it. I love my daughter fiercely and know she loves me too but why would any woman give another pans for a present? I'd have liked Lily Allen's latest CD.

The pans are, it's true, a fine set of kitchen cookware. The best money can buy in fact. Pippa has the complete set too. Mine are the loud orange version. I know it's a signature colour of the products but I can't imagine why. I've only ever known one person who actually liked orange and she'd a leaning towards Buddhism and fruit teas which might explain it. Pippa's are in turquoise. They complement the navy toned designer units and polished grey steel of the large and immaculate 'heart of the home' family kitchen she's so proud of.

Christopher, Pippa's business lawyer husband, is on a trip. He's in Hong Kong. He is, I came later to appreciate, the catch Pippa fully intended to land when she chose philosophy at Durham.

'Philosophy love? What on earth will you do with a philosophy degree?'

'Mum, Durham is about the *opportunities,* not the silly degree!'.

I don't know how any 18-year-old has such clarity about her direction in life. I certainly didn't.

Christopher was in the final stages of his MSc in International Law and Finance with a job lined up when they met at a university tennis event. I'd never known Pippa to be interested in sport of any kind. They married after her graduation. Rose was born a year later. Two years on, his career in ascendancy, they're trying for a second. 'An heir and a spare' they joke, only I'm not sure it is a joke and I think Pippa's disappointed her first child is a girl. I'm disappointed we raised ours to think that way.

The pregnancy efforts are apparently why the mountain of cheese I've laid out in the buffet is a no-no. I ate cheese when I was pregnant with both my children but times change. Christopher works for an international kitchen company. I'm guessing the pan set was a freebie. They have a gorgeous old house. It used to be a vicarage and has walled gardens to die for. A footballer lives next door and Pippa has become a play-date chum with his WAG and their little girl. Pippa was right, she never did need the philosophy degree. She's always been a clever girl.

'So Matthew, how *is* your love life these days?'

Angela's drunk the full bottle of sparkling wine she brought with her but has located some cans of lager to top up with. 'I bet all the girls over there in cellophane valley want a piece of you eh Matthew?'

I don't know why she teases him but once she gets a drink in her, she always does it. Matthew blushes, drops his paper napkin and his mini-sausage roll tumbles towards a delighted Rose as he goes to retrieve it from the carpet. Pippa swoops in hawklike to stop the child consuming pork offal and gluten.

Matthew visits fairly regularly but not usually for birthdays and whatnot.

'People in the States use aeroplanes like we use trains love' Andy said but popping to East Yorkshire in March is much more of an effort than a weekend trip to Honolulu. I'm not sure a fifty-eighth birthday is a milestone deserving of five thousand miles of travel. Matthew looks awkward and I feel achingly sad that he probably wishes he hadn't bothered coming.

I still have Matthew's trophies on display. 'Bin them Mum' he said but of course I couldn't do that. I still have the newspaper cutting too *'Local Boy's Perfect Paso Doble'*. His classmates called him 'Pufta-Dobble' till the day he left school. I sometimes wonder if I should suggest he tries journaling about the bullying but I don't actually know if he has pain he needs to honour or a need for a more conscious relationship to it after all this time. I can't imagine what he would think if I asked him. I haven't told him about Melody Skyhorse. He hasn't come out which is confusing and disappointing.

At university, Matthew was headhunted by one of the giants of Silicon Valley. As soon as the hired cap and gown were returned to Ravenscroft and Co we were driving him to the airport. I wasn't ready for him to go. I cried in the car. Neither of us were ready to talk about why he was really leaving.

Sometimes when we video call and after I've said hello to his 'flatmate' Yuuto I try to draw him out

'Have you boys been into San Francisco recently?' I might ask.

He sometimes calls from his laptop at the dining table

and right there behind him on the fridge I can see a rainbow flag magnet and a flyer for some venue in the Castro. I've seen a documentary about the Castro district on TV. I make an effort to try to understand his life so I can be ready for when he does tell me and we can have a hug and go shopping together. It's usually at this point Yuuto finds some other thing to do than to talk to me. His beautiful honest face cannot carry lies. I wonder if this is related to the importance of honour in his Japanese heritage and wonder too if I'm being a bit racist in thinking that.

Once, shortly after they moved into their flat together - an entirely economic decision Matthew said several times - he showed me around. He carried his phone room to room and used the camera to pan around. Most of their stuff was in boxes.

'Just one bedroom then?' As an invitation to start the 'gay' conversation it wasn't the best approach and Matthew looked utterly panicked.

'Americans call it flexing mum' he said showing me the sofa bed in the open plan lounge unconvincingly trying to persuade me it was where he would be sleeping.

'Is that a Mapplethorpe poster on the wall?' I wasn't trying to force his hand but it was an impressive image. Matthew was surprised and a bit flummoxed I even knew who Robert Mapplethorpe was. Thinking about the exhibition Andy and I once visited in the Tate Mod I suppose he could've been in a lot more of a kerfuffle had he made a different poster choice. I remember Mapplethorpe art mostly for imposingly large erect penises and I wonder how Matthew might have explained one of those on his wall without saying the 'g' word. I noticed the poster had been taken down once he showed me the flat tastefully furnished. I didn't ask him about it but I keep chipping away at trying to make it safe for him to tell us. Andy thinks my chipping might be making it harder.

When invites were issued I told them it wasn't a big party but a small early gathering to welcome in the spring.

I'd never intended to make a big deal of it because who cares about being 58. To be honest, until the actual day itself I thought I was 59 and it was Andy who reminded me. I remember my dad once forgetting how old he was and teenage me finding it hysterically funny. I was counting months towards the excitement of becoming sixteen with late bedtimes and permission to smoke and simply could not imagine how anyone could forget how old they were. I told dad he was a moron. To give him the credit I never gave him at the time, he laughed along with me even though I was being brattish and rude. I miss Dad so much. I'm glad he and Mam won't have to hear about the cancer. He would've laughed about me forgetting my age though.

It was just us four, plus Angela and Rose of course. Christopher was invited though he couldn't come. I wasn't expecting him to anyway. He's often on what Pippa always emphasises are his *international* trips so everyone appreciates his work is far too important for Barnsley or Scarborough. Yuuto was invited but of course he didn't come. I wish Matthew would let me like him out loud. I wonder if he's out to his family.

Angela's latest boyfriend had, at Andy's insistence, been invited. It turns out, as I'd suspected all along, he had a wife and two children in Ilkley who he'd failed to mention on Tinder. My party was Angela's relationship wake which explained her speedy downing of the Prosecco.

We'd intended to give them the news. Andy and I had it planned. After the cheese was nosed, grapes fingered and pastry had gone hard I was going to call everyone to attention and do a 'good news/bad news' speech. Nothing heavy. We were just going to call it a lump and avoid words like tumour and cancer. I thought the lottery win would somehow soften the blow of the news of Eric. Any-which-way it actually went these were the people closest to me. The ones who *should* know, who had a *right* to know. Only, as Angela complained because there was no karaoke machine, Pippa with a manicured, plastic nailed finger dug non-organic southern fried chicken poppers out of Rose's mouth and Matthew's body language evidenced an ache to be back in the safety of America - or indeed anywhere else - I reconsidered. I didn't tell them about any of it. Neither Andy or I felt a right time.

Pippa offered to drop squiffy Angela home on her way to take Matthew back to his Premier Inn. We still had a single bed set up in what was once his bedroom but since we put in a desk and a computer had become our home office. Most middle-aged couples whose kids have left have a home office these days. Matthew said he wanted to give us our own space but I guess it was that he wanted his. I miss Matthew so much.

'Well, that went well' Andy said as he scraped the mini toad in the hole canapés into the swing bin. Both of us ended up with tears of laughter streaming down our faces. We laughed and laughed until it caused Andy to get a pain in his side and then we laughed at that as well. It was the best moment of the awful day. I don't know what I'd do without him and now, because of the lump, I'm aware he's probably thinking the same thing about me. I would do anything in the world not to be hurting him so badly.

We've an appointment with the specialist in a few days. I think we were getting our laughter in while we still can.

Choosing a Path to Take

Whether a glass is half full or half empty is simply a perception. The choice is yours.

Everyday Grace

The Consultant gets straight on with it.

'You have Ductal Carcinoma in Situ. The good news is it's ER-positive, very small, hasn't spread which means it's treatable'.

Dr Mhoya, waxes lyrical about the breast reconstruction she recommends. A full mastectomy is apparently the best option for my particular tumour because although relatively small at under two centimetres it's in the middle of my breast.

'My team will remove the breast tissue, a lymph node or two and unfortunately your nipple will need to go but that shouldn't be too much of a problem'. She tells me how they will go on to reconstruct my breast. Depending on what's found in my lymph nodes during the operation which she assured me appeared 'beautifully clear' in the needle biopsy results, I'll need radiotherapy, chemotherapy and hormone therapy afterwards.

'It's a straightforward operation and your prognosis is excellent' She assures us making it clear she considers the reconstruction element part and parcel. I've a distinct feeling she prefers the creative aspect of the operation. I wonder if it's more artistically satisfying to her than the human butchery of boob removal.

Apparently, my rounded tummy - what Andy affectionally calls my 'bread basket' - is perfect to use to replace my breast tissue. It will be harvested in a strip and folded into the sac of skin left after my breast has been removed.

'Think of it as a tummy tuck for free' she chirpily suggests.

Similarly, she is far more pleased than I've ever been about my wobbly bottom. On Instagram, I could probably have had a million followers but why the world had gone mad for bums or photographs of them is beyond my understanding. I stood with my hospital gown agape while Dr Mhoya sat behind cupping my dimpled cheeks appreciatively and advised us that it had a textbook muscle to fat ratio. She actually patted a cheek as she stood to wash her hands before sitting at her desk. She'll suck out the fat, pump it into the breast sac and over a short space of time, it will marry with the tissue to create a realistic looking and feeling breast. In my head I hear 'ta-dah' as she says this. When the scarring has settled down I can have a nipple tattooed on.

'It will be a perfectly serviceable breast'. She says.

I'm not sure what 'perfectly serviceable' means. The last time my breasts were called into active service was to feed Matthew. As I had no likelihood of breastfeeding again it seemed like a lot of effort for the achievement of boob symmetry but Dr Mhoya didn't concur.

'Oh, it isn't an effort, it's all part of the breast cancer care service' she tells us making it sound like a complimentary car valet after an MOT.

I once saw a YouTube video of an actor portraying twelve different emotions using only facial expressions in under a minute. He was good at it. Dr Mhoya does the same kind of thing when I tell her I'm unsure about reconstruction. It seems to me it is unnecessary. She tells me, a little frostily, I should take time to consider my options but not take too long because my cancer is 'a ticking clock'. She makes clear she does not think I'm making the correct choice.

'But why wouldn't you want to keep your figure? You don't have to decide now dear, talk it over with your husband, decide together and let my office know within the next few days so we can book you in'.

As Andy and I leave her office I feel cross she'd called

me 'dear' and imagined it was anyone's decision to make but mine. I don't think I'm going to have chemo either. I haven't discussed it with Andy yet but in my heart, I think it's not the right choice for me.

Both Andy and I have a bit of a cry in the car. My heart breaks for Andy. I can't remember the last time I saw him cry.

I decided to still go to the hula hoop class despite Eric and Dr Mhoya. I'm trying to live in the moment. Melody Skyhorse says this is about letting go of both the past and the future and experiencing every moment as a gift. What with Eric and the money everything has become a bit wobbly and a place of far too many 'what if' moments. Whether discussing either the cancer or the money there's an awful lot of daunting unfamiliar. The only decision Andy and I have made so far is not to make any big decisions. I imagine a lot of people dream of big wins but we've talked about how much our lives could change and it's scary. You imagine having the big house or the first-class travel but you never ponder about the things in between like where that big house will be and the faff of buying all that new furniture, whether you actually want to go to Disneyland or whether you will leave work and then miss your job. You don't spend time thinking about death either. One way or the other, our lives are going to be different forever and that feels like a big weight. I'm sure Melody Skyhorse would be impressed that in the middle of all that kerfuffle my self-care involves hula hooping.

Since I was a girl, the hula hoop had me beat. I can dance. I've always loved dancing and, if I say so myself, I'm good at it. One of this month's lessons from Melody Skyhorse is that we need to see and love our own qualities. Rhythm is one of mine. I like to think Matthew gets his from me. When he was a boy and we went on holidays Matthew would lead me around the floor. People used to watch us and I was proud of him of course but also, a little bit proud of me too. We had such fun until he got to the teenage years of being embarrassed by his parents. Still, despite my adequate samba and enthusiastic jive I can neither cajole or demand that my hips find the correct formula to keep a hoop up. I should be able to do it. Five-year-old girls do it effortlessly but not me, not at five years old or since.

A few years ago, passing the hospice shop in the high street they had one in the window. It was stripey and adult sized and only three quid. On an impulse I bought it. It would be good exercise, I told myself. After moving back the living room sofa to give me space to practise I was forced to admit defeat. The hoop would not hula. It spent most of the week on my carpet before it ended up back at the charity shop.

The email booking confirmation included instructions to wear comfortable clothing such as t-shirts and leggings - leotards were not necessary which was a good thing as I neither owned nor intended to ever own, one. I hoped the class wouldn't be full of the kind of women who did. I'd give it a go but if they were all size four gym bunnies I'd be out of there faster than the hoop off my hip.

Theresa is as nice in person as she was on email even if she is wearing a full, lime green, lycra body stocking over her tiny slim form.

'Don't be a soft lass! Of course you aren't too old and I promise you'll be spinning the hoop by the end of the first lesson'.

I like her immediately and I believe her too. Some people have that kind of vibe don't they? There are eight of us in the class including her. Even with so few of us, it's going to be snug. As instructed we put our belongings around the edges of the small attic room, each of us awkwardly careful not to trespass on the little space claimed by someone else. Theresa wanders among us all graceful and light-footed. She has a collection of hoops over one arm which she selects from, measuring the size by holding it next to our thighs.

'It should stand floor to your belly button. Have a go

with mine, to begin with but as with all tools, it's better if you have your own. If you're comfortable with the size and weight, you can buy either directly from me or online. Online is a bit cheaper than mine but I sell at the best price I can'.

Theresa has an easy laugh and a soft Liverpudlian accent which I wasn't expecting because accents don't come across on email. The group is made up of a couple of pretty girls who are possibly early twenties. The older I get, the less I can differentiate between sixteen and twenty-five. All the girls have such amazingly sophisticated eyebrows these days and they make it hard to tell. They wear lycra of course and look comfortable in their bodies but awkward in the community centre. Three women, in their early forties or thereabouts, also arrive together. One of them is a bit chunky and struggled to get up the stairs so I wasn't sure how she would get on with a hoop but I admired her tremendously for giving it a go. She isn't in lycra but Jeans and a David Bowie t-shirt. I hear one of her chums call her Jo. I hope she likes the class and sticks with it which is a bit mean because without even seeing her try I judgementally imagine we can be bad at it together. There's an angular chap with the toned and fatless body of a whippet. I hadn't expected to see a man in the class. He has a profile as sharp as a knife, all cheekbones and solid jaw, fashionably stubbly. He has a little patch of tightly curled chest hair peeking out of his vest top. He's captivatingly handsome - like men on aftershave adverts on the billboards. I don't want to stand next to him once the class gets going. I can tell just by looking he'll be good at it.

Theresa invited us to give our names and say something interesting about ourselves. Jo's group all work at the same school. Jo teaches maths and likes crime dramas and old-fashioned trifle with sponge in. Raquel plays the flute. She does country and western line dancing on Tuesdays. She once did a skydive to raise money for dolphins and broke her leg 'It was a bally nuisance for the line dancing' she

43

said. Cecile is from Seychelles, teaches English and loves singing. She has a phobia of horses since one bit her on the shoulder. She's the tallest woman I've ever known and has a perfect figure-eight shape - big on top and bottom but the teeniest tiny waist. I know we're not supposed to judge women on their bodies these days but she's mesmerising to look at. She has the kind of energy that feels loud even when she isn't saying much. I can tell just by looking she's used to and comfortable with being noticed.

'I'm Wendy' I say, 'and I like cooking'. It's an odd thing for me to say because I don't and I'm rubbish at it but the other thing that came to mind was the cancer and I thought that might spoil the mood a bit. Mr Gorgeous says he is, as I suspected, a dancer. His family are from Nigeria but he was born in Batley. His name is Tony. He's the only person I've ever seen who can make leg warmers look good.

With the exception of Mr Gorgeous, most of us have the fluidity of a folded ironing board when Theresa gets us to wiggle and jiggle about. We need to move the hoop with the part of the body nearest to it so she tells us we should get in touch with which part it is. There's more to it than I'd realised. A hoop on the waist needs legs, arms and hips to be relatively still or gravity - our enemy, Theresa tells us, will mess us up and our hoops will hit the deck. She makes it look so easy and actually talks and walks around the room spinning her hoop while she instructs us. She is amazing and Mr Gorgeous is elegantly competent. He's not a beginner. The rest of us look like we are wired into the mains current. We can shimmy side to side or have one foot forward - either is OK Theresa says, but neither are yet working for any of us. If we want a more intense work out she said we can stand with our legs close together but whichever stance we choose it's important to isolate the waist movement. It's like body Lego and trying to get all the instructions in order is much easier said than done. She walks around us one by one, gentle hands on a waist here and a hip there, shifting feet and smiling a lot. We all concentrate so hard but the hailstone clatter of hoops hitting the floor fills the room. I wonder how the creative writing class on the ground floor is coping with the noise. And then I did it. Four circles. I kept it up for four circles before I started thrusting my bum and lost the rhythm.

'There you go!'

Theresa smiles broadly and I'm ridiculously, stupidly happy. Jo is beaming too. She's moving her chunky self like a goddess and her smile is lighting up the tatty attic room. At one point every single person in the class has a hoop going and it's absolutely marvellous. I feel happy. I feel invincible. I feel cancer-free. Melody Skyhorse talks about lives half-full with space for more instead of being upset about what we think is missing. In the class, there's nothing missing at all. Gladness wraps me like a blanket and blessings are easy to count. I kept the hoop up for the first time ever and it feels important.

'Give yourselves a big round of applause' Theresa says. The young girls are a bit half-hearted about it but the rest of us clap and cheer as if we're at a football match. I even high five Mr Gorgeous without feeling daft and he allows himself a proper smile. The class was the best, most delicious fun. Some of us place an order with Theresa for our own hoops which she promises to bring with her to our next class. Jo offers to bring tea break biscuits. Seizing the moment, I point to her Bowie t-shirt and tell her Andy and I saw his 'Sound and Vision' gig back in the '90s. 'Me too!' she says, smiling broadly. 'Me and you are going to have to educate Raquel about his genius because she says he's a drip'. Raquel pokes her tongue out at us both.

'I'm going to spend some winnings on a hoop' I tell Andy when I get home. He knows it is tongue in cheek because nearly four weeks since Abdul and Jenny's visit, and despite the advisors they arranged for us, Andy and I still have no idea what to do about the money. Years ago, when we won two thousand on premium bonds, we had the gas fire that looked like a real coal fire installed. We loved the gas fire and how cosy it made the living room. Winning that much was such a treat and we had a list of home improvements we planned to do so deciding how to spend it was easy. It was in and out of our bank account in no time and it was a satisfying spend. Winning nearly eight million pounds doesn't make any sense. We've dipped into it for some bits and bobs but the numbers don't change much. When you can buy just about anything, it's overwhelming. All those things you sometimes dream about - beach cabins on stilts over a tropical blue sea, a kitchen extension, a canal boat - seem dull once they don't have to be dreams. Dreams are supposed to be made of things that take effort and not just luck. When they don't you are left with not much to aspire to. There should be a winners support group because I'm not sure how to get my head around having such a stupid amount of money. It's easy to understand how it messes with people's heads. Andy and the kids are what matters. What I wish I could spend it on, for them and for me, is getting rid of the cancer.

As an interim, we text the kids and tell them we've had a win on the lottery and have deposited a treat into their bank accounts. It took us ages to decide what was enough of a sum to be a proper treat but not enough to turn their lives upside down. Cancer news, which had not yet been shared, would do enough to sideswipe them both so a hundred thousand pounds each, for now, seemed about right.

KALEIDOSCOPE

Burden in a Name

*Explore labels. We name to frame understanding - but
what understanding is being offered by the name given?*
Everyday Grace

Melody Skyhorse says the words we choose have power.
I've never thought about it before but I guess even scary
words like 'blood' depend on perspective. You wouldn't
want to be without it, but neither do you want to see it on
the carpet. No parent should ever have to tell their child they
have cancer and we did consider not telling them for a while
on the grounds of what they don't know can't hurt them but
it's too big an un-truth to live with. Telling the kids is going
to make them sad. It's the last thing in the world we want to
do. We've asked them both to come over. Andy and I spent
a lot of time planning how best to tell them but I'm not sure
we got the right words in the right order because it was such
a hard conversation.

Pippa, like Dr Mhoya, doesn't understand why I'm not
interested in reconstruction. It must be hard for a daughter
to hear her mother has breast cancer. She doesn't take the
news well. Her anger fills our living room. She directs it,
towards me as if I'd done something wrong, which I
understand but could do without. It's unfair to be having the
conversation with them both on the day before Matthew
flies back to America but time was against us and it had to
be a face-to-face discussion. Matthew scrunches his eyes
and curls his shoulders around like a hedgehog as he always
does when Pippa flies off the handle.

'The tumour is less than five centimetres which is small
as breast tumours go. The good news is, it looks as if it
hasn't spread'.

It feels a bit peculiar talking about my breasts with my
children. Matthew silently does his best to stop his bottom
lip from quivering but I see it. He looks like a little boy and

it hurts my heart. Pippa does not silently lip quiver. It isn't her way.

'This is fucking insane Mother. What do you have to say about this dad? You absolutely *must* have it re-made. Why on earth wouldn't you? On what planet would you just choose to have your boob lopped off? You'll look ridiculous. Of course you must have it rebuilt. What does your consultant say? He must've told you not to be so stupid?'

Pippa assumes my doctor is a man but it's not the right time to get into a discussion about what Melody Skyhorse calls 'the toxic standards of the male gaze' and how sexism does women no favours. I'm not sure Pippa can accommodate that not choosing a fake boob is a part of reclaiming my true warrior woman self although, it isn't that at all really. I like the idea of being an Everyday Grace warrior woman but the truth is, the idea of a non-real breast feels a bit icky and all those operations unnecessary. I don't want any more messing with my body than Eric needs for eviction purposes.

I shouldn't have mentioned Eric.

'Eric? You call it fucking Eric? You've both gone mental and need to speak to someone!'

Poor Pippa flies off into out-of-control mode and winds herself into a terrible state. She deals with fear the way she always deals with being unsettled. Pippa prefers order. She either ignores things as if they aren't there or gets in with an attack first. Melody Skyhorse calls things that work but are not the best way to go about getting needs met 'functional dysfunctions' but while they might make life less challenging - at least for Pippa if not for us - they can't do away with cancer. She can't deal with it so she focuses on what she can focus on which is being cross with me and her dad. I accept how she copes but her shouting feels like being sandblasted.

'Your lovely strappy shift dress, the one you got for Greece, will slip off your shoulder if you don't have a breast. How embarrassing would that be?'

I tell her looking chic is the least of my concerns. She's right about the dress though - one of the few outfits I kept. It will have to be evicted too.

Matthew initially says nothing. When he does, quietly and so different to Pippa's ranting he says, 'Are you going to die Mum?'.

It breaks a damn and all four of us, my lovely family, cry and cry and cry together. We never got around to talking about the money we'd given them or our lottery win. It didn't seem important.

What you don't know until you are in what people call 'a life-changing situation', is how much telling there is to do. I'm going to have to tell work that I won't be coming back. It makes me a bit sad.

On the shelf with Matthew's trophies, there's the award I got from the tourist board a few years ago. It was a black-tie event. Andy was down with a tummy bug so Angela came with me. It's a simple glass rose for my 'Contribution to Inclusive Tourism' is engraved with my name but it was handed over by some MP whose name I can't recall. We had to pose for photos as he passed it to me and I was so proud. After I'd been up to the podium to collect it, Angela told me the halter neck on my evening dress made me look like I had swimmers' shoulders but I didn't let it spoil my night.

Melody Skyhorse says to move forward we must consider whether a relationship - whether to chocolate, a person or a workplace - continues to be useful. If not, the tie should be snipped. As much as I've enjoyed my job, I can't see it in my future. It would be a faff for the management covering my patch while I have treatment and being a millionaire toilet cleaner is too bonkers for me to contemplate.

Andy says I should stay on sick leave. I can see his point. I'm entitled to three months full pay and I don't suppose there will be any problem getting a doctor's note but with almost eight million pounds in the bank, we don't need the money so making a clean break feels like the decent thing to do.

Giving back my name badge and security lanyard is an experience. My manager cries. She says she's terribly sad I'm leaving. I'm fairly sure it's because she suspects I'm about to pop my clogs. She sympathises when I tell her I don't want a leaving do. I've always found those little goodbye gatherings truly awful. There are usually a few shop-bought sandwiches and some warm white wine. They're always held after work or in the lunch hour so no one wants to be there. Cancer gives me an opt-out. A huge bunch of lilies arrives at our house from the team. They remind me of the flowers at my mother's funeral. Jamila the Princess Diana toilet attendant sends me a scented candle in the post and the card says I should pop in to see her next time I'm in her patch. Not many people get invited to lavatories so her note does make me laugh. The candle smells of cinnamon and vanilla, like her toilets.

Melody Skyhorse is a fan of the universe and says it's always acting exactly as it should. It's funny how the universe works sometimes. Andy and I had never thought about retirement but unexpectedly a round of redundancies came up at his company. He's the best transport manager in their team. On his watch lorries never end up in Belgium or Vienna without a load to bring back. I'm not the only person in our family to have won an award at work but Andy got vouchers for Marks and Spencer's which are more useful and don't need dusting. Ordinarily, I doubt they would've even considered him as someone to pay off but he only has to mention breast cancer and it's enough to have everyone bending over backwards to accommodate. I think people are nice that way but Andy said one mention of the C-word made them worry about their own mortality. They wanted him to be away from them as if he was infectious. Like me, he never mentioned the lottery win because while I might be content to turn my back on sick leave entitlement he had no intention of walking away from the redundancy package.

Melody Skyhorse talks a lot about the law of attraction which, as I understand it, is about the universe sending things our way. All we have to do is mindfully invite good stuff in. Looking back, Dad had a similar idea. He used to say 'money breeds money' but he certainly didn't imagine people like us could will it to come our way. Asking the universe to help us leave work hadn't even been on the table but we've become not only retirees but comfortably off ones too - though, to be fair, not many people would call having cancer comfortable.

It feels as if there have been a lot of difficult conversations in our lives lately and heaven knows, none of us need any more but once you start, you have to see it through. The not-lies-but-not-truth-either between Matthew and us was untidiness that needed attention. Andy suggested we role play it first, which was good in theory, but I'm not very good at acting. I went first while he pretended to be Matthew. Every time we tried it I sounded so formal.

'Well, here's the thing Matthew...'

'Your dad and I....'

'We need to discuss something important...'

Andy said it sounded like I was telling him off which is the exact opposite of what we wanted to achieve. We decided to ring him together so he knows we're both on the same page but we gave him a few days to settle into being home first. When we ring it's lunchtime in California but for us it's been all day of fretting. It was easier telling him about the cancer. We still hadn't cracked the role play when he answered the video call.

When Matthew comes into view with his lovely boyish face I don't even know how to begin so I make a right pig's ear of it.

'Matthew, I - that is me and your dad - want to have a grown-up and difficult conversation with you...'

The terrified look on his face tells me he's preparing for

more bad cancer news. I see his eyes begin to tear up which starts me off.

'No, no Matthew, it's not the cancer I - well me and your dad - want to talk about … well, not directly anyway…'

Andy chips in with the bit we agreed he would say which we thought would be reassuring but it muddied the waters. With hindsight, I'm not sure Andy should've read it off our 'things we need to cover' crib sheet.

Matthew looks confused and confirms that yes, he does know his dad and I love him and always will. I can tell he wants us to get on with it.

'So here's the thing Matthew: Your dad and I know you're gay and we want you to know we know so you know we know and we're fine about it. Also, we need to tell you - that lottery treat we gave you - we're rich as well'.

I hadn't intended to throw in about the lottery win but if we were clearing out clutter, the fib about it being a small win needed attending to. Matthew looks a bit bewildered which is not surprising really.

We talk for a long while and it's lovely. It hurts to hear he kept his sexuality from us because he didn't want us to be disappointed in him. How on earth could we be - especially as we knew already - but as Andy said later, this is his stuff, not ours and we don't have to take it on board. Matthew gave 'an' explanation, not 'the' explanation. Andy's wise sometimes. In a way, I wish we had more to be disappointed about. Kids are supposed to disappoint parents occasionally, aren't they? Pippa has given it a fair crack of the whip what with the teenage smoking and the ex-boyfriend we're not allowed to mention but Matthew never has. Andy says I shouldn't go looking for problems and Matthew is not much of a rebel - apart from being gay.

We all laugh when Matthew tells us what we already know. He and beautiful Yuuto are a couple.

'Three years. We met at work' he says. I don't guilt-trip Matthew about keeping it from us but I'm sad he felt he had to.

He tells us about them both starting the process of applying for dual citizenship. 'It's not a biggie mum. We like California but it's more about making visas and travel easier'.

Andy tells Matthew about the visit from Abdul and Jenny and shaking hands in the conservatory and we all laugh. Andy tells him about us both leaving work and he says 'jeez' over and over as if he is becoming a real American.

What Andy said about Matthew not coming out being 'his stuff' doesn't sit right. When I think about it I wonder why I'd left that ball in his court. His being worried about our potential disappointment was prompted by something. Homophobia isn't always about queer-bashing is it?

Power for Beginners

*The universe vibrates with powerful forces which shape
our world and how we live within it. Cultivate intuition for
vibration, and transformational power will follow.*
Everyday Grace

I ring her and try but Pippa can't be persuaded to come and
give the hoop class a go and she still thinks it's a strange
thing to have taken up but instead of being negative she said,
'don't overdo it Mum'. I tell her I'm listening to signals
from my body so I can re-balance dis-ease but she sighs like
she wonders if I'm mental.

'Come round and spend some time with me and Rose'

Invitations must be issued by Pippa. She isn't a fan of
the quick pop round. She's a bit modern like that.
Christopher's in Zurich and Andy's still serving his notice
so when I do visit, it's just the three of us. We're in what
Pippa calls the family room. It's a kitchen diner with a half
lounge alongside and patio doors out to the garden. The
rhododendrons are starting to bloom. Rose's toys are on her
playmat in the corner of the room. Each and every one is
noisy, even the books have an in-built jingle. I don't know
how Pippa stands it as Rose moves from one plinky noise
machine to another. Pippa looks beautiful - glowing in fact.
It comes to me all at once. I remember it from last time.
She'd something to tell me and that's why I'd been invited.
Melody Skyhorse would probably have called it women's
intuition but it was more I noticed how Pippa's fingers have
become plump and bumpy around her platinum wedding
and engagement rings.

'You're pregnant aren't you?' I said and it's a little bit
heartbreaking when she apologises for what she calls the
bad timing and says that she isn't going to let it get in the
way of taking care of me. It's arguably always the role of

the mother to take care of her children because even with cancer treatment lurking I spend the rest of the visit reassuring her that I'll be there for her.

Later that day at my next class only the older women and Mr Gorgeous turn up. He's still coolly standoffish as Jo, her two chums Raquel and Cecile, and I test our new hoops. He doesn't giggle with the rest of us when Theresa hands them over. I'm stupidly excited to have my very own. Mr Gorgeous is wearing tights and to be honest, they're snug and quite distracting. I'm not sure men should ever wear tights. In the week since the last class, I'd lost any ability to keep the hoop up and it clatters to the floor. It's hard not to be disappointed. He of course keeps it on his elegant waist perfectly.

Cecile has the most magnificent bum. It's mesmerising. You could serve tea and scones on top of it. Theresa jokes she shouldn't have any trouble keeping the hoop up.

'Oh yes lady, watch and weep!' Her laugh is loud and saucy and fills the room. She doesn't take offence. I envy how comfortable Cecile is with herself. I think she might be one of those women Melody Skyhorse talks about who honour themselves. Exuberance is a nice quality on some people. Raquel sticks her tongue out a little when she concentrates and has a v-shaped frown of lines on her forehead when she hoops. You can see she's the determined type. I bet she was a prefect at school.

Jo is friendly. In the break, she tells me the three of them have a thing where at the beginning of their new school year in September one would suggest a new challenge for them to do.

'We've done it for years. This was Cecile's idea. Last year it was Raquel's idea to give the Yorkshire three peaks a go. Cecile gave up after Pen-Y-Ghent.'

Jo said she felt she couldn't let Raquel down so she went the whole hog and did the other two as well.

'It was an absolute fucking nightmare' Jo said.

She uses the F word like an ordinary, garden-variety word. They aren't like any teachers I can remember.

The lesson is about recovering a falling hoop and goodness knows, it's a lesson we all need. I don't say it out loud, but in my head I hear myself saying 'I'm fucking sick of picking mine up off the ground'.

'Keep your thighs still, rock your waist and bend your knees just a little bit and speed up!'

Theresa assures us this will bring the hoop back up our body and if we want to give the 'booty bump' a go we could allow the hoop to go a bit lower and swing it around our bum. Cecile has something of an advantage. Eventually, allegedly, we'd be able to move the hoop up and down our body but the clatter of hoop on flooring makes it crystal clear all of us have some way to go with this particular skill.

It's so easy to brood about the things that make us unhappy but we hardly ever spend time figuring out the things that make us happy. It turns out this is one of them. I drop my hoop every ten seconds. My hips get it just right for the smallest moment before they disconnect from the intention in my head and it all goes to pieces. Despite being a million miles away from the booty bump I feel giddy with joy and face-achingly smiley-grateful for it. Melody Skyhorse says we should take care to notice and learn from the feelings and elements of positive experiences rather than let them pass by. I guess the idea is if we notice good times, we can do more to repeat them and reduce the bad times. I suppose it's a bit like going on holiday but back to the same place as last year because you know you can have a nice time there. I'm determined to remember the class, later, when I'm boob-less because I know I'll need all the positive energy I can draw on. I aim to get back to it. Even Mr Gorgeous laughs at the sight of a room full of huffing and puffing, madly wiggling women and I wonder if he's less standoffish and more a bit intimidated by so much oestrogen.

Our school gym teacher used to say, 'horses sweat,

humans glow' and there's a lot of glowing at break but cooling off gives us chance for a chat.

Mr Gorgeous is in rehearsal for a show opening at some festival or other. He'll be working with a gymnast for the performance.

"It's a call and response piece between us. She's a gymnast on a Cyr wheel'.

Theresa says a Cyr wheel is a giant hoop. Mr Gorgeous says he's at the class so he can be ready for his part in the performance.

'I mirror her movements but with the smaller hoop. It's a piece about being gentle and strong, black and white, backwards and forwards, contrast…. You should come and see it'.

When he tells us about it he's passionate and animated and I see a different side to him. It sounds strange and modern. Andy and I went to see The Nutcracker to get a bit of culture. I was bored half to death and the tapping of the hard pointy ballet shoes on the boards was distracting. I didn't mention my reservations but like everyone else, I say it sounds like a must-see show.

Raquel takes charge of the situation.

'Well yes of course we will. I'll arrange transport - are we all in?'

Jo and Cecile nod along with the plan.

Theresa's up for it too 'I'll need to sort a childminder but will definitely come'

I've never been to a festival so I'm not sure what I'm signing up for but caught up in the moment I get the devil in me and tell them to count me in.

Melody Skyhorse says energy has a life force and we can gain or be depleted depending on how we adapt to it. She encourages us to grow from what she calls 'incredible instants' and I feel excited and touched to be included in the plan. I haven't yet told them about the cancer and hope treatment doesn't get in the way of the trip because going feels less like a change of scenery and more about being the kind of person who has adventures.

Mr Gorgeous is called Tony. 'Anton' is his stage name, but his mum calls him Antony he tells us. He's a lovely young man, not standoffish at all. A bit more shy in real life than you might imagine of a performer. I wonder if Matthew and he would get on.

My instincts were right about Jo. She's a warm woman. I don't understand how new friendships work. At my age, single people might be looking for new partners. Death and divorce are a bonus for those dating agencies that advertise on social media and in women's magazines. We used to call them lonely hearts adverts but I guess no one wants to admit to being lonely. People are not usually looking for new friends though. Over time friendships seem to become stable and fixed and not many of us have new-chum-needed vacancies. Even if we did, the effort to make new friends - with all the 'being on best behaviour so they like you' required can feel too much. That might explain why some folk end up collecting cats and stacks of newspapers to fill life gaps instead. Jo's going to become a friend. I liked her a lot at our first class but by the second, when I don't even know her surname, I'm sure.

Melody Skyhorse says women should trust our intuition and feel vibrational energies close to us. The lesson was about self-defence and avoiding muggers by reading our environment and feeling the hair prickles on the back of our neck. She wasn't talking about making new friends but, when we chatted at break, I felt I'd known Jo for years. If we can pick up bad mugger energy it makes sense we can notice a lovely fizz of hitting it off with someone. It's not usually like me but I throw caution to the wind 'Jo do you fancy going for lunch sometime?'

Straight away she tells me about a local pub she knows of which does a fabulous veggie Sunday dinner. She'll book it for two o'clock and see me there. I'm not surprised she's a vegetarian - I suspect most teachers are.

I've been looking forward to lunch with Jo like a teenager going on a date. I order the veggie roast too because I want Jo to get positive vibes from me and don't want beef Wellington to put the kibosh on a friendship before it's even begun. Funnily enough, she apologises to me because she isn't a real veggie - just a flexitarian which I thought was something to do with allergies but she explains it's being veggie off and on. It's about being healthy and reducing the impact on rain forests or some such. The roast has a funny texture for my liking but the Yorkies are fat and delicious and we both tuck in.

'I hope the hula hooping burns this lot off' Jo said grabbing a handful of midriff.

We didn't stop talking for the rest of the afternoon.

Like all new friends getting to know each other, we've loads of material to talk about. She tells me about her recent relationship break up and how awkward it was that her ex was promoted to be her new line manager. I tell her about Angela and how I don't want to see her much anymore. Melody Skyhorse says showing our vulnerabilities is honesty-in-action so starting as I mean to go on, I tell Jo I'm possibly not a very good friend.

I also tell her about Eric.

What's great about Jo is that she doesn't start patting me on the arm or welling up with tears at the mention of the cancer. She carries on tucking into the roasties and asking me questions.

'Breast reconstruction wouldn't be for me either. I would want everyone to see cancer doesn't have to be a killer. Imagine how great it would be if every woman who was diagnosed with breast cancer could see all the survivors just by looking for all the one-breasted women. Thumbs up for the amazon women!'.

Jo's the first person to listen like she's interested rather than afraid. She asks me about my options and we talk about what choices she would make if it were her. I think this is what Melody Skyhorse means when she talks about people being mirrors. It's clever how all this stuff works, once you start thinking of it. Chatting with Jo, I feel more confident about the choices I'm making and it feels good.

I thought amazons were Pygmies but she tells me about Greek mythology and about women who had breasts removed so they could be better archers but we don't dwell long on cancer. It's the first time I feel normal since my appointment with Dr Mhoya. I want to be an amazon woman. Jo tells me I will be and I believe her.

A few days after my lunch with Jo, Andy and I see Dan, the financial advisor recommended by the lottery people. The money has been barely touched because it's hard to know where to start. If you win enough for a new conservatory or a bit of landscaping that's fairly straightforward because you can talk about how long it's taking or how nice it is with neighbours and the like. It's much more complicated when you could buy a small island. You can't talk about that or it sounds like showing off so the money is sitting in the bank… We've paid off the mortgage but we would've done that with Andy's redundancy payment anyway and we only had seven years left so it hardly made a dent. Like Abdul and Jenny, Dan repeats it isn't a lot of money and I wonder how anyone could believe such a thing.

'If you were younger would've advised you to keep working. At your age, if you don't go mad with it, you'll stay reasonably comfortable'.

Dan also advises against buying a big house. He tells us many winners regret it and end up selling at a loss which makes sense because big houses take a lot of cleaning and whatnot.

'Please don't start giving money away because nothing is more certain to bring out the scam merchants and loons.' Dan does not have a positive opinion of people who might be in need.

'Enjoy the money, but don't go spending as if there's no

tomorrow or you could end up regretting it'.

We leave Dan's office assuring him we've no real yearning for a yacht and will most definitely avoid Las Vegas. I'm not sure why we feel the need to reassure him but in any case, we've no idea what on earth we will do with so much money.

On the way home I ask Andy to wait in the car while I nip into the Glowing Girls sportswear shop. I treat myself to some leggings and trainers to wear at my class. I think Dan would agree it was a suitably moderate spend.

It wasn't as intimidating going to the class the third time. We started with the warm-up stretching which had all of us except Mr Gorgeous out of puff before we even began the lesson. Me and Raquel have taken to the step position with one foot back, but Jo and Cecile lean towards standing with their legs side by side - what Theresa calls the parallel position but is just ordinary standing. Same as at the last session she tells me off about my elbows being too low but with everything else going on it's hard to focus on the location of elbows. All of us can just about spin our hoops on demand though only Theresa does it effortlessly. I can spin for at least six circles. Six! Theresa started us off with exercises to help us focus on the hooping points on our body. If we spin to the left, we lock onto the back of the right hip and the front of the left. If we go in the other direction the lock points are reversed.

'Concentrate on the sweet spots and bump the hoop every time it hits that spot' she says. When we can instinctively do this without thoughts getting in the way, we've cracked it.

Raquel pokes her tongue out as she gives it a go but Cecile and me can't find our sweet spots. It's where the hoop touches when it circles the body but it's hard to feel exactly where it is. Theresa grabbed pinches of both of us to show us where she means.

I can't imagine being able to go in the other direction but somehow Cecile manages it and gives out such a yell we all drop our hoops and have to start again.

I don't know how it happens but if one of us messes up, we all do. Theresa says every time we fail, we fail better but once we get it we will just *know*.

'And after that, you can all apply to join a circus' she deadpans.

We all laughed and it carried on after break - when she tried to get us to shimmy and speed.   Shimmy involves putting your arms inside the hoop and penguin wiggling your shoulders. The hoop will travel up and down your body depending on how much speed you manage. When you speed up, the hoop raises, when you slow down it sinks to your hips. Try as she might, Cecile can't do an alternate shoulder jiggle and keeps shrugging them both together at the same time. It doesn't matter what your starting position is, shimmy and speed makes us all look like we are possessed. Poor Jo has to sit down and says she's having a heart attack. I can't remember when I last laughed so hard. Hula hooping is completely bonkers and just about the best thing I've ever done.

I've had my admission date so the group will finish the term without me. Theresa's lovely and says I can carry over my fee and join her next course but not being able to learn with my new chums feels like my first cancer loss. When we went for the nut roast, Jo told me about cancer losses. She said her friend kept a 'cancer loss' jam jar. Every time something bad happened because of the cancer, she wrote it down and put it in the jar. It was her way of noting what had happened but not carrying the loss around with her. When she was told she was all clear, she burned the scraps of paper on a bonfire. I liked the idea. I hadn't told Jo but after our lunch, I started my own jar. I hoped I would get to have a bonfire. Not being able to come to the sessions anymore meant they would go all on without me and be good at it and I would be left behind. I wouldn't even be able to practise.

I wait till the end of the class to say I won't be coming for a while. I don't want to put a downer on the session or give the impression it's all about me but it's right to say something. I avoid the C-word because it always causes that look - halfway between 'bring out your dead' and 'find me cotton wool to wrap you in'. I say mastectomy instead and they all get the picture. Mr Gorgeous - Tony - gives me a hug which is unexpected and lovely.

'Do not, even for a second, get the idea you are bunking off our outing lady. I was born to be on VIP guest lists and I plan for us all to be there'. Cecile's laugh is typically exuberant but there's a soft warmth to her words and I can feel the kindness in them.

Jo says we should all go to the pub. Theresa has to get back because her childminder has essay work to do and a university deadline to meet. Her daughter is the same age as Rose and is called Clover which is a lovely name. I wonder if she has a partner. As everyone is packing up their stuff, she pulls me to one side. I expect her to say something about the cancer. People always want 'a quiet word' to talk about cancer.

'I'll be over in a tick' I tell the others and Jo offers to get me a glass of wine.

They go into the Hope and Ruin carrying their hoops, waving 'see you next week' to Theresa. Theresa tells me she isn't sure she'll be running more classes next term.

'I'm only just covering the costs of the community centre room so I'm not sure it's worth me running more. I'll give you a refund for the classes you can't take'. As she tells me she looks upset and demoralised and it makes me upset too. I gave her a hug and tell her not to be so daft. I wouldn't dream of taking a refund.

Seeing the Sunshine

Notice when joy is in your soul. When we tune into the light, the bounce, the fizz of the essential experience of happiness we are nurtured. In identifying the source of joy we can seek to replicate it in our every day.

Everyday Grace

Making new friends has nudged me into thinking about old ones.

Melody Skyhorse advises to follow our inner voice because apparently we have untapped wisdom there for the taking. Mine must be well hidden because I don't know what to do about Angela. I'm fed up with her but when I mull on it, I don't feel wise, I feel mean.

To be fair she hasn't done anything wrong as such and she isn't different in any way to how she always is. When I told her about the cancer she cried but it was all 'what will I do without you', assuming I would die and this would be bad - for her. It's hard to generate much sympathy. A couple of days later I get a parcel in the post. It's a silicone breast prosthesis complete with a self-adhesive nipple. There's a card, 'Sorry you are poorly, Angela x'. I know she means well but it's a pink horrible thing like one of those spongy stress balls I used to get as a freebie from bleach suppliers. I throw it in the bin.

Angela's loyal in her way but whenever I spend time with her, I come away feeling bad. When she saw the decorated kitchen she said the lampshade was boring but a typical choice for me. I know it's daft being upset about an opinion of a lampshade but I am. Angela has a way of making me feel critical of myself and inadequate next to her, though her life is not one that would suit me. Matthew once suggested she was envious of my life and I shouldn't let it get to me. Angela can't ever be pleased about my new kitchen or holiday in Menorca or even going way back, the birth of my two children. She said Pippa had a flat nose. She does a bit and takes after her dad but it's not what you want to hear over a new baby cot.

Melody Skyhorse says people who 'strike out' do it because they feel unsure of the space they exist in. That makes sense to me because Angela tries so hard to be 'somebody' but I'm not sure she knows who. It pushes people away. Most of us can't meet our own needs so we don't want to have to meet someone else's. The trouble is when she points out my faults she always seems to be a bit happier with herself. I suppose I help her put a bit of light into her life but I wish she didn't have to put me in the shade to get it.

Melody Skyhorse can be contradictory. It's confusing but I'm only a third of the way into the course so I cut myself some slack. She says friends are a mirror and can tell us something about who we are. Apart from the photo of us both in school uniform when we were thirteen, I struggle to see how Angela mirrors me and I'm not sure we are alike. I don't even know if we are friends or, like the crack in a plate you keep using, we've got used to each other being there. On the other hand, Melody Skyhorse says we should have compassion for what she calls 'complex' people but I guess she actually means 'drama queens'. They help us to make sense of our own responses to drama and change how we deal with things. It's all about turning negative energy into positive or some such but Angela could, I'm sure, test the limits of even Melody Skyhorse's transformational powers.

I wonder if we all have an inclination to gravitate to people that don't upset the image we have of ourselves. It's easier not to see different points of view. I can see that for all the moaning I do about Angela, her being in my life supports me in being the one who puts up with her. If she's a pain in the bum, I'm a martyr. Which came first? It's been so much easier for me to imagine it as a one-way street.

According to Melody Skyhorse, everyone has a story

and we might accept other people's stories about us or we can create our own. I suppose it's inevitable that as we link our lives to others we pick up labels and I know mine have always included 'nice' and 'reliable'. Angela calls me 'predictable' and 'boring'. Boring or not, I'm fine with those labels because they are true. The world spins on the trustworthiness of reliability and there are worse labels to have. They may not be words with much swagger but there's light in them. I don't suppose Angela would call herself a pain in the bum. We've known each other for years and yet I can't confidently list any labels she would choose for herself. It makes me sad that I can't.

One of this month's Everyday Grace tasks is to write in our journal a list of the qualities, ambitions and activities of the person I want to be. It's hard to do and I get through nearly a full bar of fruit and nut while I pull it together.

As far as qualities go, maybe I'm a small thinker but I don't think mine need a radical re-haul. Kindness, integrity and optimism will obviously stay. Andy and I have used them as a byword for how we've raised our kids so I'm not going to dump them now, but I wouldn't mind adding a bit of oomph – power, passion, self-confidence? I don't know but sometimes I see other women and they radiate, a bit like Cecile in class. I'd like to have a bit of a shiny glow about me.

The list is about making changes happen - putting steps in place towards becoming the woman I want to be. It isn't just a tick list of silly and unachievable things like wanting to sing like Dolly Parton or become a fighter pilot or whatnot. It has to be a list with inbuilt fizz. It's supposed to make me actually smile as I write it. Mine is a bit frivolous but it does make me smile. I want to be able to hula hoop and play the harmonica but they *are* things I want to do and I want to be brave enough to do them and I shouldn't have to apologise to the universe for my ambitions being on the tame side.

As one of my activities towards becoming the person I

want to be, with the help of a book and a CD, I've already gotten as far as playing 'Good King Wenceslas' on the harmonica - well, most of it anyway. It's a lot harder than such a small instrument should be and the holes are far too close together in my opinion. I'm going to have a go at 'When the Saints Go Marching In' next, despite what Andy thinks.

With statistics being what they are, none of us should expect to be fit as a fiddle for the whole of our lives but we do don't we? We never imagine it can happen to us but when it does we discover life is more complicated than we'd ever thought. I grasp what Melody Skyhorse is getting at. It's all about actively creating a positive focus so we can ride out the difficult times. Spinning the hula hoop is me being brave and frivolous at the same time. I like that version of me, especially going into battle with cancer so I pack my list into my sports bag so I won't forget what I am aiming for.

I suppose it's a bit odd using a sports bag for going to the hospital but I don't need much and the travel suitcase had a feel of long-stay about it. Toiletries, pants, a book, glasses - and my list - and I'm sorted. Also in the bag is a button-fronted nighty for easy access to probing medics. It's hideous. I cry when I roll it up to put it in the bag. Andy pulls me into a bear hug. I drip snot and tears onto his shirt but, heaven knows, it isn't the first time and both of us know it won't be the last. We've talked about it of course. I have cancer. People die of cancer. I might die. Dr Mhoya suggests my chances are good for the best outcome but I suspect she always says this to her patients. It seems unlikely she ever comes right out and tells patients they are buggered. We asked her whether going for private treatment would get better outcomes. Judging by the raised eyebrow we'd surprised her. The treatment would be exactly the same she assures us. The biggest difference for the vast amount of money it would cost seems to be for 100% linen duvet covers in private rooms and meals on china crockery.

Andy and I grew up with the NHS and we trust it, besides, Dad would turn in his grave if he knew we opted out of what he believed was a right his generation fought so hard to get. 'Duvets and bone china?' he'd say 'not worth the invoice they're written on'. He was a fan of Aneurin Bevan. Dr Mhoya didn't push it when we said we would stick with the NHS. I guess she doesn't think we're the sort've people who can afford to go private.

We've written wills. It feels like a grown-up thing to do. I told Andy there'd be no Dignitas hemlock for me - he has to do everything in his power to keep me alive. I have hope. A cancer cure can't be too far away and I want to be ready for it. All considered I love being alive. It's funny how cancer focuses the mind. I've never seen myself as someone who loves her life but, for all its flaws, I do and I want to hang on to it more than I've ever before realised. It's my ambition to stay alive. It's on my list. It wasn't the easiest conversation for Andy and me to have, but we're both the kind of people who like things to be in order. I can see where Pippa gets it from.

At bedtime, the night before I go into hospital and when Andy is having a shower I take off my bra and stand in front of the wardrobe mirror. I've never been topless on a beach. To be , when other women are, I'm always glad of a good paperback to hide behind, and now thongs are all the rage I wonder where it will end. Thanks to Eric I never will be topless on a beach. When I was talking to Jo in the pub the thought of women showing their scars was so empowering. I told her I was going to be one of those Amazon women and we chinked our wine glasses together in a toast 'one-breasted and proud!' I said. In front of my mirror, looking at my paired breasts for the last time I think I probably won't be. Andy comes up behind me smelling all linen clean with his skin damp from the shower. He slides his arms around my waist and we stand together, a familiar and snug fit, just looking into the mirror for a while. I guess we are both saying goodbye to my boob but we don't say the words.

When we get in bed he gives my cancer-free breast a gentle kiss. He doesn't kiss the Eric occupied boob because he says Eric doesn't deserve it. We have a little cry together but it's OK. We're ready for the eviction.

FOCUS

Shade and Light

Challenging times present important opportunities to expand our wisdom, learn about ourselves and others, and open doorways to abundant kindnesses.

Everyday Grace

Generally, I don't expect the world to give me anything which is probably because of my dad who was a 'you sow what you reap' kind of man. For Dad, this was about being a good person. He used to say honesty, kindness and hard work make the world a better place and come back to you in spades. Melody Skyhorse says the same sort of things but calls it aiming for the achievement of karmic balance with the universe. My dad wouldn't have much truck with karmic balance because he wasn't the sort to believe in the universe but they're on the same page. I'm aiming. Before they even put the needle in the back of my hand I've decided to wake up not missing a breast, not having got rid of cancer, but instead *having* a breast, *having* a life, *having* a healthy future. Feeling thoroughly wise is much better than feeling scared.

As I come round from the operation I'm still a bit drug addled so I struggle with the buttons trying to open my nighty to show Andy the neat bandage pad. Our eyes are drawn to the drain out of the space which once homed the now evicted Eric.

'If only we still smoked - that would be a perfect place to rest the ashtray in bed'.

He always knows how to make me smile. I love Andy so much.

The ward staff like you to be up and about quickly. Dr Mhoya put some kind of special anaesthetic in when she operated so it wouldn't hurt when I woke up and, to be fair, it doesn't as much as I expected it to. I smell a bit like I'm sweating gin. At the ward round, surrounded by fawning acolytes she fills me in with how it's gone.

'I was able to leave the muscle on your chest wall but had to nip out the lymph glands which looked a little iffy. We may need to take more. We'll schedule radiotherapy to sweep up any cells that have made a break for your bloodstream'.

The white-coated junior doctors hang on her every word, nodding like poodle puppies, eager to please.

'The patient declined a reconstruction' she tells the baby docs. My lack of gratitude was obvious in her tone. I can see their uncertainty about how best to respond. They think it's a test.

'Because of her age?' offers one young man.

'Why is that relevant' asks a young woman who looks to me to be twelve years old.

'Are you being sexist?' she adds crisply. I thought that too so would've liked to see him be allowed to answer but Dr Mhoya said they had lots of beds to visit and should discuss it further at their case meeting.

They swarmed off to another bed further down the ward so I never got the chance to ask any more about the lymph glands. I imagine cancer cells are like angry wasps after their nest has been stick-poked and it's not a comforting image because I'm as scared of wasps as I am of cancer. I don't see the point in wasps. Nazis of the insect world. I wonder if chopping it out is the same as poking it with a stick.

Shortly after Dr Mhoya, a nurse came over to fill me in on the detail doctors don't bother with.

'We'll have you out of here in a couple of days' She says. 'Your drain will be removed by a district nurse. Most of the stitches will dissolve on their own but she'll snip out the ones holding the drain in place. The nurse says I'll be given painkillers to take home, to expect to be sore, and take it easy until my two-week follow-up appointment. It's all very efficient and not what I expected. I thought I might at least get a bit of bed rest, but they don't allow this anymore because it costs too much and causes thromboses. I wonder if private patients get to stay longer and check out when they feel ready, like in a hotel.

When they tell me it's time to go home I leave the ward in a transport wheelchair and Andy's allowed to bring the car right up to the door. He helps me get into the car because the seat seems so high and the doorway gap so small. I can't fold myself in and he has to lift each of my legs, one at a time into the footwell. I'm sat too far forward in the seat but however hard I try to slide back my drain pulls. It's exhausting. I can't plug the seatbelt in one-handed so Andy helps but the black strap falls right across where my breast used to be and it hurts so much. I cry with great heaving snotty sobs and even the high-vis jacket-wearing parking warden gives us a few moments. I guess he sees it all the time.

Pippa and Rose are waiting when we get home. Christopher is in Chicago. Pippa cries as she clings onto Rose who is overly interested in my drain tube and Rose starts crying too because she wants me to play. I want to tell Pippa not to cry and it will be alright but Melody Skyhorse is big on allowing the expression of grief without jumping in and offering advice because of our own inability to cope with distress. The truth is, I'm not coping with their distress and I'm not coping with mine. I just want to sleep for a while and wish they hadn't come.

Pippa is noticeably pregnant. She has a lovely gently rounded swell of belly and I throw a hope out into the universe that with Eric evicted I can be here when the baby's born. They've decided on names already.

'We've decided on Garvey if it's a boy and Ruby for a girl. Christopher wants a boy of course'.

I've never heard the name Garvey as a first name and think it's a bit showy but that's Pippa's way sometimes. Pippa has never heard of the political activist and I've never heard of the pop star so we have a confusing conversation about inspiration. She plays me a track by the pop person's band on her phone which is lovely.

I'm not sure why Christopher wants a boy 'of course'. Pippa says it isn't sexist to want a boy, it is about having one of each, the different experiences of raising a boy and getting to choose cute baby jeans instead of dresses. I'm not sure baby clothes choices are the real story. I am too tired to argue about it. Melody Skyhorse says dishonesty causes little fissures of distrust between people whereas being truthful can be fraught but worth it in the long run. It makes complete sense but where Pippa is concerned, I leave the gender choice fissures ajar. At the best of times she's easily irked if she believes anyone has expectations of her. She'll always reject advice regardless of how it's given or whether it's good advice. I've come to realise it's best to let Pippa follow her own path because she gets to her right place eventually. You can't force trust. Still, it makes me sad my beautiful girl seems to think her sex isn't 'heir' good enough.

Andy offers to make us all a cup of tea. He avoids joining in because as much as he adores Rose, I think he's quite keen to have a grandson.

The tea in the hospital was British Rail strength with a whiff of plastic beaker about it. My first cuppa at home is nectar. Pippa nudges me to have a Bourbon but two-layer biscuits are too much of an effort. Andy entertains Rose on the new garden slide. Pippa used to show off during her pregnancy with Rose. 'Never had morning sickness, and I positively glowed' she'd tell people as if it was a personal achievement. She doesn't glow now. Christopher is off negotiating contracts, as per, and I can't lift so much as a kettle to help. As she gets ready to leave I tell her to take care of herself and rest but she snorts it is me who needs to rest. 'Pregnancy is not an illness mother' she scalds but the words sound like something she has heard on TV. I notice how swollen her ankles are.

It's funny that in those first few days after the operation I spend so much time reassuring others about how well I am. Cancer seems to terrify. Everyone has a response to it, none of it positive and mostly they want to avoid it with euphemism or are keen to move on. They tell me how I've beaten 'the big C' and how I'm now on the road to recovery. I notice how few people actually use the word 'cancer' and I guess this is because they associate it with death. They want *me* to think I'm a survivor but they have some doubts I will be and are hedging their bets. Even at the hospital people tell me how to manage my wound but the nurses and doctors insist I must have a positive mental attitude and won't let me talk about the possibility of death. 'There's no reason to consider your cancer might become terminal at this point' Dr Mhoya said but the fact is, I *am* considering it might be terminal and I want to be able to talk about it without having to reassure everyone else.

When I leave the hospital every man and their dog ask to come and see me. Andy's done a sterling job of keeping people at bay with explanations of tiredness. The house looks like a funeral parlour there are so many flowers. It's stifling. Kieran and Donna brought an organic frittata round which was practical and delicious and we haven't seen any rats for a while so all is well on the neighbour front.

Jo doesn't need me to reassure her.

'Are you scared you're going to die?' She asks. 'I'd be scared shitless'.

Jo's a breath of fresh air and I'm so glad to see her. I know it's her way of asking how I'm doing. It's unbelievably refreshing to not feel a need to say the right things or protect her from terrors about Nazi cancer wasps breeding in my cells.

'I keep having a nightmare about being buried alive and trying to claw my way out of the coffin' I tell her.

'That would play havoc with your manicure' she says. 'You should tell Andy to chuck a mobile phone in with you just in case'. We talk about dying and end up laughing. I'm not sure how it is that talking about cancer and death can still lead to a lovely afternoon but it does.

It turns out Jo's been diagnosed with type two diabetes 'Because I'm a lard arse!' she laughs but the laugh has a hollow ring to it. She's been for an eye test and all's well so far vision-wise but she has problems with her feet being numb. Jo is undeniably a well-padded woman but I'm shocked when she tells me she has food issues.

'Binge eating disorder they call it. No one would ever tell an anorexic all they need to do is eat a pie and yet everyone is always telling me to eat less and exercise more. If it was that simple I'd be a supermodel.' She laughs again but the laugh never reaches her eyes.

'If you're an alcoholic you can at least stop drinking and stand a chance of getting better. It's so much harder being a food addict because I can't stop eating can I?'

I feel bad about Andy having brought the chocolate eclairs out with the coffee.

It just goes to show, you never can tell what is going on for other people. I tell Jo when we first met she looked so comfortable with herself I wanted to be like her. She tells me she thought I looked scary and I laugh so much my boob drain tugs. I've never been described as scary before and I like it. I tell her I'm a bit terrified and she says she is too. Fear's easier to manage when you're not alone.

Jo fills me in on news from the class. Everyone can keep their hoops up and they've even walked around the room while they kept them spinning. Raquel can walk around and turn in the other direction without losing the spin, which is impressive. They're working on moving the hoops up and down their bodies and we laugh about how both Jo and Cecile will manage given their shapes and the distance it has to travel on Cecile. Jo talks about their boobs getting in the way but it isn't even a little bit awkward. She hasn't forgotten my missing breast and she's not labouring a point. It's good to be having ordinary conversations because since leaving hospital I've felt nothing but awful. Jo's visit is a tonic. Mr Gorgeous, as we still call Tony, is as anticipated on day one, the star of the class. 'He looks so elegant'. There isn't a jot of envy in Jo's admiration. She says she's so proud of him and I know exactly what she means.

Strangely, after I got out of hospital, I stopped caring about getting better. I don't mean I wanted to be ill. I felt as if I had absolutely no say in what was going to happen, one way or the other, so there was no point in staying positive. I wouldn't say I was depressed but giving energy to most things seemed like a waste of time. I felt like my battery was flat. Andy, on the other hand, was like a cat on a hot tin roof. He was trying to stay upbeat and positive but I could see he was coiled spring tight. By the time my first post-op appointment came around, he'd started to be snappy. I didn't take it personally but I couldn't seem to find the energy to help either. Neither of us were sleeping well. It wasn't like us at all.

I'd been careful to keep the dressing as dry as possible and there'd been no sign of weeping. So, the first time we see the actual scar is at my first post-operative appointment with Dr Mhoya. The nurse peels back the dressing and it nips. I hold my breath and watch Andy. His face barely changed but the line of tension that had been living on his forehead since we were at Pippa's disappeared so I know he's going to be OK and so am I.

When I look down I see three or four spidery stitches where the drain is fixed, a couple of steri-strips and some greenish-brown bruising. It smells of antiseptic. At first, it's confusing because it looks as if she's left some of my breast but Dr Mhoya says it's swelling which will go down over time. There's a dark red scratch line going down from my armpit to the middle of my chest. It looks healthy and tidy and I remember the Amazon women Jo told me about. I can live with being an Amazon.

We ring both the kids to tell them so far so good. Because Matthew is so far away we video call him.

It's a bit weird when Matthew asks if he can see the scar. He was breastfed but we didn't walk around naked in our house so it is a peculiar boundary test and it messes with my head. I tell him I'll call him back after I've thought about it but, in a way, that made it more weird. With hindsight, I should've just lifted my t-shirt but you live and learn. So anyway, I call him back and lift my t-shirt. I don't have a dressing on because Dr Mhoya said it would heal better if I allowed air to get to it. She advised wearing a soft crop top type bra for my other breast but in the house I don't bother. The mostly dissolved stitches are still a bit itchy.

Matthew has a look of his dad. I see his relief at my absent breast site and my relief at his relief makes the weirdness of the moment go away. I lean in towards the laptop camera so he can get a good look at the scar while holding the t-shirt over my non-corralled floppy boob. I've no intention of flashing that on screen because that *would* be weird.

'It's tidy Mum. I thought it would be horrible but it's neat'. We have a bit of a laugh about Dr Mhoya's fabulous needlework skills and that she could make patchwork quilts for a hobby if she ever got fed up with lopping off boobs. I assure him it doesn't hurt. Matthew asks how his dad is doing and it takes me by surprise because it strikes me it's the first time anyone has asked how Andy is.

'Perhaps you could have a man-to-man chat with him to check' I suggest to Matthew and it's a funny little moment because I haven't asked him to help in a grown-up way before though he hasn't been my little boy for a long time. It's time I learned more about the man he's become. Cancer is all kinds of teacher if you let it be and I'm surprised to realise, that's my thought, not Melody Skyhorse's.

It turns out Yuuto's mum in Japan has had a double mastectomy. She's sent me a message which Yuuto says roughly translates to mean 'two heads create wisdom'. I realise it's her way of saying we share a special kind of knowing about what's happening. She doesn't speak English and I don't speak Japanese so I don't imagine we are going to be friends but I'm touched by her message of support to me via her boy. Melody Skyhorse talks about ideas, actions and thoughts never being stand-alone but instead being like the ripples of a stone thrown into a still pond and I figured out what she means. Cancer has given me a connection to Yuuto and his mum that would never have been there otherwise. In a peculiar way, it's lovely. I ask him to send her my love and thanks.

Matthew and I chat for a bit longer about nothing important but after the scar showing I feel closer to him than I have for a long time. Intimacy creates trust I suppose and that too ripples. When we come to the end of our video call Yuuto appears in view, behind Matthew with his arm casually draped over my boy's shoulder. They have a physical ease with each other which has been obvious to me for a long time but they've never been so comfortable showing me it before. I'm so glad. I guess the message from Yuuto's mum means she knows they're a couple too. I want to ask how long he's been out to his parents but I don't want to spoil the moment for any of us so I don't. We blow kisses goodbye and I call his dad to come to the laptop and speak to his son. They speak for ages.

Forgiveness

Do not identify with suffering. Compassion is our greatest healer and brings happiness, wellbeing and love into our heart.

Everyday Grace

Melody Skyhorse says our journal is a sacred site for reflection, gratitude and love so I don't think we are supposed to write about how bad we feel but it seems like a good place to off-load. I don't want to burden Andy. He's putting a brave face on it and keeping his own counsel but I know he's worried. Everyone has something to say about survival because cancer focuses the mind on how lovely it is to be alive but most of us keep thoughts of death to ourselves. Andy and I will have the 'worst-case scenario' chat about cremation or burial at some point (for the record: cremation. I can't be doing with the thought of worms). We're not putting it off so much as trying not to binge on the awfulness of putting stuff in order. We agreed from the off that difficult discussions are better out than in and we've lived by that. I must put him right as well about the afterlife thing and tell him I won't haunt him if he gets another wife. I wish I'd never joked about it now. I need to set his mind at rest, just in case. I'll make sure he knows it's OK to find someone else if I pop my clogs but, in all honesty, I'm not sure I mean it. I'm not sure whether Melody Skyhorse would call that an authentic reflection or not loving enough. I can hardly bear thinking of him going on without me.

Before the operation, you get so many leaflets telling you how to prepare you could wallpaper a bathroom with them. Advice about the kind of toiletries to use, when to bathe, clothing to wear - I guess Pippa read that one because she bought me leggings and a loose top. Loungewear she called them but in my, they're just fancy pyjamas. They even gave me one on how to have sex. I read them all because it's hard not to feel greedy for anything that might get me closer to not dying. One of the leaflets said something about 'challenges' but that's the kind of word I associate with traipsing across the arctic for charity or having to learn how to use a guide dog. Having a breast removed is, at the end of the day, just an operation and I fully intended to be back on my feet in no time. So, I never thought about it as a challenge. Only, it turns out, it is. I feel terrible.

It's like being halfway between crying and kicking something hard, not that I could kick anything. Even my coffee mug feels heavy and going to the toilet is an effort. The tiredness is not like anything I've ever known. The dressings nurse advised it was the drugs leaving my body. I wish they would get a move on. I can barely hold a conversation before I drift off and yesterday I told Andy we should get a cat and I'm allergic to cat hair so where that came from, heaven knows. I'm all over the place. I smell bad too, chemical and sour.

When I look down, the pyjama top has a space where my boob should be. I remember what Jo said about Amazons and how a missing breast 'changes the narrative of being victims' because it shows us all we can survive cancer. I can see how that is a good thing but I don't like the space. I feel like a stranger to myself. The shape of me is different. I know I'm no supermodel but I liked my body how it was before because it did the job. I knew how to hang clothes on it, how to pull my tummy in when walking to the pool on holiday, and which bits Andy especially likes. It's only one breast, and I have another but so much more seems to have gone with it. Andy says it doesn't matter to him and I'm still beautiful which is nice but the thing is, I want it to matter. It matters to me! I feel ugly. I feel horrible. The leaflet says we should take sex after surgery slowly. Whatever Andy says about me being gorgeous, I can't ever imagine having sex again.

Melody Skyhorse says to properly heal you need to forgive whatever it is that has hurt you which sounds great in theory but I'm not sure how to *do* forgiveness. Thinking you forgive something is like saying you're going to go on a diet. Full of feel-good promise but actually doing it is a different kettle of fish. Given how rubbish I'd been feeling since the op I could've done without my efforts to forgive being so well and truly tested.

It was a shock when they rang and I wasn't prepared for it. He chatted as if we were friends which threw me.

'Wendy, hello! So good to talk to you. I am so very sorry to hear about you having cancer that must be awful but I guess your lottery win has given you something to look forward to. How will you be cheering yourself up?'

He spoke so quickly with a bounce in his voice like a radio DJ. I hardly had time to think, 'erm no … sorry, who is that?'

When he said he was a journalist I didn't know what to do so I put the phone down but that day the local Courier ran the news story anyway.

'*Local Family Lottery Fortune Tragedy*'

I wonder why it is newspapers are so fond of house prices and labels. According to the Courier, our house is worth a lot more than we thought. They've added a hint that as an ex-council cleaner and lorry driver we've done well for ourselves but I'm certainly not 65. Blooming cheek! Last week the headline news was that local youth had set fire to the community centre bin shed. You can see why the win and cancer together were more interesting to write about. They took an awful picture from Pippa's Instagram page I think because it's cropped out of one of her wedding photos. I'm wearing The Dress. Both Andy and I have those wedding photo rictus grins which you have to hold for ages while the camera person fiddles around with settings and such. I supposed it could've been worse and been one of the holiday pictures of us around the pool, holding porn star martinis. I wouldn't have wanted to be in the paper in my swimming costume - not that I want to be in the paper at all.

The thing is, we weren't being secretive about either the money or the cancer but I do think we should be able to decide who we tell and when. I don't know why so many young people want to be famous. The news story went with the angle of comparing the so-called tragedy of the cancer with the 'amazing' good fortune of the win. It ended by saying we were planning a luxury holiday to celebrate my 'all clear' which he made up because I certainly never said such a thing.

Only a few hours after the paper came out we had all kinds of phone calls, including someone from the local TV news, but Andy said 'no comment' like they do on those crime dramas and put the phone down. Donna popped round with a marrow which was nice but she doesn't mention the Courier or our win at all and just says she hopes we're glad she has sorted the rat problem and is sorry I'm poorly.

'Maybe a hot tub would be a nice way to get better' she says.

Perhaps that's what she would buy if she came into money. I wouldn't spend a lot of money to sit in water till you wrinkle like a prune but each to their own.

Someone once wrote 'the devil is in the detail' and that's how I know Angela is behind it. There were five people in the room when I told the silly story about thinking I'd won 78 thousand pounds. The journalist makes Andy and I sound like we're a sandwich short of a picnic when he re-tells it. Pippa would never talk to the press, especially not the Courier, and obviously Rose didn't. When you take Andy and me out of the picture, that leaves Angela.

According to Melody Skyhorse it's important we don't think of ourselves as victims because this makes us focus on how cross and upset we are about something. As I understand it, we're supposed to try to work out how the thing that upset us came about and forgive with compassion so we can't be hurt by it anymore. I can't work out why Angela would betray us and can only think it is because she wishes she won the money. I feel so angry with her I can't even say how angry I am. If I put it into actual words I am scared it will turn into the kind of horrible words you can't take back. I'll aim to forgive her though I'm not sure I can, but I can forgive and be compassionate to me. I'm not going to let myself fall into a swamp of being livid because it will harm me more than her. The Courier story couldn't have come at a worse time. Angela knows about the cancer but not about how terrible I've been feeling recently. I don't need to add anger to it too. She hasn't asked but to be fair, I haven't told her either. My dad used to say, 'once bitten, twice shy'. She won't get the chance again. Enough is enough. We're done.

We get quite a trickle of letters and cards hand-delivered through our letter-box in the days following the newspaper article. At first it's something of a novelty. Lots of them are kind and friendly. We have a few nice get well soon messages from people living in our avenue who we don't have much to do with, apart from Christmas cards. I can't remember if Robert and Helen live at 26 or 50 but it was nice of them to send a helium balloon. I guessed the 'congratulations!' message was about the win rather than cancer. We get a hat-trick of sympathy from the local priest, vicar and rabbi offering support if we need it. I've never heard from any of them before. The vicar throws in a reminder about the church roof repair fund so it's hard not to be cynical. Five days after the story ran, Marcus the postie dragged five big sacks out of his van and up the path.

'Next time you sell your story, give us some notice so I can go on leave' he said, sweating as he dragged the last of the bags to our front door.

We read all the letters which might not have been the best idea but when someone's poured their heart out explaining their problems it didn't seem right not to. It must be hard asking strangers for money and you can't blame people for trying. There was a lot of pain in those letters - and a few that went straight in the bin. Andy and I won't be financing the search for extra-terrestrials within the Labour Party any time soon. The insurance lacking surfer in a coma needing air transport home from Thailand pulls on my heart-strings. Poor boy. His parents must be worried sick. Jesus and pets feature in a lot of the letters. The dogs needing expensive operations are the most difficult and I have to hand these over to Andy to deal with. I'm not, in all honesty, sure about the merits of doggy wheelchairs.

Pippa said we should put them all straight in the bin unread but it's a good job we didn't. Cecile had sent a parcel of spices and a card.

'*At home, we say there's no ailment or woe this dish can't salve*', the card said. The spices are golden yellow and pungent, their perfume conjures up thoughts of tropical beaches and palm trees. She's sent a family recipe for Seychelles fish curry. Fish curry is a bit adventurous for us. The card says 'sorry you won't be back at class for a while. We'll miss you', which is so nice. It's a bit of an unusual present I suppose but personal and touching, especially as I hardly know her really. Raquel and Theresa chipped in and sent two lovely eco-friendly scented candles in the same parcel. They were from somewhere called Jade's Precious Crystal Sanctuary, one pecan waffle, the other vanilla bean. I'm not sure what the difference is between an ordinary candle and an eco one but they smell heavenly. I've never had such an exotic parcel. We also got a card from the big win chap in Burnley. He'd bought his local pub and invited us over for a pint and a gastro meal 'on the house' so that was nice.

At the end of the last of the bags of letters, we decide Pippa was right and we wouldn't be reading anymore. Strangely, they'd helped lift me a bit, even the sad ones gave me something other than my missing boob to focus on. Andy and I decided we would focus our charitable giving in one place to simplify things. You would think cancer support would be the first thing to come to mind but I'm fed up of thinking about the disease and they focus a lot on death for obvious reasons. I've already had flyers from them about will writing. In the end, thinking about how Matthew was bullied, we set up a standing order for the local young people's LGBTQ group. If the money can stop one young person from going through what he did, it will be money well spent.

I'd forgotten she was coming and was nearly rude to her when I heard the knock at the door. She had to show me her ID lanyard before I'd let her in. She was very understanding and said she wished more people asked for ID. 'People are far too trusting these days' she said.

The dressings' nurse is one of those cuddly, down to earth types it's easy to be undressed in front of in my living room. If she's read the Courier story she doesn't let on. She traces my scar with her finger, gently and stops for a closer look at the drain site. She says everything is as it should be with no signs of infections which is good news. I try to do one of those grateful nods but she isn't fooled.

'You don't have to put a brave face on with me pet. It's important you get to know your scar so you know if things aren't right with it'. I cry when she points out how well it's healing. She tells me to take a breath and with a snip of a single stitch takes the hideous drain out. It doesn't hurt and she covers the hole with a tiny dressing. There are some dark marks that look like car crash bruising but she says it's the iodine they use in the op and it will go as soon as I have a shower. I'm dying for a shower. She gives me some exercises to do which she says will help me get my shoulder movement back and keep my chest muscles strong. I'm not sure why I need strong chest muscles but I don't ask. I've to roll my shoulders forward and back three times a day which is a bit like the penguin shoulders move at class. It will help with the blues as well, she says.

'It's common to feel down after a mastectomy. Have you

thought about joining one of the breast cancer survivor support groups? You can feel isolated after the op and other women who have gone through the same as you are the best source of advice and support'.

She hands me a leaflet.

'It was helpful to me after my mastectomy'.

She must've seen me looking at her chest because I had no idea. I thought the pink ribbon broach was just part of her job. There are no spaces in her jumper where a boob should be.

'Reconstruction'. She tells me.

It makes me remember what Jo said about invisibility. I'm not sure I'm ready to chat to complete strangers and I am sick to death of thinking about cancer and wondering why it decided to choose me but she was on the nose about feeling isolated. I crave non-cancer normal where I can ignore operations and tumours and scars. Melody Skyhorse says healing requires us to be empowered in our suffering. I guess she means don't pander to it by letting bad thoughts rule our lives so, after the nurse leaves, I ring Jo and invite her round. She says she'll bring buns.

Anchor Vitality

The power to live and grow to your optimum capacity depends upon your ability to focus. Be present to your innate, essential wisdom to choose your best path.

Everyday Grace

It's still a bit of a challenge travelling in a car because the seatbelt sits exactly where I least want it to. Seatbelts are not designed for women with breasts but they don't work too well for one-breasted women either. I promise to hold onto it instead of clipping in and Jo promises not to crash while I'm unclipped. Andy agreed with Jo that going back to the class, even if just to watch, is a good idea. Truth be told, I guess it's Andy's way of getting me to stop practising the harmonica - there is only so much he can take.

The stairs up to our attic practice room are hard work and I can't say the creative writing class students look pleased to see us as we pass them making a brew in the kitchen. Sharing the space with noisier than ideal bedfellows is the nature of community centres I expect. I bet they wish the Wednesday knitters had our slot.

'Write beautiful words people!' Cecile gives the scribes a friendly hello and wide smile as she passes them on the stairs. I wonder if they think she's being cheeky but hopefully, they can hear the warmth in her tone. It's the way she is. She's jazzed up her hoop with silver and gold tape. It looks fabulous. Mine's at home. During the session, I work at being Melody Skyhorse 'mindfully present in the moment'. I think she means enjoying the moment without wanting it to be something else but it's hard not to feel grumpy I can't join in.

Jo's lost a bit of weight. I noticed it when she came round but it's more obvious when she isn't wearing a jumper. She's looking well despite having caught nits off the kids at school. An occupational hazard apparently. She says it's the first exercise class she's ever enjoyed. Cecile has mastered how to move the hoop from shoulders to hip and up again on repeat. When I was watching online videos about hooping techniques, almost all the girls are stick thin but watching shapely Cecile is a joy. She looks beautiful. I thought about suggesting she posted some videos of herself as an inspiration but didn't in case she thought I was being pervy about her or implying she's fat. I remember when the assistant at the shoe shop touched my toes a moment over-long and said people would pay to see what he called my gorgeous feet. I suspect he was in the job of his dreams. I've never been in the shop since.

Raquel can talk while she hoops and doesn't get out of breath. She has a lovely back and forth technique and looks all poised and elegant. The way she holds her arms is so purposeful as if she could have a martini in one hand and an old-fashioned cigarette holder in the other. I always imagine she looks like a headmistress but she isn't a teacher as it turns out. She's a finance manager. She said hanging around with teachers, along with the risk of nits, is another occupational hazard she's had to learn to live with.

Theresa's taking the group through a lift-up which she says is a classic and simple but impressive hoop move. She makes it look as effortless as waving at a friend across a street. It involves raising the spinning hoop up the body, right up the arm and catching it in the hand.

'It's important to catch it at the bottom of the hoop and not the top' she says.

She might as well not have bothered with the instructions because everyone is terrible at it and I have to protect my chest from flying hoops. Jo's might have left a little dint in the wall. I heard the creative writers leave early.

I'm sad and glad to be at the class, all at the same time. Cancer takes away the positives of looking forward to anything much. The other day, Andy said he would give every penny of the lottery win back if we could go back to the day before we got it, when I didn't have cancer - or at least, we didn't know I had it. Having cancer is lonely and it's not money that helps. People do. I'm sad I'm behind with the moves but ever so glad to be back with the gang.

After class, when we go to the pub, the creative writers are in the pub garden before us. They've found the best spot to catch the spring sunshine. We say hello but they don't look friendly. I faff about what to have because of all the drugs I'm on. Cecile says 'one glass of wine won't kill you'. Everybody agrees and it's a nice moment. None of them are making a big deal of me being one breast less. It's so lovely to be able to laugh. I think, what the heck, what's the worst that can happen and if that isn't being mindfully in the moment I don't know what is. I only have a single glass of wine but I'm a bit squiffy when Jo drops me back off at home.

The next day, at the clinic, I have to have a blood test and I hope the alcohol doesn't show me up as being irresponsible about my recovery. Dr Mhoya makes clear she thinks I am irresponsible and doesn't even mention blood alcohol levels. She's of the opinion my reservations about chemotherapy are foolhardy and speaks to me very slowly as if I'm dim.

'At your age and considering there was some evidence of cancer cells in your lymph nodes, I strongly suggest at least four cycles of treatment'.

She says 'strongly suggest' like it's more of a diktat than a suggestion.

With hindsight, I'm not sure telling her I just didn't fancy it was the best way to explain my thinking because it sent her eyebrows skyward. She wasn't unkind and I know she's trying to do her best for me. I don't feel easy about the idea of chemo. I know some people swear by it but my intuition screams that poisoning myself will do me no favours in the longer term. It might kill the cancer but how much of me will it kill too? Andy's less sure and says he would try cutting his leg off if there was even a chance it might do something to make sure I survive. We agree survival is an absolute goal but isn't life about more than simply existing? I want to enjoy it too and being horribly toxic on the off chance it might give me a bit longer on the planet pushes all the wrong buttons. Melody Skyhorse is big on the idea that we have to trust ourselves to be our own guides. I think intuition trusting should be taught in schools. After all my years on the planet, for the first time I am trying to do exactly that and I think she is right. I agree to have hormone therapy. I'm not sure that's the right choice either but intuition is about probabilities rather than certainties. Agreeing to hormone therapy and telling her I'll think about chemo calms Dr Mhoya's dancing eyebrows down from her hairline so we all leave the meeting feeling like we got somewhere. Andy does look worried though. No one has given him any leaflets and I wonder why. He's going through it as much as I am.

Almost as soon as we stepped through our front door when we got home the phone rang. Matthew's taken to calling a lot more often than he used to. I don't know if it's because he's getting some time in with me just in case the worst happens, or whether it's easier now he doesn't have to hide his life from me. Whichever it is, it's lovely. I assume he is ringing about the clinic appointment but he doesn't mention it and is waffly and vague.

One of the strange things about having a lot of money is that people are embarrassed about it. Thanks to the Courier everyone knows we had the big win but except for the letter writers, most people avoid raising it. When Matthew was a child he had no problem asking for a raise of his pocket money so you would think asking his millionaire parents now he's an adult would be easy. Because he was waffling about cash flow and speculation it took me longer than it should have to cotton on that Matthew had a point to make but eventually I catch on and interrupt him

'How much do you need?'

Dan, the lottery man, advised us to keep our capital fixed

in a safe but sure investment that would give us a decent monthly income. 'Avoid dot com' he said but Matthew says the internet is still a growth area. It's funny when experts have such different views but at the end of the day, Matthew is family. I guess Dan would say listening to family is a bad investment idea but, to be honest, I didn't give Dan a hundred per cent of my attention. If he was really good at his job he'd be living off his own investments on a private Caribbean island so I didn't pay too much mind. I went with my heart and Matthew.

Matthew and Yuuto have what he calls a 'side hustle' which I think is what we would call a second job outside their proper one.

'We were looking for something to help us prepare for applying for dual citizenship but there was hardly anything out there so we made an app' he says. I'm out of my comfort zone when he talks about artificial intelligence, bots and user interfaces but I know what apps are and he and Yuuto have developed one in their spare time.

'It has real potential Mum' he tells me.

'Think of bots as digital bees that gather information pollen. The app will pull it all together and create a tailored, focussed list of possible questions for a citizenship test anywhere in the world'

Their app will help people know if they are likely to pass or what to study to make sure they do.

'Making the app was easy Mum, it's getting people to download it that'll be the challenge. Once they use it, we know it'll get traction because people will tell others about it'.

He's as excited about it as he was about his first games console. Matthew and Yuuto have been working on its development for a while and it's almost ready to launch. Getting it noticed is where the effort and money needs to go next. They've invested the money we've already given them but extra will allow the launch to be bigger and help the app take off.

'We can give you money Matthew or lend you it if you'd rather' I tell him but he says he isn't looking for handouts. 'It's an investment Mum and we're confident it will build a healthy return for you'. We're barely making a dent in the capital so I'm not sure it needs building. I told him I'd talk to his dad and get back to them but I know we'll help out. After all, he and Pippa will get all of the money one day.

Not long after we end the call Pippa turns up. There doesn't have to be any particular reason for Pippa to visit but there usually is. Before she's even taken Rose out of her pram Pippa wants to talk about what she calls my 'falling out' with Angela. Angela's been in touch with her and from the sounds of it, moaning that I am being unfair.

'You can't know for sure it was her Mum. It could've been anyone going to the papers. Maybe one of those new friends you are always on about lately'. She raises her fingers to do the air comma thing when she says 'friends'. I wonder what she would think if I told her at least two of them have nits.

Angela and Pippa have a peculiar relationship. They don't always get on but Pippa has known Angela all her life and shared history creates strong, if sometimes elastic, bonds.

Once Pippa reached six years old and developed her own mind, she stopped calling Angela Aunty. She wasn't a proper Aunty of course but she's the nearest thing I had to a sister. It has an ear missing now but Pippa still has the Steiff teddy bear Angela bought her. Matthew didn't stop calling her Aunty until he was 18. Angela said it made her feel ancient and asked him not to.

I don't expect the kids to take sides in my issues with Angela and I'm glad Pippa cares enough to defend her. To keep the peace, I tell Pippa I'll ponder on ringing Angela but I know I'm not going to.

I can't help but notice there's something not right about Pippa. I'm not sure what but there's no pregnancy glow about her. She looks tired and just the effort of the Angela conversation seems to have taken more energy than she had to give. I test the waters by telling her about Matthew and Yuuto's app and she says the right words but there's little interest. She hasn't asked about my hospital appointment either. When I ask her how she's doing she says she's fine but, when I offer her some cheese and onion pie for lunch she gets cross with me about how unhealthy it is and how I should know better.

'For goodness sake mother, anyone would think you are actively trying to kill yourself but please do not try to take Rose and me with you!'

It's all a bit out of proportion for a bit of white flour and dairy.

I wish Christopher was at home more.

VIBRATION

Manifest

The universe is always listening. Positivity creates beneficial rewards, the more we ask, the more bountiful gifts the universe will deliver.

Everyday Grace

I only really think of places like Chatsworth being famous houses so I've been looking forward to going to one, albeit not so grand, just off our by-pass. Raquel said the TV series followed a group of people with dreadlocks and Staffie dogs on string leads who chipped in and bought land to self-build six eco homes. Theresa and Wolf, her partner, were one of the couples building. None of the group were builders but they were working together and sharing skills. At the end of the series, two of the wood-framed houses were finished and Raquel said they looked 'jolly charming if somewhat rustic'. Raquel had been invited too but a line dancing clash and the call of the cowboy hustle won out.

When we arrive, I can see what Raquel means. We park in a building yard in front of a house with a bright yellow painted door and grass on the roof. When Theresa invites us in and I introduce her to Andy she gives him a big hug which throws him. We both realise at about the same time he needn't have worn his smart trousers. Wolf has dreadlocks but he and Theresa don't have a dog.

Theresa and Wolf's house is a bit of a mishmash of batik and bean bags. It has all the essentials - windows, electricity and plumbing but it's short on interior walls and is a long way from finished. The shared gardens at the back are a delight and full to the brim of things growing but all in together, with courgettes and dill right next to citrus smelling roses and buddleia. When Wolf offers to show us the gardens we say we would love to because you can't really say no.

'Mixing it up keeps a healthy bug life' he explains. 'Would you like some French beans to take home? We've a glut and you can have too much of a good thing.'

Theresa said that two of the original self-builders left after some kind of acrimony about whether the group were a collective or something more anarchic. From what they said, I think Wolf and Theresa wanted a house to live in rather than political world overthrow *per se* so they seemed glad the anarchists left. Theresa said it was a shame as they'd taken their building and astrology skills away, though I don't understand why star reading is as important as the loss of power tools.

'Motivation went out the window once the arguments started. The ecosystem of the whole project became unbalanced and building work has stalled' she says. It sounded exactly like something Melody Skyhorse would say and I imagine she might live in a place a bit like this, only posher, with walls.

As they show us around the garden Theresa tells us when it was a patch of land, she, Wolf and their daughter Clover lived in Wolf's van, parked in the same spot their house now stands. It must've been hard caring for a baby in a van. Their house was the third to be occupied and despite being unfinished, it's toasty warm thanks to hay insulation. I've never heard of hay as a building material. It sounds a bit itchy but there's no smell of the barnyard about it. I don't know if Andy's being polite but he and Wolf get into a conversation about bale needles and load-bearing and other boring stuff so Theresa and I leave them to it and join the other guests. I thought Andy had been invited for my benefit but wonder if it was to give Wolf a bit of male company. Andy's never fazed by meeting new people.

Theresa gives me a chair which, I must admit, I prefer to the idea of the beanbags, and I sit next to Jinx in hers. Jinx is their friend and babysitter. She's doing a PhD in something I didn't grasp. Jo explains it's related to maths but it still goes over my head. Jinx is a bit scary and severe-looking which is odd for a babysitter and it's hard to read someone who wears mirrored glasses. I don't know if I warm to her or not. Her purple hair is spectacular though. Theresa and Jo sit on the floor cushions. Clover, Theresa and Wolf's daughter climbs onto Wolf's knee when he and Andy come over to join us.

Usually for the first half an hour of any dinner party guests work out how to get in a flow with each other. There's always a sense of 'what now?' until ice is broken - or the wine - kicks in. Maybe it's the impact of floor cushions that stops that happening because I feel completely at home since we took our coats off. Jo helps bring stuff from the kitchen and plonks it down on a large pine table. Theresa says 'help yourself' so we all do.

To the best of my knowledge, I've never eaten vegan food in my life but it's delicious!

'Malay curry. All the veg we grew ourselves except the mushrooms. We haven't cracked mushroom growing yet. We aren't those preachy types but we do think it's better not to eat bits of animals. I'm surprised you still do given all the carcinogens in meat'.

If I'm really honest it did sound a bit preachy. Theresa says the curry's creamy because of coconut milk and that's a revelation because when the chap on the beach macheted the top off a coconut and stuck a straw in it on holiday it was disgusting. I tell them about the spices Cecile sent as a get-well gift and Theresa tells me about the healing power of turmeric being well known. It wasn't to me but it made me realise how extra thoughtful the gift was. I'm surprised to see Clover tucking in. She's the same age as Rose and there's no way Pippa would ever give her curry though when you think about it, I'm sure people in India do it all the time.

'She's eaten the same as us since she came off the breast. I can't be doing with all that pureeing malarkey'.

Pippa never breastfed. Theresa's idea of mothering would scare Pippa half to death.

It is all a bit hit and miss. No table and no serviettes and we eat off non-matching plates on our knees. Andy has thirds. When we were invited to supper I thought there'd be olives and oil to dip bread in, but it's not a bit like that. There's no pudding either but Theresa says she has some dope brownies if we fancy one. I almost fall off my chair. Jo says she can't because she's driving and I also turn one down because we don't do drugs but Jo laughs out loud 'I'd make a bet you've have more high-grade NHS opiates lately than anyone else in the room!' I suppose she has a point. It's all relative.

Theresa shows us pictures of when she was a trapeze artist with the famous circus, travelling all over Europe. She's twenty feet off the ground dressed as a jewelled, spangly blue sea creature and is doing the splits between two ribbons wrapped around her ankles. She looks breathtaking. I had no idea.

'We met on tour' Wolf says. 'I was crew. We'd been just about to take the show to Hangzhou when Theresa realised she was pregnant'. The beaming smile on his face as he tells us makes it obvious that he wasn't remotely disappointed about having to pull out of the tour. Theresa clearly feels the same 'Clover's the best thing to have ever happened to me. The money we earned helped us buy the land for this place. It's a shame it ran out though!'

Wolf brings us some camomile tea. He seems like a lovely man and he's done the cooking. Obviously, Andy cooks but only for us. Never for guests. When I think about it, I'm not sure why because neither of us are the kinds of people who think women belong in the kitchen. I certainly don't - he's a better cook than me anyway.

Because of Wolf's thin tatty dreadlocks, I thought he might smell a bit grubby but he doesn't at all. I'm not sure, however hard they try, white boys can carry off dreadlocks though I'm not sure if we're allowed to say that. Andy looks unexpectedly at home on a bean bag and it's good to see him and Wolf getting on like a house on fire. Why the weight-bearing capacity of lintels is so interesting I'm not sure but I suppose work gives men something to talk about. I don't think it's polite friendly either. Andy does look genuinely interested when

Wolf shows him the half-built internal wall next to the kitchen. I thought it was meant to be a decorative feature but it's just unfinished.

Clover hasn't been put to bed. She drags over a cushion and comes and sits in front of a wood-burning stove which looks like an old oil drum too rustic to be safe and I'm glad it doesn't need to be on. Personally, I wouldn't have flames around hay walls but then, I wouldn't have bean bags either.

'Read this one Jinx'. Clover holds up a book with a Cat in a Hat on the cover. Jinx is surprisingly nimbler than I am at getting off her chair but then she's younger and her chair has leverage arms.

'My feet are in my shoes Jinx and I'm ready to go'. The little girl says and both of them giggle. When Jinx giggles she doesn't look so unapproachable.

'Where are we going today Clover?' Clover snuggles into Jinx's lap and they open the book.

'I love that story!' Jo says and joins them both on the floor. It's a proper book that doesn't make a noise when it's opened.

I know children develop at different paces but she seems self-assured compared to Rose.

Theresa tells me she's tried to make the finances work but can't. She won't be running the classes next term.

'I want to but the community centre isn't available'.

We both wonder if the creative writers might have complained. Jo overhears.

'Could we book our school hall? I'm sure Raquel could sort us a deal. We had a Taekwondo group use it last term'.

Jo goes back to Jinx, Clover and her book. Theresa looks downcast.

'I just don't have the funds to lay out in advance for a full term. I might not get enough sign up to cover it so…'.

Theresa shrugs her shoulders. I suggest a big publicity drive might bring more people in.

'I can't afford that either. It's chicken and egg'.

When we leave, Wolf offers us each a brownie to take home and Andy said we would have one! I'm convinced we'll be stopped by the police and Jo can't stop laughing.

'Did you *never* have a misspent youth? You're so funny Wendy'.

She teases me but it's different to when Angela does it because it makes me feel liked, not judged. I laugh along with her but I'll be keeping an eye out for police cars all the same.

'You don't need to get a cab Jinx'. I say, 'we can get the chair in our car.'

Jo leaps in and says that hers being a hatchback is better for loading but she isn't looking me in the eye so I can see there's more to it than avoidance of paint scratches on the bodywork.

Jinx is far cooler than Jo and not at all flappy but I'm unconvinced by the casual

'Oh thanks Wendy but Jo's is closer to mine so …'

There's a definite little spark between them and it's obvious as Jo helps Jinx into the front seat of her car and starts to fold the wheelchair.

Jo catches me looking and gets so flustered she struggles to get the chair to fold. She gives me a 'stop it' glare and we both grin. She knows I won't be letting this drop when I next see her.

We had such a lovely evening, even without a table and whatnot.

When we get home Andy and I throw caution to the wind and share the brownie. Apart from sleeping well I never noticed anything which was a disappointment. When we get up I tell Andy we should get some buy veggie sausages for tea.

I've not been able to stop thinking about how deflated

Theresa looked when we discussed the classes not going ahead. Melody Skyhorse says that if a decision needs to be made we can use magic to help. At first, I thought she meant reading tea leaves or the like but she says magic is 'the accumulated wisdom available from within our tribe'. It took me a while to cotton on that she just means 'ask people' though to be fair, I think she means ask the right people the right questions. When I mention my idea about helping Theresa with her chicken and egg conundrum, Andy, as supportive as always gives it proper time. He listens carefully, asks a lot of questions and tells me it's worth exploring if I want to go for it. He would tell me if he thinks it's a bonkers idea.

'You should speak to Pippa. Get her opinion'. We both laugh because if there's one thing we can be sure of, Pippa will always have an opinion. Melody Skyhorse says important decisions need to be informed by different perspectives so I ring and ask if it's OK to pop round.

Pippa's right about freshly ground beans. The grinder rumbles and the kitchen smells like buttery toast. The coffee's delicious and worth savouring but her intuition is faultless. She wipes the bean dust from the kitchen work surface and sits down opposite me, waiting for me to explain my visit.

With hindsight, I could probably have been a bit clearer in my thinking about investing but I'm not sure being clearer would have made much difference.

'You are going to do *what* Mother?'

Pippa calls me mother like an exclamation point. 'What does Dad have to say about all this?'

If she hadn't inherited her dad's unusually long toes, I could imagine she'd been swapped in the maternity hospital. Neither me nor her dad have ever given her any reason to think my decision making can only be trusted if it's supported by him. I've never deferred to Andy because I've never needed to, so I don't know where she gets her ideas from. Probably those glossy magazines she reads.

'It's a small investment and even if it doesn't make any money, I won't lose much. It's low risk. Could you be excited about it?'

Pippa is not of a mind to be excited.

'You have to be careful not to let those weirdos you are hanging around with take advantage of you. It's a well-known fact cancer messes with your hormones and at your age it must be worse. No wonder you're foggy.'

Pippa thinks I should know better than to trust strangers and give them money. Mostly she focuses on my allegedly menopause/cancer addled thinking rather than the investment potential of hula hooping. Rose comes over for a cuddle. I reach into my handbag and pass her the ten-hole harmonica. As she sucks and blows it makes a satisfying racket.

I told Pippa about Dan the investment advisor and how Matthew had helped me work out what was important.

Dan advised Andy and me to put money into investment bonds. He chatted away about 'terms' and 'premiums' and 'capital growth' and I switched off. I wonder if he thought I was too thick to understand it but I'm not, it's just that what he seemed to find fascinating, I found quite boring. He told us it was important to be conscious of the gains and risks before we invested. It sounded like a right faff and I was of a mind to leave it in the savings account and spend it as we felt like but he didn't share that opinion.

'You need to make the money work for you' he said.

Dan's idea of making it work is about using the money to make a lot more money and avoiding anything that might make a loss. I understand where Dan's coming from but Melody Skyhorse says enjoying the bounty of life can be a singular activity but bounty shared leads to infinite joy. I don't tell Pippa about Melody Skyhorse's contribution to my pondering but I do tell her about how her grandma used to say, "sharing is caring" which is along the same lines.

'We could have just given Matthew a chunk of money - we would hardly have noticed a dint in the capital but he didn't want hand-outs - he wanted support'.

I tell Pippa that Andy and I have thought it through. For us, 'making money work' isn't about giving it away or necessarily making more money but about how and where we invest. We want it to make a difference and we want to spend money in happy ways.

'Well go on holiday then like normal people!' she says.

Although Pippa went off on one, it was helpful which I knew it would be and why I asked her. I'd been contemplating what else I could do to share the bounty in a way that didn't involve sensible but dull offshore bonds. Pippa might sometimes have a sharp tongue but she has a sharp mind too. Something else she gets from her dad. All the reasons she could see for not investing in hooping gave me bullet points for thinking it through for myself. She thought of a lot but one, in particular, hit a nerve.

'You can't buy friends Mum'

She wasn't being cruel but we both grasped that was a bullet point needing unpicking. After she put Rose down for her afternoon nap, she made another coffee and brought out the biscuits.

The money's scared Pippa.

'I'm not being funny Mum but you and Dad are just ordinary people. I don't know who you are as millionaires. I wish we could all just go back to like you used to be before you won the money'.

To keep the peace, I don't say I think her fear is more about the cancer than being millionaires but I do think that. Pippa says she's worried we'll be exploited. Drawing on 'the tone' she uses for Rose when she puts her on the naughty step she says we should listen to the experts rather than spend money willy-nilly. She's happy about me supporting Matthew because her opinion is family should come first, but my fledgeling idea about financially supporting the hoop class falls into the willy-nilly class of daft.

'You hardly know these people Mum and how will you

ever get a return on an investment in a hula hoop class?'

Pippa manages to combine 'frustrated and impatiently intolerant' with 'sad and disappointed at her tragic parent' into one single look when I tell her 'I guess it all depends on what is meant by a 'return'. The hula hoop class has been one of the best things I've ever done in my life'.

One of the things Pippa could be happy about was our plans to buy a new car. She suggested one of the same type her footballer neighbour owns - he has three; sporty for him, tank with child seats for her and cheap and cheerful for their nanny. I don't know why any UK urban car needs bull bars but both his and hers have them.

'We're open to all options so long as it has an inbuilt sat-nav and heated seats.' I told her. To me a car is a car. If it goes and doesn't ever break down on the motorway, it's perfect. I don't want something which draws attention or has gadgets and gizmos I'll never be able to learn how to use. I still don't know where the fog lights are on the one we have now.

We've never owned a brand-new car so when we go shopping we make the most of the day. Sharif, the salesperson, is a lovely young man and very attentive. I wonder if he's seen us in the Courier but Andy says I shouldn't be so cynical and maybe he's just good at his job. He lets us take two out for test drives. One of the cars is a huge all-terrain thing and will be a beggar to find parking for, the other looks like a giant bug. They both have the sat nav I want though. We decide to buy the new model Skoda which may not be as fancy but ticks all the right boxes. Sharif pushed to sell us something a bit more swanky so we chose the special edition metallic blue paintwork. In the end, we're all happy.

To celebrate buying a brand-new car we go to Carlito's for pizza - on a Wednesday afternoon! It is such a lovely sunny day we even sit outside. Apart from holidays, we've never dined out on a Wednesday afternoon. I wonder if this is what it's like for film stars and famous people. Carlito's calzone is to die for.

Andy is licking the spoon of the last of his tiramisu when my phone rings. As soon as I see Donna's number I know something's wrong. For some reason, my first thought is that her chickens have died. It's odd how the mind works. I think most people have the number for the next-door neighbour but on the odd occasion we need to be in touch we text. We save chatting for emergencies like when they locked themselves out. We were away in the Lake District and she wanted to ask if it was OK for Kieran to climb on our extension roof to get in through their bathroom window.

When someone starts a phone call by apologising closely followed by 'but' it's never going to be a positive call. I struggle to make sense of what Donna's saying. She can waffle on at the best of times but says she's rung the police and a locksmith on account of our house having been burgled.

I've no idea why I rang Abdul the validator chap from the lottery but he'd said we should ring him with problems so I did. He comes straight away, which is nice of him, but once he gets to our house I'm not sure what I expect him to do.

'I'm sorry to say this is not the first time this has happened'.

While I'm with Abdul, Andy lets the constable out of the front door. She gives a cheery 'bye' as she leaves which in the circumstances seems to me to be a bit over jolly but she's young. She smiles at the man from the Courier standing at our gate pointing a camera. How do they hear so quickly? I can see some of our neighbours are out too. Everyone notices a police car in their street. The policewoman wasn't over sympathetic. She handed me a photocopied leaflet about what to do next. Both she and Abdul give the vague impression the burglary is our fault because of us being in the paper. I'd half a mind to go out and give the man from the paper lurking by our gate a few choice words but Andy says he's just doing his job.

Abdul scans the room and lifts a cushion from the floor. He puts it back on the sofa which is kind of him, I'm sure it's not his job to tidy up. He places the cushion so I can see the zip but I try not to fret about it because there are plenty more important things to worry about than cushion orientation. He reiterates what PC Carmichael had already told us - we should photograph everything for our insurers. No one else will be coming from the police because, from their perspective, it's 'just' a burglary. There will be no fingerprinting or anything but she'll have a chat with our neighbours.

'It's not exactly CSI Crime Scene' PC Carmichael laughed but I was expecting some sort of investigation and not just a crime reference number. I'm not sure laughing at our burglary is professional either. It seems heartless but maybe police people get hardened to awfulness.

Abdul tells us about one of the first big lottery winners. They went to get their cheque presented at a posh hotel in London. It was going to be handed out by some game show host who I can't recall but apparently they were chuffed to bits to be meeting him. The next day, when they got home, not a stick of furniture was left in their home.

'Everything gone, Granddad's war medals, photographs, furniture, kettle - everything. It'd been picked clean'.

Abdul says the burglary was devastating enough but the lack of sympathy on the grounds they could afford anything they wanted to buy was what hurt them the most.

'They bought a fortress of a place with high walls and an electric gate. They said they would never trust anyone again. It was terribly sad'.

We didn't have much of value to take and, if I'm honest, not much is out of place, the burglar was a bit half-hearted. A few drawers and cupboards opened and turned out. A panel was kicked out of the back door and they crawled in. I'm guessing it was an opportunist rather than a proper criminal. I had a little tin box with a few bits of jewellery. My mam's wedding and engagement rings are gone. They aren't worth much and I never even wore them but it feels like I've let Mam down. I'm not sure what else has gone but as Abdul leaves, I thank him for his advice and assure him I'd remember to note everything down and try going round pawnbrokers. I didn't know there was still such a thing as pawnbrokers.

I was glad when Abdul said he wouldn't stay for a cup of tea. I want to try to get the house back to normal but I doubt it will ever feel the same again. I know what those other lottery winners meant. The burglary boils down to Angela. Was it Oscar Wilde who said the bitterness of old friends is worse because they know how to hurt? Anyone would imagine finding out about cancer is the worst thing that could happen but maybe they've never had strangers forcing their way in, poking about in private spaces. Burglary is a lot like cancer in that regard. Our lovely home feels poisoned and it hurts more than Eric ever could.

Melody Skyhorse is big on the power of positive thinking to bring back balance and a positive upward forward trajectory. Back in the day, we used to dance to a song 'the only way is up' and everyone used to thump the air on 'up'. Andy always missed the beat and thumped half a beat behind. We used to laugh and pretend argue about where was the proper place to punch the air but we both agreed that 'up' was the place to aim for.

As soon as Abdul leaves and trying to think positively. I get on the phone and book people in to come and sort alarms and such. It's never entered my head to have an alarm but the house feels like an unfamiliar place. I have to give it a proper deep clean to get every last bit of the burglars out. The bedside tables had to go because that's where my jewellery tin had been. The thought of them being in my bedroom touching things was so bad I told Andy we had to sleep in the spare room until the alarm's fitted. At first, I want to change our bed, the carpets - everything, maybe even the whole house, but Andy said getting rid of things we like is a bit daft.

113

Wolf came round to help Andy fix the back door. Theresa sent a rolled-up bunch of dried sage with instructions for a cleansing ritual called 'smudging'. We lit it till it smouldered and as instructed, wafted it around each room saying 'I cleanse my home of negativity' but in all honesty, my heart wasn't in it. Sage smells like a sock bonfire when it's burned so we'd to open the windows.

In the end, we decide to splash out a bit on brand new fitted wardrobes. Freshen the bedroom up with something the burglar had never touched.

After the burglary, I've been mulling about positive thinking and the only way being up. Melody Skyhorse says we're responsible for how our lives are and capable of creating the life we want to have by proving it every day by our actions. It was one of the things that used to put me off about her lessons. I am not responsible for cancer. I didn't choose to win the lottery - or be burgled. I misunderstood what she was getting at. Life happens, but how we respond to it is our choice. It took me a while to cotton on. George Michael used to wear a t-shirt that said, 'choose life' and I've decided, I will.

Choose Life

*How we navigate our life journey is up to us. We might
choose the safe, easy and predictable route but the
unknown path presents untold opportunities for
excitement, exhilaration, learning and creativity.*

Everyday Grace

We're on the VIP guestlist for Tony's show. I've never been
a VIP in my life! Raquel arranged a communal purse and
we've all put sixty quid in it. Theresa's skint – no one minds
subbing her and there's no fuss about it. Theresa doesn't
make a song and dance of it either which is nice. She'll
reciprocate when she can. I bet Melody Skyhorse would like
Theresa's style.

Going to Leeds is exactly what the doctor ordered and
Raquel's planning hadn't anticipated me dying before we
got there. Cecile insists we travel first class on the train
which I wouldn't have even thought of even though I
could've afforded a limousine for all of us - though that
would never have occurred to me either. From the minute
Andy drops me at the station and the five of us set off we
have such a laugh. Even though it's daytime and we're on a
train I allow myself a red wine when the trolley comes
round. Raquel pays for it out of the communal purse. I
thought you only got those cute singleton bottles on 'planes.
There's a vicar in the carriage with us. Judging by his
frequent sighs as he tries to read his Telegraph he's not
happy to be sharing it. To be fair, it probably didn't help
when Cecile offered to buy him a drink to cheer him up. I
had doubts about the train but Raquel took charge of getting
us here. She's something of a woman of the world and says
parking in Leeds is impossible during Pride weekend.

Raquel booked us into a lovely flat above a pub which
has a paved terrace. It's stylish with rugs and chrome

gadgets. It has one of those coffee makers with a steam spout to make froth. I expect the flat seems even nicer when it smells of fresh coffee. It's a shame we only bought a jar of instant with us. I take some photos to send Pippa because I know she'd love it but decide not to send them in case they make her grumpy about my trip again. She says it's too soon to be exerting myself, though I keep telling her the doctor says I am fine and I feel it. I wish she'd come with us.

The owner shows us around and says we're welcome in his pub downstairs anytime but it's not a hen party sort've place. Jo and Theresa laugh but I've no idea what the joke is given we aren't a hen party. They serve breakfasts from 10 am daily if we fancy it. He says there's no call for earlier breakfasts but if we are either early risers or not-go-to-bed-ers there are plenty of places where breakfast can be had.

The girls let me have the single room on the grounds of me being in recovery which makes me sound like an alcoholic. What with the scar and everything I'm glad of a space of my own though I feel a bit of a fraud. Cecile and Jo take one twin room whilst Theresa and Raquel take the other.

After our host leaves, we sit outside on the terrace. Cecile pops open a bottle of Prosecco and Raquel raises a toast to the end of their school term. On the terrace below ours, two portly men wearing leather trousers chink glasses of their own and have a lingering snog which is something else to tell Andy about.

The next morning after breakfast we set off for the parade. I'm not sure what I expected the Pride parade to be but I've never been a part of anything like it in my life. There are great waves of people as far as the eye can see in every direction. Thousands of people and rainbow flags everywhere being waved and worn and hung from windows. On the side of the road there is a queue of lorries, busses and trucks waiting to start the parade. Each is bedecked with all sorts from DJ's and discos to people dressed as snowflakes handing out bottles of iced tea. About three floats down from where we are I see an open-top bus with most of the cast of the soap opera Angela loves.

'I didn't know they're gay!' I say to Jo.

'They're allies' she says. 'Like you'.

I've never thought about myself as an ally but I suppose there's a big difference between passive and active support. I like that Jo considers me an ally so I suppose there's more to being a friend as well. I'm determined to be a deliberate ally from now on.

There's a fire engine painted in rainbow colours. I'm not sure whether the men dancing on top of it are actual firemen or one of those male stripper groups. They have very little on so I expect they're glad it's such a gloriously hot day. They're ever so handsome and I am not the only one who thinks so judging by the whoops and hollers from the crowd every time one of them wiggles his bum to the music coming out of their cab. The atmosphere is so bouncy. It feels as if I'm inside a great big lovely, happy laugh. People of every description are bopping around to music blasting from the huge tinsel covered speakers on almost all of the lorries waiting to start the parade.

The noise is all mixed up and bouncing off the walls of the shops on either side of the street but it isn't hard on the ears. I can feel it pulsing in my chest like a heartbeat. People on one lorry are handing out what I think are sweets so I take some from a person in a huge yellow wig who says, 'have fun you saucy minx!' and blows me a kiss. It turns out they're condoms so I feel a bit daft.

There's a float with topless women drumming. Along the side of the lorry, a draped banner says 'Aysgarth Amazons'. I guess they wouldn't be topless if they minded people staring but I do stare because at least two of them have missing breasts.

Drag queens in the highest of heels are shaking buckets and walking around the crowd. I've no idea how they can walk in the shoes but they look incredibly glamorous and most of them have much better legs than me. I see one person holding a placard that says 'Jesus had two Dads' and Jo runs over and kisses a woman holding one end of a street-spanning 'Queer Teachers' banner.

'Is that someone from your school?' I ask.

'Never seen her before in my life' Jo says.

A group of Morris dancers wearing sashes that say 'Fish City Dykes: Hull' wave ribbons and throw themselves about. They're accompanied by a woman with a shaved head playing 'The Girls I left Behind' on a fiddle. I didn't know there were lesbian Morris dancers.

Raquel goes over to a stall at the side of the road and buys a multi-coloured face paint stick. She swipes rainbows over all our cheeks. Jo buys us all whistles but I wish she hadn't because I'm not a fan. Whistles hurt my ears; I don't know how dogs cope. Another stall is selling t-shirts. Jo buys one she says is a 'classic'. It says 'dip me in honey and throw me to the lesbians' and right there in front of everyone she just whips her top off and swaps it for the new one. Some of the t-shirts are extremely rude and, in my opinion, not suitable for wearing but there's one that says, 'proud of my gay son'. I want to buy it but don't. I wish Matthew was with me at Pride. I don't know if he has ever been to a Pride festival. Imagine not knowing that? I haven't been much of an ally to my son.

I've no idea what the signal was but the lorries set off on a slow crawl and the crowd give out a cheer that can probably be heard all over the county. Like a swarm, people start following the float convoy in a blur of colour and noise and joy. There is so much joy you can taste it in the air. It tastes like candy floss. We walk alongside a samba band and everyone nearby is bouncing along in step to the drumming. Raquel starts a little line dance move to it and dozens of people join in. I see a tv crew filming us and give a little wave but the camerawoman pans to an old lady on a mobility scooter. The sign attached to the front says 'queer before it was fashionable'.

'Isn't this FANTASTIC!' I shout towards Jo, smiling so

much my face hurts.

'Yes, it's great but it used to be a demo against homophobia. They call it a celebration now so it's every man and his dog. The gay politics ripped right out of it but hey, times change'.

Jo's on school holidays and needing a break from being a teacher but I don't really understand what she means. Melody Skyhorse has this thing about maps. She says we tend to get stuck on our life maps and we feel safe on them because our life is known and predictable. She encourages Graces to step off our path and try a strange one, or someone else's because un-walked paths open all kinds of doors to what she calls 'new vistas'. I think she means different points of view are good for us. When we get home, I'm going to ask Jo to explain. If I am going to be an ally I owe it to Matthew to learn about his map. I've expected him to live on mine and his dad's path all this time.

We walk, stop and start, for miles. I've no idea what the various hold-ups are but in a way, it doesn't matter because each time we stop a party starts. People lining the streets cheer and wave flags. We pass one group with nasty banners about sin and damnation but instead of being nasty back, when we pass, everyone blows kisses at them and shouts 'we love you' which is nice and I join in. I drop the condoms I still have in my hand into their donation bucket.

My feet are throbbing when Jo says it's the end of the parade. I don't know how she knows because the crowd is still dancing and moving but most of the floats are out of sight and there's a run on the beer tent at the side of the road. Jo's sweating cobs and fanning herself with a corner of Cecile's rainbow flag. We sit in a row on a kerb drinking extortionately expensive cans of pop from a burger stall. I assume we'll all make our way back to the hotel but Jo says the party's only just started. Raquel offers to take me back to our accommodation which is kind but I suspect she wants a bit of a rest herself. She's a bit glum when I want to stay. Theresa offers to go and get us all a falafel wrap as an energy boost. I'd prefer a burger but she has youth on her side and can cope with queuing. The wrap is delicious as it turns out.

'What do you call two teachers, a one-breasted woman, an acrobat and a finance worker sat on a kerb surrounded by rubbish?' Cecile asks. Raquel joins in

'I don't know, what *do* you call two teachers, a one-breasted woman, an acrobat and a finance worker sat on a kerb surrounded by rubbish?

'Fuckin marvellous!' Jo shouts at the top of her voice and we all dissolve into a fit of giggles.

We plan to have a gentle pub crawl on the way back to the flat and maybe drop into our host's place but every single venue is rammed to capacity and neither my aching feet or chest wall can cope. We buy a couple of bottles of supermarket wine and sit in a park near a duck pond. Swigging wine out of the bottle in a town centre park sounds like a slippery slope but it's lovely. The sun's setting and turning the sky pinky blue, it's July warm and loads of people are doing the same. We plonk ourselves down on the grass next to a group of men. One is playing the guitar and another has a hand drum. Cecile joins them for a song and gets a massive round of applause. A couple of hula hoopers are showing their moves alongside someone juggling. There's something of a rustle going on in bushes with lots of people coming and going. I assume they're having a wee but Jo gives me a look, laughs and says I've lived a sheltered life. When I catch on I must admit, I'm a bit shocked. One person asks if we're interested in buying drugs but is good-natured when we decline and wishes us a happy pride. Mostly though, people are just laid on the grass enjoying the perfect evening.

We get back to the flat quite late. Theresa isn't with us. She'd hooked up with Tony and his theatre friends and said she'd see us in the morning.

I thought going to Pride was just a run-up to Tony's show but it's the best thing I've ever done in my whole life.

The next day we rest up and Jo and I spend a lovely afternoon on our balcony. I'm not comfortable with the word yet but Jo says queer watching does her soul good and it does mine too. There are a great many beautiful people when you take the time to look.

In the evening we join the queue outside a huge marquee. I'd expected Tony's show to be in a proper theatre so the tent's a surprise. It's in a fenced enclosure filled with smaller tents and stalls selling beer and food. Theresa calls it a pop-up festival venue which is exciting because I've never been to one before. It is a weekend of more firsts than I could ever have imagined. There's a cocktail bar in a red van that has a birdcage top. A glamorous girl on a swing is inside it. I am not sure what she's doing other than looking lovely. Tables are filled with people and all I can hear is sparkle.

Raquel walks to the head of the queue and talks to an alarming looking woman guarding the red rope hooked across the tent entrance. I see Raquel pointing towards me as she talks. The woman in huge platform shoes and a purple beehive hairdo stares at me. It turns out that despite the skull tattoo on her neck she's lovely and not a bit scary. She's Welsh. She moves the rope back so we don't have to stand in line and walks us all to one of the booths which edge the venue. She tells us her mum is a breast cancer survivor too which I guess is what Raquel was telling her about. Getting into the venue early and without queuing even though I don't have a stick or a wheelchair like some of the others she has shown in, is a bit of a cancer bonus. I admire Raquel even more than I already did because she's the kind of woman who isn't afraid to take charge.

I'm in the most incredible place I've ever seen and it's a tent! It's much bigger than it looks from the outside. It's all mirrored with draped red velvet brocade and stained glass and looks like I imagine a 1930's Berlin salon might. It's not like any tent I've ever seen before and it's disorientating. It reminds me of Dr Who's Tardis.

We have a perfect view of the stage. As people start pouring in and taking seats Tony appears in a flurry of hand waving and hyper-chattering about rehearsals going wrong and loving Theresa for being a great teacher. It's hard to keep up with what he is saying. He hugs me a bit too tight so it hurts my scar but I try not to let on. He's lathered in make-up with red cat eye contact lenses, blue lips and the longest eyelashes I've ever seen. His costume is plain pale pink, all-in-one, long-johns. Dry ice smoke begins to fill the tent, the lights dim and the audience settle. Tony plants a kiss on all of us, says he will see us after the show and disappears behind a black curtain next to the stage as a drum roll is sounded.

It's fair to say the show isn't like any cabaret I've ever seen before. An old lady, who I only later realise is a man raps to '*it's a long way to Tipperary*'. When Jo said she's peed herself I'm not sure if she's joking because I know some women do. It's the funniest act I've ever seen and I wonder how actors make these things up.

Next two beautiful young men, climb out of a bath of water and do a saucy acrobat routine involving trapeze swings hung from the top of the tent. Drops of water fly all over the place and into the crowd but no one seems to mind. Later a man with a monkey puppet over his naked genitals does a strange ventriloquist act. It was a very naughty monkey. Some people get up to go to the bar when Anton and Delice, or Tony and Denice as we know them, are introduced by the MC. I wish our teachers would step in and tell everyone to sit down and be quiet, which I know is silly. I think some people imagine dance will be boring but the noisy room becomes still and quiet once they start their performance. Tony has a small hoop like the ones we use in class, but Denice, wearing the same make-up and a blue onesie, has the biggest hoop I've ever seen. It is at least five foot tall.

Denice, standing inside the ring, makes it spin on the stage. It twirls around in movements which are balletic and

122

delicate despite the size of the massive metal Cyr wheel.

'Can you do that?' I ask.

'I taught her' Theresa says.

Tony mirrors Denice but his movements with the smaller hoop are bold, thrusting and masculine in contrast. Each of them moves separately and so differently through the dry ice mist but it's as if they are joined together. The routine looks like love feels. It's mesmerising. For the finale, Denice spins around and around inside the ring faster and faster on a tiny spot on the stage while Tony moves his hoop around his waist with his arms reaching in prayer to the sky. The guitarist slaps the body of his guitar with a loud bang and each hoop falls to the floor. The tent explodes with applause and I'm so proud I could burst into tears. Cecile, Raquel, Theresa and Jo are hollering and clapping so energetically I have to cross my arms to stop my body from jiggling.

We're invited to a party in the tent after the show and we have such a marvellous time and dance till late. Tony and Denice are as good at moving off stage as they were as Anton and Delice on stage. Denice, it turns out, is Tony's partner so he isn't gay after all. I probably need to go back to Melody Skyhorse's lesson on making assumptions and how they help us hide behind our versions of reality.

Jo does an enthusiastic version of the bump with a girl who has two-tone hair and a bustle. She's a fire-eating act which explains why she smells a little bit of paraffin. She swallows swords too. I wonder how anyone discovers they have either talent or ambition for such a thing.

Gloria Gaynor is blasting out of the speakers and as I sing along, I have never in my entire life felt more determined to survive.

When we gather at the table for a mid-tune rest Tony says our hula hoop group should do a show with him and Denice at the Brighton Fringe festival next year. Egged on by one or two spritzers we all think this is a marvellous idea.

'I'll sort somewhere to stay!' As usual, Raquel is on it

and says she'll liaise with Tony about finding a venue.

'I can sort getting us into the official programme!' Cecile chips in closely followed by Jo's new chum who says if we want a fire eater she's in too. We have such a giggle planning our ridiculously fanciful hula hoop spectacular as if it was a real thing.

I know my shoulder is going to end up aching like mad but I don't care. I dance and dance and dance like no one is watching which is something Melody Skyhorse says we should do but I've never understood what she meant before.

When we get back to our flat, I see I've missed a call from Andy but it's too late to ring him back. I'm going to tell him he needs to come to Pride next year. I go to sleep trying to work out how I can explain the genital monkey ventriloquism to him.

As soon as we wake up sorting the flat and getting packed up is a priority so I leave ringing Andy until we've had breakfast in the pub downstairs. I can't face a full English.

When I ring he picks up straight away. Pippa has lost the baby.

Change and Growth

Like the seasons, change comes unbidden but inevitable.
Do you huddle up indoors or dance in the cold of the
snow? As a small seed can break through frost crusted
earth, you too can grow from the myriad opportunity
change offers.

Everyday Grace

It's odd that sometimes the days seem so short that you can't
fit everything in and yet they can seem endless when you're
counting down to a holiday or something nice. When people
say time is relative I don't understand what it's relative to
but the journey home seems to take forever. Andy came to
get me and I'm glad to be in the car. I wouldn't have wanted
to put a dampener on the train journey back. We can't
discuss very much because Rose is in the car seat. Children
have such finely tuned antennas for atmospheres. I do my
best to be jolly and entertaining but she's not fooled and
despite every grandparent trick we know, grizzles all the
way back to Pippa's.

Pippa looks like a ghost of herself.

'Thanks for collecting her dad'. She takes a still
grizzling Rose from Andy and rests her on her hip. Rose
bury's her face in her mum's tee shirt adding snotty tears to
the coffee stain.

It was good of Pippa's neighbour to take Rose. When the
chips are down people can be so kind. Andy had dropped
her there before taking Pippa to the hospital and collected
her later.

'She's had breakfast but I could take her up and give her
a quick bath and change while we're here'. Andy reaches
out to take Rose but Pippa shrugs a no and holds on to her
as we walk into the kitchen. On the worktop, there's uneaten
toast on a plate, a dirty cup and a folded-up wodge of

paperwork next to leaflets about stillbirth. The air is thick with emptiness.

'Maybe we could have Rose for a couple of days Pippa'. I offer 'Or I could stay and make you both lunch. You could come and stay at ours …?'

Pippa is unreachable. I've never seen her so shut down and so un-Pippa-like. There's no anger, no tears and just a great big colourless void of pain I can't seem to cross.

'They say it was an infection' is all that Pippa says.

It's obvious she's exhausted but Pippa does not want us to have Rose and when we leave I feel utterly helpless.

'We have to let her take the lead in this love'. Andy says 'she needs time to process what's happened. She knows where we are when she needs us. Let her deal with this her way'.

Andy's right about needing to process. Loss has such power over us and most of us are rubbish at navigating a path through it. Pippa had leaflets. I wonder what the world did before leaflets and I do hope they help but I'm not sure he's right about leaving her to deal with it her way. I wonder if we are far too good at leaving people be? I wonder if this is a thing we tell ourselves because we don't want to interfere or worse, don't know what to do? As far as Pippa's concerned she's very good at giving messages of being in control and I go along with it because she can be intimidating but I know she's hurting. I know it with every fibre of my being and what mam leaves a daughter to deal with hurt alone? I notice I still have parade glitter sparkling on my shoes and it's falling into the footwell of the car.

'Take me back Andy'. We're just navigating the second roundabout, almost back at ours and I can tell from the way he sighs, Andy thinks I'm making an error. He shakes his head a little but keeps on going round back towards Pippa's. He parks up and goes to unfasten his seatbelt but he's also been at the hospital and up all night. He's wearing tiredness like a worn-out jumper so I tell him to go home.

Pippa isn't anything when she answers the door. Not annoyed, surprised, glad or upset and that's how I know it's right for me to be there. Pippa cares about everything. When she doesn't is when she needs the most care of all.

I follow her into the lounge. She absentmindedly picks things up and puts them down again before sitting down on the sofa next to a now sleeping Rose.

'They said she wasn't a stillbirth Mum, she was a miscarriage, but I held her. She was born. She was born Mum. She was real'. Pippa looks too tired to even cry.

Rose is still in her grubby yesterday clothes. Her lovely little face is crusty with dried cereal. I bathe her and put her back down to finish her afternoon nap. When she's drifted off I lead my broken-hearted daughter into the bathroom, bathe her and put her in bed too.

Five days after she lost the baby Matthew and Yuuto arrive at Pippa's. It's not the best circumstances for meeting Yuuto in real life for the first time but we're so glad they both came. Christopher's at a critical point in business negotiations in Delhi and can't come home.

'We'll take care of her mum', Matthew promises. Matthew and Pippa are so different and it can be difficult to see the love in between the bickering but it's there. I think she's glad her brother came but it's hard to tell because she's wearing grief like armour.

Making the most of Matthew's unexpected visit, and after he pressed for me to do it even though I trust him with my life, I made an appointment to see an 'Innovation Investment Consultant' at the bank Abdul put us on to. For complicated reasons I can't be bothered to engage with to do with tax, Matthew says he wants Andy and I to be partners in their business and not investors and he wants me to be crystal clear about the implications.

'I have no idea what to wear to see an Investment Consultant' I've rung Jo for advice. 'I got rid of most of my work clothes'.

Supermarket fashions have stood me in good stead for years - good value for money, serviceable for work and casual. Handy to put in the trolley alongside the weekly shop too. Two birds with one stone. After the clear-out, I'm a bit short of clothes but with the post-op different shape of me and without work to set the blue skirt-white shirt combo parameters I don't know how to re-stock the wardrobe. Melody Skyhorse has little to say about replacements other than buy what brings joy. I've no idea how to buy joyful clothes. Jo suggests a shopping trip and that we should make a day of it in Leeds. I'd only planned on having a bit of a splurge in M & S so a day trip with a chum sounded like a good way to add joy to new clothes buying.

It's one of those glorious summer days when Jo collects me. The sun is shining making the day feel like an adventure waiting to happen. We park up in Leeds town centre which is lush with loads of shops and Jo knows exactly where she's heading. We stop outside a shop window with nothing in it but a rail bearing a single pair of ivory-coloured cropped trousers and a fuchsia pink blouse. Jo points to the outfit.

'That would look great on you'.

I wonder if she has a bit of sunstroke because the outfit is paparazzi chic more suited to women in Paris than East Coast of Yorkshire me.

'Come on, you have to try it. This place has gorgeous clothes' she says and drags me into a shop that looks like a clinic. Nothing in the minimalist window has a price tag so straight from the off you know it's for posh people.

I have a sneaking suspicion Jo hasn't been in the shop before but being with a lottery winner seems to give her the confidence to go in too. As it turns out, neither of us should've been worried. The shop assistant looks like a fashion model and is top to toe in expensive-looking clothes but she isn't a bit snooty. She even gives us both a glass of wine which I've never heard of in a dress shop before.

I've been in meetings of course because a whole county's public toilet provision doesn't manage itself, but never *investment* meetings I set up. Jo says if I look the part I'll feel more confident so although I don't go as far as the outfit in the window, I do buy a gorgeous, cornflower blue jacket and geometric design shirt. I'm going to team them up with the Capri trousers still hanging unworn in my wardrobe. I've never worn anything like it because pale colours were not serviceable for the cleaning industry but it looks smart and makes me feel … taller. I was right about the absence of price labels though. The cool shop-girl must be paid a lot more than I once was. We had a delicious lunch in a little Indian street food place in the indoor market which happened to be right next door to the very shoe shop all the trendy girls at school used to go to. It took me over forty years to be able to buy something there. Funny how life is sometimes.

On the day of the meeting, Andy's going to some eco-building workshop with Wolf and isn't going to come. He says I'm more than capable of managing things, which is true, but in all honesty I know he's keener for a day in the country chucking hay bales around with Wolf than putting on a suit again. He doesn't miss the suits but I think he misses his workmates. A few days before he had been out for a drink with the lads from the company.

'How was it love?' He was back earlier than I'd expected.

'A bit strange if I'm honest. There was a bit of joshing about the Courier story from Keith and Roy. Roy kept banging on about me being 'Mr Moneybags' and asking if I'd be emigrating to Barbados. He wouldn't let it drop. Once we caught up on redundancies, useless Dennis still sending lorries to Antwerp via Mexico and young Tim having a heart attack we ran out of things to talk about'.

Work friends, even if we spend every day for years with them, are for the most part bound by work rather than friendship. I feel as if I know Dennis, Roy and the others because I heard their names off and on, for the best part of the fifteen years Andy worked there. I saw them at his work's Christmas do's but I can't recall the names of any of their partners or their kids.

As Andy told me, I could see how sad the night had made him. He hasn't made any more plans to meet up with them again though he said they all promised to keep in touch. I'm guessing that will mean the odd Christmas card. I'm glad Andy has offered to help Wolf finish their house. Theresa is too since he did a good job of re-hanging their sticky front door. Wolf and Andy make a good team.

Wolf and Andy's workshop is in the grounds of some country house miles away so he's had to take the car. Matthew and Yuuto collect me in a cab and neither are wearing suits. I wonder if it's a California way of doing things and if I'm a bit overdressed but when we get to the bank, the 'call me Cathy' Innovation Investment Consultant is as poshed up as I am. She's wearing pillar box red tights which strikes me as a bit unexpected for someone who works in an office. Not everyone's ankles could carry them off but she looks great. She tells me she loves my outfit which is nice.

None of the chairs in Consultant Cathy's office match but despite that, she seems to know what she's talking about. She bandies about all the words you might expect about risk management, portfolios and expansion. Matthew and Yuuto bounce right back with marketing, branding and analysis so they're all on the same page. They have a knack for making exciting plans for Matthew's business sound as dull as dishwater but they're full of energy. Matthew must've seen me glaze over a bit.

'Are you OK with all of this Mum, is there anything you need us to go over?'

I wonder if children always underestimate their parents.

'It seems to me Cathy's financial and strategic advice alongside her analysis of business trends will enable the company to be efficient and profitable in a challenging and competitive market. Therefore, her advice to me is that investment via a limited partnership is a sound proposition.

I don't believe there's anything we need to go over but thanks for making sure Matthew'.

I couldn't help myself. Consultant Cathy has a lovely chuckle.

There's lots of paper involved and signatures needed for the silent partner investment into Matthews and Yuuto's business but once the pens are all passed back to Cathy she takes a breather, ready to start again.

'I believe you have something further to discuss Ms Wooldridge?'

Matthew and Yuuto offer to wait for me at the coffee shop around the corner. If they're curious about why I have another meeting with Cathy they don't ask. From the smiles on their faces, I guess they're more focused on their business than mine.

'So...' says Cathy. 'Nice boys. IT is a growth area and financially I don't think you have anything much to worry about there. Now let's talk about your other project'.

Thankfully Cathy doesn't feel the need to take me through the simpleton guide to investment detail of earlier when I tell her about wanting to give backing to Theresa's hula hooping class. It turns out she used to love hooping when she was younger and thinks it's a wonderful idea.

'People are so bored of paying a fortune for machines and gym membership. Hooping's cheap but cheerful. I think it has real potential!'

How to give money seems relatively straightforward but I had no idea there were so many different types of business models to choose from. She recommends a partnership that instinctively feels like the right choice.

She talks me through the need for a good business plan.

'Clarify your thinking, spot potential problems, identify your goals and know how you will measure your progress.'

I wonder if Consultant Cathy is one of Melody Skyhorse's Graces because that is exactly what she says about personal self-development and becoming the person you want to be. It's funny that it works for businesses too.

There's even a pre-prepared template for writing the plan. Melody Skyhorse doesn't offer a template which is a shame because I'm sure it would work for universe type goals too.

Cathy gave me a lot of useful paperwork and I promise I'll tell her when our next class is up and running.

'Please do, I'd love to come!'

A couple of days later Matthew takes Yuuto for an overnight visit to York. I imagine the Jorvik time travel ride might be a bit tame for someone more used to California. They plan to visit the museum and the Shambles which seems like something a coach tour of pensioners might do but they seem excited about it, so what do I know?

I've been putting off having a chat with Pippa about Christopher and having Matthew staying at Pippa's has made it easier to avoid. I know she's being looked after but difficult conversations don't get any easier by being left so while the boys are on their jaunt I go round.

Pippa looks pale and sad. I don't want to make things worse but Christopher is still not home and the long and the short of is that I think he should be. We both started to pootle about in the kitchen, me making a cuppa and her absentmindedly wiping over the already spotless surfaces. I realise I'm looking for a gap that feels right. I could look all day without the right gap turning up so I grasp the nettle and ask her to stop wiping and sit down because I want to talk about the Christopher situation. She gives me a look - still an essentially Pippa look - but there's tiredness in her eyes.

'I'm sure his work is important Pippa but so are you and Rose'. I tell her I don't want to be one of those parents that interferes but her poker rod straight back makes it clear she thinks I am. She is brittle.

'I am completely fine Mother' she says but of course, what she means is *'I am not going to discuss this'* and in calling me 'Mother' instead of mum she means *'no trespass'*. As hard as it is, I refuse to go along with this story. She's not fine and we both know it. There has been far too much 'going along' over the years, mostly by me but by Pippa and Matthew too, and often it hasn't got us to the places that really matter. I've come to realise that as a family we've held truthfulness in high value, so long as being truthful doesn't make anyone too uncomfortable. It comes from a good place but it's not truthfulness at all. Where is the value in that?

Melody Skyhorse is big on what she calls transactions between people and ownership of feelings but Pippa can be harsh when she expresses hers so I'm mindfully - and carefully - trying to stick with focusing on how I feel as the best way to navigate tricky ground. It could go either way.

'Christopher *is* a good man Pippa. I worry sometimes that you're lonely and I want you to help me stop worrying'. I'm not sure where the idea of lonely comes from because I thought I was going to say bored or fed up with him being away all the time but I'm glad I stuck with me being the one who needs help. It takes the pressure off. Rose is having fun pushing a Marmite toast finger in between the sofa cushions but Pippa doesn't seem to notice which is a sure sign she's awry.

'Oh I don't think the sofa wants your lunch Rosey-tosey'.

I take the toast and pretend to nibble it and of course, Rose wants to have it back to eat. Pippa doesn't seem to hear me call our granddaughter Rosey either though it is strictly forbidden to give her a nickname. I had to fight to be called Grandma which Pippa says is old fashioned. Christopher's mother is Nana but I could not imagine me being a nana so I put my foot down. There was no issue about Andy being Granddad but Rose calls him Pop-pops of her own accord. I don't know where that came from but she's a creative child and she can be as determined as her mum when the fancy takes.

'I love you Pippa. I try not to interfere but I wonder sometimes if you see this as not caring and the opposite is true. I'm only happy when you and Matthew are. If there's anything I can do to help you, you only have to ask'.

I would die for Pippa and it makes me sad that I can't remember the last time I told her I loved her. The clock ticks in the background and we sit still for what feels like a long time. I'm not sure how to fill the space so we both watch Rose resume her sofa stuffing. Pippa does not want to discuss her relationship with Christopher, how she's feeling about losing the baby or anything at all. The air between us is still uncomfortable prickly crisp when I get my coat on and leave with Pippa's 'bye Mother' a curt full stop on the visit.

When I get back to ours, Andy is resetting his new wrist gadget step counter. I don't know why walking needs to be complicated with technology but he says it's motivating. Andy's taken to having a brisk walk around the block before tea so he doesn't get a retirement fat roll. I suppose spending time with a strapping lad like Wolf might have been a bit of a nudge to watching the waistline too. His teatime walk foray into middle age exercise has led to the wrist-worn fitness monitor and a new bike. He's also decided to build a garden pond. To say both of these things are a bit left field is an understatement. He has never mentioned any interest in cycling or nature and I wonder if the brownie is to blame. After the veggie sausages, he seems more open to new ideas.

'Please have the good sense to abandon any thoughts of wearing Lycra'.

He promises he won't and I'm relieved because once middle-aged men put skin-tight nylon on they seem to become boorish road Vikings. I wonder if it's because the outfits are so exposing. I don't know why jeans and t-shirts aren't enough like they are at hoop classes but maybe it's all about the show. Part of the pantomime of being yellow jumper aspirational and shroud avoidant. Either way, if he dons embarrassing shorts we'll have an issue. Especially those with a nappy in the back.

The pond is a lovely idea. Melody Skyhorse raves about the benefits of running water and how it helps to balance different types of energy. It will be a nice addition to our little garden but I'll need to consult the rules about where water should be. In the right place, positive energy floats in, in the wrong place it flushes out. Getting Feng Shui wrong can be a disaster apparently. It's hard work being mindful but not as hard as digging the pond out.

Neither of us are good gardeners. We buy something and stick it in wherever there's a space. This works to varying degrees. Our passionflower is huge and abundant with beautifully smelling flowers - only Kieran and Donna get the benefit because we planted it on the wrong side of the garden. It grew over the fence. We have a bit of stalk at our side but it seemed churlish to cut it down because it has decided to bloom for them and not us.

'In the early evening it smells heavenly' Donna told me. It was hard not to be a smidge put out.

I suggest we should ask Yuuto how to turn it into a bit of a Japanese themed type of pond but Andy says it might be a bit racist to make assumptions about his knowledge of ponds based on his culture so we decide not to. We don't even know if he likes houseplants.

When Andy gets back from the retail park the car seats are down and he seems to have had a good time spending a bit of our winnings.

He is surprisingly enthusiastic about the bike. It's black with red on the crossbar, has thin wheels and is what, back in the day, we used to call a racer. That is the extent of my knowledge of bikes and to be honest, also the extent of my interest and I zone out when he tells me about the latest disc and brake lever gear shifts. I realise this is his way of telling me it was expensive. I'm glad he got a helmet and a high vis jerkin. He said there were some cool looking women's bikes and hinted at a possibility of us doing a ride together. There are few opportunities to positively play a cancer card but on this occasion, I was happy to do so. If ever I start being interested in shoes with cleats, I'll know the cancer has spread to my brain.

I help Andy unload bags of things I don't recognise which are allegedly essential for a pond. Lots of plants and an impressive looking fountain which he says aerates the water so it doesn't turn into a smelly swamp. I remind Andy we don't have electricity in the garden but he says we'll get it put in because we can afford to. I'm going to look up where we need to put the plants in the garden this time so we don't have another passionflower debacle.

Andy is a changed man since he left work. Melody Skyhorse is big on not putting things off until tomorrow and doing what you love today but she never says much about how to pay the electricity bill while on a journey of self-discovery. One of her lessons was a guided visualisation. She suggested we use our mind's eye to summon what we wanted to achieve but added the caveat it shouldn't be a million pounds or some such, but something we could make happen through our deliberate actions. I've not taken much to visualisation exercises because I either see myself swanning about like Kate Winslet on the bow of the Titanic or ambling around Tesco. I'm missing something. I never imagined coming into a big sum of money which is ironic when you think about it. I'd never imagined not being at work because ordinary people work, don't we? When I look at Andy humping the bags of sand out of the car boot, he looks happy. Wolf is coming round to help him build the pond as a favour for Andy sorting their door.

It's funny it took a nudge as big as cancer to change how we live our lives. People talk about all the things they would do if they won the lottery, and some people do buy racehorses and swanky huge houses with swimming pools but it's not for us. I feel sure Melody Skyhorse would approve that our lives changed direction because when we were forced to face up to mortality we realised how valuable life itself is - and that you can't buy it. That is not to say the money hasn't helped. We could've afforded a new bike and a bit of landscaping without the win though I'm not sure either would have happened without us meeting Theresa and Wolf, but not to have to budget for the spend is partly what adds to Andy's contentment. Eric has given him more than enough to worry about.

I guess Andy's decided to focus on the positive and I'm glad of it. We've both been trying so hard to take care of each other. I've tried not to be too scared to protect Andy from feeling he needs to look after me all the time while he's been making sure I'm OK. He always does, of course, it's the kind of man he is, but there have been more cups of tea in bed, more baths run, more 'how are you feeling today love' and, if I'm honest, it's a bit suffocating. As Melody Skyhorse is fond of saying, 'fear blocks positivity and creativity'. Seeing Andy prattle on about his handlebar-mounted mile counter and the importance of putting stepping stones in ponds to ensure creatures can get out is a sign for me he's not as scared as he was. His shoulders are less crunched up and he's moving like he's put down a heavy weight. I hate that my body has caused him to feel so afraid.

To the best of my knowledge, neither of us have ever seen a hedgehog in the flesh but it's lovely seeing him and Wolf take so much care to prevent them drowning in our new pond.

I'm planning my own spending too. I haven't spoken to the others yet but when I have another go at visualising what I hope to make happen I see Theresa, Jo, Cecile and Raquel in the picture. Theresa is key because she's the one with all the practical skills. If she's not in, the plan is kiboshed before it even gets off the ground. I may be wrong but intuition tells me Jo's itching for new challenges and I think she'll be up for it. I hope so. Cecile and Raquel I'm less sure about but with them involved I feel as if we could conquer the world. I hope they'll come on board.

The *Everyday Grace* lesson on visualisation says if we focus on our goals we achieve the benefits hiding in our creative subconscious and activate the law of attraction. Andy went to the big shops in the retail park and I don't even think he had a list. It seems fair enough that starting a proper business should take a bit more of an effort than installing a garden pond. The idea for the hula hoop business has been lurking about in my head since Theresa said she couldn't afford to book the hall. I've never been the sort of person to have starting my own business ideas and I can barely keep the hoop on my hip. It's a mad idea but thinking about it gives me a little gurgle of excitement. I read in the paperwork Cathy gave me that 90% of new businesses go under within a year of opening. Despite that, I remember how smiley Cathy was about coming to a class - like I feel about my hoop class. I have absolute faith, I don't know where it comes from but I do. In my heart, I truly believe that investing in the hoop classes is a great idea and it will be a success. I can't wait to talk to Theresa about it.

Two days later and the basics of the pond are in. Andy has gone off on one of his fat roll pre-tea evening walks. When the phone rings as I mash the potatoes it pops into my head that Andy has been run over or had a stroke or some such because who rings at teatime? It's a relief to see Pippa's name on the screen.

'Mum… I don't know what to do'. Her voice cracks into small quiet sobs. Melody Skyhorse says being honest about feelings will give us a positive sense of wellbeing but hearing my girl cry, I feel a little break in my heart. I'm sure I sound much more grounded than I feel when I promise to help.

CHANGE

Creative Security

Consciously build and grow your world and fill it with abundant graceful energy.

Everyday Grace

It's funny how we all kid ourselves that we are in control. Melody Skyhorse says the only constant is change but mostly we're comfortable thinking things are always going to stay pretty much as we expect them to be. 'Let's go to Portugal next year' we say, or 'when we retire, let's get a nice bungalow in Filey' but we never build in any caveats, do we? We don't imagine ill health, world wars or tsunamis on the East Yorkshire coast. I don't think anyone would have imagined getting cancer and a lottery win at the same time.

When Pippa rings I can hear her heart breaking 'will you come Mum'.

It's reasonable to assume a pregnancy will go on to be full-term once you get to four and a half months because they usually do so I don't blame Pippa for the beautiful nursery. When I get there she's sat on the floor, eyes red-rimmed, next to a stuffed patchwork elephant holding the remnants of a broken hanging mobile. I join her on the floor and we sit quietly for a while. Eventually, and in a tiny voice I barely recognise she speaks into the cosy but redundant room.

'Mum I need to move all this. I can't…. I can't have it here… I need it not to be here…'

After I put Rose to bed we fold up the baby clothes and put them in boxes to go into the loft. The house is unbearably tidy. Pippa reeks of sadness. There are no baby jeans. She knew she was carrying a girl but hadn't told me and that hurt a little bit.

'Christopher said as I'd lost Ruby there was no point in

coming back early. He said he can't leave his company in the lurch right now so ...'.

It breaks my heart to hear her call the baby by name. I let her talk at her own pace. She doesn't need me to be critical.

'She was perfect Mum. Perfect. She had eyelashes and eyebrows and hair. She even had little half-moons on her tiny fingernails. The skin on her back was soft and downy. She was like a little porcelain doll and I could feel her like a butterfly in my tummy. I don't know what I did wrong'.

Andy and I have reminded her several times that the hospital said it was an infection and not her fault. I recognise an anxious need to stop her talking about the death of her baby as if this will make the grief go away. We used to say people needed to move on which seems to me to be the most cruel of ideas. I'm learning from Everyday Grace because instead, I encourage Pippa to tell me every tiny detail about Ruby in the hope that remembering some of her loveliness will help both of us deal with our sorrow.

'Isn't the light on the wings lovely Mum?' I'm guessing Raquel organised sending the beautiful, framed photo of an iridescent blue-winged dragonfly resting on a wheat stalk. For once Pippa doesn't rant about 'the weirdos' she believes my new friends to be. On the back, there's a little scribble from Clover. Pippa and I hang it on her kitchen wall.

'Christopher wouldn't like it there Mum, but it's not going to be his concern anymore. I've told him not to come back'.

For years Pippa and I have seemed to speak a different language. I wonder if mothers and daughters always do. I wonder too how the shift to a woman-to-woman conversation occurs and was it me trusting her more, or her trusting me that made it happen?

After we've dismantled the cot and put it in the loft, I help pack some of Christopher's things. I'm not sure salmon-coloured socks are a good look for anyone. It's the second wardrobe I've decluttered this year. By the time we finish, it's late.

'The spare room isn't made up Mum. Get in with me'.

It's the first time since she was seven years old I've shared a bed with my daughter.

The next day Andy collects me. I haven't told Pipa about my hospital appointment. She has enough to deal with. I don't expect she minds me leaving. We need space even in the most difficult of times and she's taking hers by emptying Christopher's bedroom drawers. Pippa says it is all amicable but a part of me doesn't want it to be. I don't know why he's not fighting like hell to save his marriage to my lovely girl.

When I get to the hospital the first appointment is in radiology where I lay on the table to be zapped with x-rays. My body already feels fizzy and troubled as if the hateful cancer wasps are buzzing under the skin. The technicians have stained pinpoint radiotherapy targets into my skin. It didn't hurt. They can barely be seen, but *I* can see them. They shouldn't be there. Melody Skyhorse says life circumstances are a resource to learn from so we shouldn't seek to avoid or escape even the most challenging ones but I've had my fill of the learning opportunities of cancer. I hate the dots.

After the first session, Andy and I go to the clinic. Dr Mhoya has her smiley pert look about her. I've noticed that so long as she believes we agree with her every word she motors along, all efficient, her words confident of the space they take in a one-sided conversation. She looks at us when she speaks but I'm not sure she always sees us. She sees a job or a task or a disease.

My mam used to use an expression 'a face like a slapped arse' and Dr Mhoya has that exact expression when I say no - I've decided not to have chemotherapy. The watching doctor-in-training emits an air of shrinkage. I'm guessing she's already had lessons on stroppy patients and doctors who must be obeyed because she curls in on herself waiting self-protectively for the fallout.

'I'll continue with the five days of radiotherapy Dr Mhoya, but I'm not going to go ahead with the chemo'.

Andy and I have researched it on the internet. I'd bet doctors hate Google. Drug therapies for anything seem to be a bit of a hit-or-miss gamble. Look at thalidomide. I think cancer is probably caused by toxins or poison from something or other so it makes no sense to put even more poison into my body. One website says chemo can give you an extra five years but for two of them, you'll be sick. I'd rather have a shorter but vomit free three years. It's all about probabilities. I guess I'm banking on better odds and Dr Mhoya is a worst-case scenario kind of person. Perhaps her job makes her that way but it doesn't instil confidence when you think about it.

I don't want the radiotherapy either really. X-rays didn't do the poor folk in Chernobyl much good but Andy and I decided it's a reasonable compromise and we're hedging our bets.

Melody Skyhorse says we should be mistresses of our destiny and not hostages to fortune. I've never thought of myself as someone who makes choices about destiny which makes our appointment with Dr Mhoya a bit of a surprise for all of us. I'm not sure Dr Mhoya imagines patient empowerment is the good thing her NHS Trust mission statement suggests. I suspect she would be much more comfortable with patients happy to be hostages to fortune.

'With respect, I must make clear I never suggest any treatment strategy unless it is absolutely essential. It's nothing short of a foolish decision not to have the full course of treatment'.

When anyone begins a sentence with 'with respect' it is immediately obvious respect does not underpin what's being said and the observing junior doctor-in waiting looks so anxious I want to give her a barley sugar and a little pat on the arm.

Dr Mhoya prickles for the rest of the appointment. She reminds me of my old school headmistress but I'm not turning my waistband over to make my skirt short these days and her crispness is not scary at all. I won't be intimidated. Every now and again I see her trying to catch Andy's eye as if trying to rope him into a 'let's sort her out' conspiracy but Andy and I are on the same page and he won't be snared. I think he is a little bit scared of her though.

When we leave the clinic there's an autumn chill in the air. 'Well, that's that then' Andy says as we leave the clinic pulling his scarf tighter. I hope we've made the right decision.

Andy's been helping Wolf to plaster unfinished walls. On the way home, we pop round to drop off bags of clay. We haven't told the kids I'm not having chemo because I'd never hear the end of it from Pippa and Matthew would worry. Theresa and Wolf don't even put fertiliser on their cabbages so we know they'll understand.

'Have you thought about trying cannabis oil? Its use in treating cancer is well researched. It might help'.

Wolf knows someone who makes it for medicinal use. He says you can use it rectally, in capsules. Andy thinks we should ponder it but after the terror of the car ride with the loaded brownie, I don't see myself as a cannabis-using sort of woman, especially up my bum which, even to me, sounds like a bit of a waste.

We don't hang around after Andy and Wolf unload the boot because Clover is a bit grumpy and wants her tea.

'Theresa are you free to come to ours on Saturday? I've a couple of ideas about how we can still have classes next term. Bring Clover - we're minding Rose'.

I feel all buzzy about having an actual business meeting in my house. Abdul and Jenny's visit was about business but Andy and I were fish out of water at that meeting. I didn't tell Theresa the others were coming. I just said to Jo, Cecile and Raquel to come round and mentioned buns so they can't be blamed for thinking I was being sociable. When I bring the tea through Raquel helps herself to an iced finger and sharp as she is, knows there's more to the invite.

'Right-ho Wendy, what's going on?'

I'd written notes on post-its so I covered all the important points but, a bit swayed by Raquel wanting to cut out the small talk, I made a mess of it by starting in entirely the wrong place.

'I want to invest some money in starting a hula hooping business and wondered if you four want to be partners'

It's quite disconcerting when four people stare at you. Jo's the first to speak.

'Thank fuck. I thought you were going to tell us you're popping your clogs'.

I abandon the post-it notes and bring out the paperwork Consultant Cathy at the bank prepared for me.

'This is a business plan she helped me draw up. It's not set in stone but something for us to build upon so everyone is happy with it'.

I hand everyone a copy and nibble a hobnob while they read it through. Raquel takes out a pen and makes notes as she reads.

'I'm not sure I'm making sense of this Wendy.' Theresa looks a bit stunned.

'It will be a partnership Theresa. We can hire a venue for you to teach in and pay you an income while we build the business. The rest of us can manage the equipment, publicity and what-not so that we can fill as many classes as you want to run every term. I think it has huge potential. What do you think?'

'It's a great idea Wendy…' there's a hesitation in her voice but before she finishes the sentence Rose and Clover who are sat on the rug beside the sofa get into a spat about ownership of a turnip crisp. Rose leans over Clover and snatches the crisp out of her hand.

'Gimme crisp' says Clover, but Rose starts shoving it into her mouth.

'Gimmmeeee!". Clover as quick as a flash lunges forward and grabs what is left of the crisp and looks very pleased with herself to have won her prize.

Rose, not happy to have lost the crisp, thumps Clover on

the side of the head.

'Waaaaaaaaaaaaaaaaagh' Clover wails like a banshee and it distracts us all while we sort them out.

I give Rose one of my serious grandma looks.

'Rose you must not hit. Now apologise to Clover'.

Theresa distracted by the kids gets back to what she was saying '….. but me and Wolf just don't have cash to invest. I'm sorry.'

Clover is still wailing like she's lost an eye but Theresa brings out some rice cakes from her bag and shares them between them and they immediately make friends again as if crisp war never happened.

Theresa never bothers too much about money so I know she isn't embarrassed about not having it to invest but I realise I haven't made myself clear so I spell it out.

'Erm, the plan doesn't need you to invest… well it does, but not money. The plan needs your skills more than money. I can invest the money. I want to put up half a million pounds'.

'What the actual fuck!' Jo says but I think she speaks for all of them and I must admit, I enjoy the little moment.

I take them through the plan. We'll be equal partners but no one can withdraw any money unless we all decide to dissolve the business. The money will cover costs and salaries until the business generates income and any profits will be shared equally.

'The worst that could happen is that it never makes any profit but for at least a couple of years salaries would be covered while we try'.

Jo needs no persuasion.

'Well, I'm in. I'll need to give a terms notice at school'. Jo's been moaning about the politics and paperwork of teaching for a while so I'm not surprised she's enthusiastic but I hadn't expected her to come on board full time.

Raquel, unlike Jo, isn't keen on the idea.

'It's a top plan and I'll help out in whatever way I can of course but I'm awfully excited about a job I've applied for at the Uni so....'

Cecile's not interested either. 'Not on my horizon and I'm not tempted I'm afraid. I already have more than enough work to do but it's a cool idea'.

I'm disappointed Raquel and Cecile opted out of being partners but with Jo in full time I think the plan is still workable.

Melody Skyhorse says bounty shared spreads good fortune like ripples in a pond. Once Andy and I bought a new sofa and tried to give the old one away but no one would take it. We had to take it to a tip in the end. Theresa and Jo won't agree to share in my bounty and be equal partners.

'Absolutely not. It could take years before we make a cent so you have to take a bigger share of the profits'. Jo is insistent and Theresa nods along in agreement.

None of us are sure the business is going to work so discussion of profits seems a bit premature but after a bit of back and forth and with Raquel's expert input we decide on a split Theresa and Jo are happy about and I can live with.

I should've bought champagne but didn't think of it so at Raquel's suggestion we raise a tea toast.

Cecile pipes up 'To the Hoop Troupe!'

The fight left both the babies exhausted so Raquel offers to drive Theresa and Clover home. Cecile leaves too while Andy puts Rose, who is staying the night to bed.

Jo and I share a bottle of shiraz. I've learned so much from Jo. She's direct and faces things straight on. It makes it so much easier to have non-fudging conversations with her. She wonders if I'm committing too much money to Hoop Troupe.

'Believe me Jo, I've no intention of dying but we have to be practical. We can't start a business and the money dries up. It would really mess things up for you and Theresa. The cancer might come back but I am sick of worrying about 'what if?' None of us can know but it is better to be positive than negative isn't it?'

Half a million is a lot but it's almost unreal money. 'I'm not worried about losing it Jo because I can't imagine how I have it in the first place!'

Jo agrees we can cover her current salary 'until the business starts paying'. I've no idea how realistic it is to imagine the business ever being self-supporting but as Melody Skyhorse often says, half-hearted energy leads to half-hearted results. We have to go for it and when I imagine doing just that, I feel a different kind of fizzing in my body. I can't remember the last time I felt so alive.

I'm not sure how the conversation about money turns to sexy tattoos but the shiraz has a part in it. It turns out Jinx has a number of sexy tattoos.

'I *knew* there was something going on at Theresa's Jo, were you flirting over Dr Seuss!' I can't help but tease her and she knew I would.

'We're trying to keep it casual so don't go making a thing of it. It's not a secret or anything!' Casual or not, Jo's cheeks dapple blush and I don't think it's just the wine

'Jinx and Jo - or Jo and Jinx has a nice ring to it' I tell her and she smiles a big beaming, wine-squiffy, smile. They're going to see a horror film on their next date. It's lovely to see her so smiley. There are a lot of new beginnings to be excited about.

Light in the Dark

Wherever there is gloom you may cast a loving light.
Transform negativity with a bright energy, grateful for the
opportunity to turn any environment into a place of joy
and peace.

Everyday Grace

The irony of one of our first big home improvement spends being on security isn't lost on me. I felt safer when I was poorer.

'See these cameras, pressure pads and outside lights? They'll do a smashing job of keeping your valuable safe' the chap from Supreme Security promises. There's an added irony because we don't have any. We never did but our house hasn't felt like home since we were burgled. Thanks to the Courier everyone knows we are stupidly wealthy and if letters we've received are to be believed, some people imagine we drink tea out of solid gold goblets and have the cash in suitcases under the bed. Kieran next door asked if we were getting a safe fitted and I said we would for our Rembrandt but he believed me. The more I said I was joking and no of course we are not getting a safe, the more he seemed to believe we were investing in old masters so that backfired.

Roland, the fitter, suggested a dog 'see, burglars can come when your asleep and dogs don't like strangers in the house so they're the best alarm you can have.' I've never imagined burglars coming while we're sleeping so I wish he'd kept that particular gem to himself. 'I should have saved myself a lot of money and gone to the RSPCA then' I said but he just smiled and whistled on, fitting the 'smart' system I'm sure I'll never be able to work.

'Don't use birthdays' Roland advises as he leaves after showing us how to set the alarm. I was going to use

Matthew's so I was stumped right from the off. Andy and I got into a right fluff trying to find a combination of numbers we would both remember that wouldn't be obvious to anyone else. It's harder than you might imagine.

'Roland said don't write it down' Andy snatches the pen out of my hand so I can't put the numbers somewhere for safekeeping just in case. The bloody alarm. We both hate it. I feel as if I have to have it - and I hate that I feel that way too. I wonder how the burgled family Abdul told us about are doing. I hope they're OK.

It was probably a bit soon to get the work done but they only had one gap before the Christmas period (a busy time for security fitting companies so Roland said) and I was having a bit of a wibble after the invasion of the radiotherapy. X-rays don't hurt and we'd read all the leaflets so I thought it would be a breeze. Dr Mhoya called it a 'straightforward sweeping up exercise'. It's not. It's awful. The nurse said I was unlucky because I got the hat-trick of sore, sick and tired - in spades. I felt worse than I did after I had the mastectomy. There have been a lot of tears. Most of them mine. Some kinds of trespass need more than a few carefully chosen numbers to put right.

The alarm fitting scratched a bit of the paintwork around our windows so Andy suggests a trip to our local DIY superstore.

'You know how to show a sick woman a good time' I tell Andy but the new car is still a novelty so I agree to go. As soon as I see his eyes land on the fireworks I know I'm there under false pretences.

'How about we have a bit of a gathering?' He suggests as if it's a new idea but I know him too well.

Andy is bonkers for fireworks. For as long as I've known him, leading up to November he has scoured notice boards and the papers for the nearest big display. For years we've wrapped the kids up and marvelled at chrysanthemum plumes, the fizz of rockets, the bang of bangers - Andy's favourite - the metallic smell of cordite and bonfire smoke.

The best one was at the cricket ground where Elton John performed. You never imagine Elton being a warm-up for a bonfire display but he was and the tickets were reasonably priced too.

'Things have been tough lately but maybe a few friends round would be nice … what do you think?'

I'm not sure at first. I worry about Atilla the hen and her chums. 'We can give Kieran enough notice to have them put somewhere quiet for the night' Andy says, trying to talk me round.

'We won't have a bonfire - just a few fireworks' he says loading the trolley with enough explosives to cause a national security alert. I'm glad we had the pretend grass laid or Andy would be itching for a bonfire too. In a different lifetime and for all the wrong reasons, he and Guy Fawkes could have been chums.

Three weeks later, on the night of the party, the weather is dry and calm. Rose and Clover run around the garden together. We don't take enough time to learn from kids. They never seem bothered about who they play with so long as they're having fun.

When Andy said, 'a bit of a gathering' he actually meant inviting 'virtually every person he'd ever said hello to'. The garden is heaving. A few of the neighbours' kids are chasing around after the littles. I've no idea what the game is but it involves ear-splitting shrieking. Thank goodness we covered the pond.

Hardly any of the neighbours we get Christmas cards from every year have even been in our garden before but I'm glad Andy extended the invite. At least no one is going to complain about the burger van on our drive.

'I can't be doing with the faff of cooking a hundred hot dogs' I complained.

'You don't have to. Wolf's chum runs a stall at festivals. I've already asked him' Andy said and I must admit. He was right. I never expected to be spending our winnings on falafel burgers and loaded polenta fries for half of the street but the van is a huge success and if anyone considers it a bit showy, they're not saying so. The polenta chips are a revelation - delicious. Ralph at 27 thought they were a bit foreign and exotic but even he was a convert.

Kieran and Donna made their front bedroom a temporary coop.

'They're listening to Wagner on volume - it drowns out the bangs' Kieran told me.

I'm sure even chickens like a change in scenery now and again but I wouldn't have chosen Wagner.

Andy's in his element and to be fair, he and Wolf have done a great job with all the fire buckets and hose pipes they set up just in case. He is a bit of a pyromaniac though, so I'm glad Wolf is overseeing security. Andy is more focused on the flares and rockets. I never imagined I'd put the safety of my grandchild in the hands of a dreadlocked person who is a fan of a hash brownie. I'm not proud of myself for how judgemental I used to be. Wolf is a most excellent fireman - much more careful than my explosion obsessed husband.

Judging by the ooohs and aaahs everyone loves Theresa's pre-fireworks show. She's such a talented woman. I didn't ask her to perform but am chuffed to bits she wants to.

'I hardly get the chance these days so it's good to have a practice'.

We clear a space and tether the kids near the Buddleia for safekeeping. Theresa lights sponges on the end of chains. When I was little Mum and Dad used to get us sparklers on Guy Fawkes night. We would write our name in the air until the sparkling stopped and dad would make us all throw the molten sticks into a water bucket. Theresa does the same thing with her whole body dancing and twirling the lit chains creating fire swirls, circles and waves ending with a beautiful spiral of flame. It is mesmerising and everyone claps. She gives a class for the kids after her show with battery lights on ropes. Clover is better at it than

Rose but that's only to be expected. Little Devlin from number 18 shows a particular flair for it. He reminds me of Matthew.

It's nice to see Pippa having a lively, loud conversation with Cecile which, from what I can gather, is something to do with parents who try to tell her how to teach. I'm glad she's starting to get to know my friends at last. At times it's felt as if she was deliberately avoiding them. They are both laughing but I wouldn't have expected a teacher to be calling parents thick dipshits. I don't suppose many parents try to interfere with Cecile's teaching methods more than once.

Jinx is gracious about having to be carried into our garden. I've never thought about wheelchair access before. There are steps everywhere. Jo knows we have a downstairs loo so I never thought any more about it when we invited them but nothing about our home is accessible.

'I'm used to it Wendy, don't worry about it'.

But I do worry about it and I'm embarrassed. Melody Skyhorse says in order to fathom people's lifestyle choices we need to try to put ourselves in their shoes. So, as part of the exercise, I'd reflected on why poor people chose to buy big tellies and butch dogs. It made me think about where feelings of security come from. It was a particularly useful lesson after the burglary and I spent quite a bit of time on it. I felt quite pleased with myself for being understanding and non-judgey about Dobermans. Wheelchairs are not a lifestyle choice so I'd never pondered that but it seems to me that nearly every single place I can see around our house has steps. If I put myself in Jinx's shoes - or wheels - it must be awful to feel so excluded all the time and exhausting trying to navigate the world. To try and make up for our terraced patio, I fetch them both a portion of polenta fries and a couple of bottles of wine so Jo doesn't have to traipse back and forth to the kitchen for top-ups.

When I mention to Raquel that I want all Hoop Troupe venues to be fully accessible she says it's my first policy decision. I don't know if people in wheelchairs can or would hula hoop but it is the principle of it that matters. I decide to ask Theresa if she might be interested in offering fire dancing classes too.

Clearing up the next day, all things considered, the garden doesn't look too bad. We'd put bins out for the glass and paper plates so the rubbish would be easy to take to the recycling centre. Almost everyone used them so there isn't much to pick up. I find a pair of fuchsia pink, high waist, size 18 knickers in one of the bushes which is odd. I'm not dwelling on whose they are or how they ended up in our raspberries. The chickens grubbing about in Donna's garden look unruffled by their mini-break in the bedroom. Donna looks a lot more ruffled and is embarrassed, I think, that Kieran had to carry her home. Everyone likes a free bar. The burger van's dripped a bit of oil on the drive which Andy said he'll power wash away so, all in all, the party was a great success.

Melody Skyhorse set a lesson based on a conundrum. We were to spend some time thinking about what we keep in by keeping things out and what we keep out by keeping things in. It was a tough lesson I found hard to follow.

Years ago, a celebrity was on the telly talking about how he invited all kinds of different people to his dinner parties because his view was that if he liked all of them, they would like each other. We don't have dinner parties so I didn't make much of it at the time but everyone got on at our fireworks party. People mucked in and had a laugh and no one minded about meat-free burgers or dreadlocks or what newspapers anyone read. For years, I've lived in the same street as half the people who came and I know nothing about them because I've never asked. It seems like such a wasted opportunity. We won't be buying a house with high walls and electric gates. While Andy power washes the oil off the driveway I take him a cuppa and see Devlin out in the street twirling his sister's skipping ropes. His mum gives me a great big smiley wave as I take the party bin bags out to the car.

Let Go

You cannot change the past but you can re-frame how you think of it. Eradicate regret. Respect and value lessons gathered along life's sometimes challenging path. Use knowledge to enter your future with positive creativity. Single small steps will lead to bountiful new horizons.

Everyday Grace

I expect Angela has had her tree up since the beginning of November. She always does and it is always as over the top as Christmas decorations can be. We disagree about the relative merits of artificial trees over the fresh lovely pine smell I always hanker for but to be fair if she had a real one it would be bald by the day itself. She won't be getting the usual invite. I wonder what she'll be doing.

I don't know how to go about Christmas this year. Matthew said I don't have to do anything special for Yuuto which is a relief. Apparently, Christmas day is celebrated as a romantic day in Japan so I don't suppose sprouts feature much in that scenario. I don't know why they feature in ours because no one in our family likes them, not even when I listened to Jamie Oliver and tarted them up with crispy onions. At the end of the day, they were still just sprouts.

They're staying at Pippa's again and we're having Christmas at hers which is new. We never did when Christopher lived there. I'm glad Pippa has the company. It's funny watching my two kids becoming friends. How does that shift happen? Well into adulthood they were at odds with each other - I knew they loved each other of course but they never got on or shared any interests. Was it our fault? There was some truth in the 'mummy's boy', 'daddy's girl' insults they used to bandy at each other. Melody Skyhorse talks about 'the evolution of relationships'. If with a blessing, we let go of how things used to be, it leaves space in our lives for fresh energies. I can see where she's coming from but now Matthew and Pippa are as thick as thieves a little part of me worries they're letting go of me.

This year I've more people to buy for than ever before, and more money to spend than I ever have and yet I've no idea what presents to buy. How do you give presents that are lovely to receive without the potential for being seen as over flashy or skinflint millionaire? It's a tricky path. I told Andy I wanted to push the boat out a bit because we can but he thought it would make the kids think I am dying so there is that. I don't think I'm dying. Not at all. Everything is going well according to Dr Mhoya and I feel positive. But cancer is cancer and if I don't get next Christmas I don't want the kids remembering my last as the year of the naff bath salts.

I've been thinking about not making next Christmas quite a bit. I suppose it is the season for it. Everyone looks forward to festivities but with one thing and another it can feel like a tense time. All that 'tis the season to be jolly' puts the pressure on when there are non-jolly things lurking. I've noticed it with Andy lately. Since the firework gathering, he's been sliding into himself and become distant. He says he's absolutely fine but I know something is awry. Unusually for a bloke, he's always liked going shopping for the kids but when I suggest a trip into town he says I should order online. As if! Where's the fun in that? I go without him.

As usual, the shops are crammed with lovely sparkly things. I couldn't help myself and I've gone a bit daft for Rose. If you can't spoil your grandchild who can you spoil? The thing is, she doesn't want for much either but I ignored the list Pippa provided. I'm not going to buy my granddaughter a mini kitchen and laundry set or the baby doll that poohs her nappy. Despite her university education, sometimes women's lib seems to have passed Pippa by. I got both Rose and Clover gorgeous little wooden bikes without pedals, a book about a princess who decides not to be one and wooden building blocks. I've never known a child who didn't love playing with wooden blocks. Both the girls are at the adorable age of being excited about Santa for the first time but I stopped at that for Clover so I didn't offend.

Theresa and Wolf aren't having Christmas as such - they're having a solstice celebration instead. To all intents and purposes, and despite their view that 'Christmas is a patriarchal capitalist event with no historical basis', it sounds fairly much like the day we will be having only a couple of days earlier. Wolf's parents will be there. I'm guessing that as a matter of principle and as their contribution to planet saving they won't have a mountain of wrapped gifts under their living yule tree. I wonder if a vegan solstice meal is different to a Christmas one? We haven't gone whole hog alternative this year but we have bought organic. Our parsnips are from their garden.

You read about lottery winners taking their families to Florida theme parks after a win but I don't fancy it. I wracked my brains but I can't imagine anything more special than the usual kind of presents we get the kids so I stuck with the tried and tested. Matthew and Pippa's matching PJ and slippers sets will make them smile. I got Yuuto a set too. It was a tradition before he came along so it's a 'welcome to the family' thing. I hope he doesn't think it's weird.

The silver handprints made from the print of Ruby's she was given at the hospital, I'll give Pippa in private, maybe after Rose has gone to bed.

Cecile, Raquel and Theresa were easy to buy for. I didn't go mad because we haven't known each other long enough yet to know if we are the kinds of friends who buy presents for each other at Christmas and it's not something you want to get wrong. The little silver lapel pin badges were three circles, a bit like the Olympic symbol minus two continents. I just wrapped them in tissue and included them in their cards so I wasn't making much of a song and dance. I got one for myself too. So they knew they didn't have to get me anything back I added a note to the inside of the card.

'*Maybe something like this should be Hoop Troupe merch?*'

I was over subtle about not inviting gifts back though because a few days before Jo and Jinx popped round with a bottle of Châteauneuf-du-Pape for us to have with Christmas dinner but they stay. I get out some nibbles and we end up opening it to celebrate the solstice. I've never celebrated the solstice before. We open the Christmas chocolates early and get through a whole tin. The four of us have a lovely evening. I was chuffed Jo was wearing her badge.

We get ever such a nice card from Jamila. There's a note saying she misses me and that her new temporary boss vetoed pot pourrie as incompatible with the council brand so she had to remove it. 'I didn't!' she added, with a little smiley face. Her family don't celebrate Christmas so it's kind of her to send a card.

Two days before the big day, Andy and I wait until the evening when Rose is asleep and take everything round to Pippa's. We put the grown-up parcels under the tree but hide Rose's in Pippa's walk-in wardrobe so Santa can bring them.

I wonder how long it will be before hiding presents will be more of a challenge for Pippa. When she was a little girl she would poke around for hours looking for hers and be disappointed when she couldn't find more. What goes around comes around. It won't be long before the wardrobe is too easy.

When we drop the presents off it's a relief to see that Pippa is looking well - happy in fact. She's sorting out the home food delivery with the gusto of a gym instructor. She's bought for an apocalypse.

'Should I come round tomorrow and help you get the veg ready?' I offer, only my services are not required. Pippa has written a list of instructions to shame an advanced military operation. Matthew and Yuuto have been given the responsibility for meal preparation. 'They're minding Rose too. Cecile and I are meeting for a festive lunch' she tells me.

We have a perfect Christmas Day. We arrive early to see Rose yelling 'he's been, he's been' and diving into great piles of presents. It isn't long before she has to be put back to bed after a too-much-stimulation meltdown. We all eat far too much food but not the pudding. No one wants the pudding. We argue about the best Christmas tune ever, eat too many chocolates and leave the orange ones. Pippa worries about when the bin men will be coming again because of the vast amount of wrapping paper she has to put in the garage and Andy falls into a stupor as an avoidance strategy when Matthew insists on a board game. It is exactly the same as millions of households all over the country. Apart from location, the absence of Angela and the presence of Yuuto, not that different to our usual celebrations, despite the money and the spectre of cancer. I'm grateful for it. Melody Skyhorse says a snow hushed landscape is perfect for dancing in. It didn't snow or I would have.

Andy and I have never especially enjoyed New Year's Eve. I wonder how many people do. When we were still teenagers we went to a house party and took ourselves down to the end of a long garden before midnight struck. All that fevered anticipation, counting down and stranger snogging wasn't for either of us. By a shed we shared a smoke with another couple already there and the four of us watched distant fireworks. There was no chit chat. After about ten minutes we heard the music re-start.

'I think it might be safe to go back in' one of them said.

'Happy new year then' said his girlfriend.

It was the last time we went out at new year. Usually, we make a buffet out of Christmas leftovers and watch a film. Because we'd been at Pippa's for Christmas Day we only had the few bits and bobs she'd made us bring home, so I cooked Cecile's curry recipe. It wasn't too difficult. It was as good an evening as any to sort out what's wrong with Andy.

Andy doesn't know when he started getting in a fug about it but I'm not the only one who's pondered on the possibility of it being my last Christmas.

'I can't shake it off Wendy. I keep thinking why you? Why us? Is it because we used to smoke? Is it the chemicals you used at work?' It turns out he's been struggling to keep his brave face on. He's been an absolute rock for me these past few months - I couldn't have been held any more carefully, securely or reassuringly but no one was holding him. 'I feel as if I'm unravelling love'. He says he's sorry for not telling me because he thought I had enough to worry about. Typical bloke to imagine that not talking to me about something obviously wrong was going to make me worry about him less. I don't think men handle mental health very well.

'Why not me Andy? You might as well ask what we did to win the lottery. As Jo always says, it's just probabilities. We're not special. We didn't deserve it. We haven't earned it. It is what it is. Completely random'. I don't tell him that if one of us has to be in the firing line, I am glad it's me. I wish cancer hadn't paid a visit to my family but rather me than Andy, or heaven forbid, our kids.

Melody Skyhorse says talking takes a lot of trust and courage. I think she's absolutely right. A big part of me wants to find the right words to make him better but he doesn't need that from me and I can't tell him how to fix anxiety. Sometimes a fix for difficult feelings isn't found by offering solutions - it is, as Melody Skyhorse says, the listening that opens doorways to new learning. I'm not sure I've ever felt closer to him and just having the space to talk seems to help him find solid ground. We dig out the leaflets and see if any of the cancer support services have anything to help. He says he might talk to Wolf too. 'Don't you go finding yourself in those brownies of his' I joke because I know that isn't ever going to be his thing but I'm glad he's going to talk to someone. On the rare occasion he admits to vulnerability he looks like he did when we were teens, boyish and gorgeous, though thankfully without the ratty moustache he tried and failed to grow.

I notice how late it is. We've talked for hours.

'How about we don't wait up till midnight and go to bed now?' He smiles back at me and gets the message. It's the right time for both of us.

'Perfect idea love' he says reaching for my hand. 'Happy new year'.

POWER

Unfurl

When we feel unbalanced it is the universe's way of reminding us we are in the presence of new ideas and experiences.

Everyday Grace

The paperwork's all sorted and Hoop Troupe is official. It feels as if there should be more of a fanfare to it but in the first post of the new year we just get a certificate to say the business is registered, which is fabulous - and a list of the records we are required to keep or risk a great whacking fine which was not quite so fabulous. Fortunately for us, Raquel's offered to keep our accounts in order in the short term. She's used to setting up spreadsheets and telling off departments for spending too much on calculators or whatnot so, for the time being, we're in safe hands on that score.

There is so much to do and an obvious first business expenditure has to be on some basics. My old desktop computer is using software so old it won't update. Jo has a Mac and Theresa's laptop died when Clover rammed a rice cake into the disc drive. We are not equipped to be the 'effective woman-led, social business enterprise' we promised to be in our business plan so some attending to is in order.

Melody Skyhorse says if we choose paths to make our pulse race it will inspire us to think more expansively. The first path I choose is to the tech superstore and Jo comes along. Some shopping is tedious - there's not much fun to be had in buying new bags for the vacuum cleaner but buying stuff for our business is exciting enough to kick my heartbeat up a notch. We decide one laptop won't cut the mustard. I am not sure going a bit mad is the same as being 'expansive' but we end up buying three business laptops and a tablet each for me, Jo and Theresa. The young sales chap thought it was Christmas all over again. I hope he gets commission and spends it on deodorant. He was a nice lad but a bit pongy. He cannot have a girlfriend and no wonder. We remember to keep the receipts to give Raquel.

Our next basic was somewhere to hold our classes. We'd arranged to meet Theresa at a potential venue at a school that hired its hall. We didn't keep receipts for lunch despite Jo chuntering on, for the whole journey, about the cost of a tiramisu being a reasonable business expenditure. Theresa is waiting for us at the Hepworth School gates.

'You look as if you've been expelled' Jo says.

Raquel put us onto the school.

'In an error of judgement a couple of years ago I signed on for a fencing class. As soon as someone thrust towards me with their sabre I screamed and ducked. It wasn't the sport for me but the hall is spacious'. As an approach to keeping fit, someone trying to stab me wouldn't be in my top ten either but I am glad she gave it a go.

As soon as I see the wooden-floored hall I'm excited. I can see Jo is too because she scrunches her mouth into a tight line and breathes noisily through her nose. She looks as if she's angry but I've come to recognise it as her impatient face. She wants us to take it but Theresa has to be comfortable with it as a teaching space. If it doesn't work for her, we'll need to look elsewhere. I feel impatient too. Theresa's on the stage having a look around. Years before me and Andy became an item I had a snog with Saul Fletcher on our school stage. I can't remember what we were doing there or where the teacher was but I remember that kiss. The stage smelled of football socks and the kiss was revoltingly spitty. It almost put me off boys altogether. I hope Theresa likes this stage.

Theresa calls to the woman showing us round. 'Emily I see the piano but do you have a sound system?'

They go behind a long black curtain at the edge of the stage where there's a wall-mounted electrical box while Jo and I look at the storage room.

'It seems perfect to me Wendy. Car parking. Central. Lock-up storage and we won't be restricted to term time. What do you think?'

As soon as we see Theresa coming out from stage left, grinning like a Cheshire cat I know she's happy.

Emily is on the school admin team and is so helpful. She takes us to an office near the main entrance to the school and for the smallest of moments I feel as if I am about to get a detention. We can rent the hall for a year and Emily gives us dates of the parents' evenings when we won't be able to use it.

'I never want to be anywhere near a parents' evening again' Jo says but Emily doesn't know she's a teacher so probably thinks she's just a bad parent.

We sign all the paperwork and promise to send a copy of our insurance certificate - the one we still need to get.

'I used to love hula hooping when I was a girl - haven't done it for years!' Emily says when we tell her what we want her school hall for.

'Would it help if I put it on our parents' newsletter? It goes to over nine hundred families. I can put a poster up on our staff and school notice boards too if you'd like'. Theresa gives her a hug and I say I'll get posters to her as soon as possible and I add it to the 'to do' list that is already starting to build.

Melody Skyhorse says when we are in the presence of a notable experience we should pause, be still and allow our consciousness to unravel the lessons being presented to us. As we leave the school with my tummy churning I don't pause and am not still. The three of us, scaring the rooks ganging up in the playground trees, shriek like banshees as we skip to Jo's car. We've done it! Hepworth school hall is going to be our first Hoop Troupe venue.

Jo offers to take Theresa home which, as Andy is there helping Wolf with something buildy, suits me too.

When we get there the floor is strewn with tools.

Clover's bashing wooden pegs into a toy bench only she's using a steel claw hammer. Wolf doesn't seem to mind. More alarmingly Rose is cutting the hair off one of Clover's dolls with a pair of real scissors. Wolf doesn't seem to mind that either and neither does Andy.

'How'd it go?' Wolf asks with a great big beaming smile. I'd noticed his smile before because he has what I call American teeth - all white and perfect - but he uses it all the time. He never seems to expect bad news. I don't know if he's naive or a sage. Theresa is so giddy she can't get her arm out of the sleeve of her coat.

'Wolf it's perfect! I can teach from the stage and it has a proper sound system. I only need a headset. There's stacks of room for hooping - I reckon we could have twenty people in the class easy - maybe a few more. I'm made up'.

Theresa's becomes far more Scouse when she's excited. Wolf helps her untangle from her coat lining and gives her a big hug while I de-tool the children.

'I'd best put the kettle on then'.

I've come to like Wolf a lot. I'm sure some of our neighbours at the bonfire party had him marked as a bit dodgy. To be fair, I might have done in the past but in their housing collective piercings and tattoos seem to be the norm. I guess they probably are in the prison population too so inking isn't a good way to judge the character of a person.

When we've told them more than they wanted to know about our new venue Wolf and Andy get on with building the wall. It's coming along nicely and Clover will soon have her own bedroom. Wolf uses one of his dreadlocks to tie the others away from his face while he works. Andy's forehead is beaded with sweat but he looks as at home in Wolf and Theresa's house as he does in ours. Andy laughs when Wolf reminds him to save some of his 'old man energy' for their trip to buy a wormery. I don't know if the joke is about him being old or buying something to grow worms but it's good to hear him laugh. Andy has a chuckly laugh which I used to say was like a little monkey. I called him chi-chi, short for chinchilla. Years later I found out a chinchilla isn't a monkey but a rodent. If Andy ever minded he didn't say.

When Wolf makes us all tea he remembers how we take it. It's funny how such a little thing makes me feel like he wants us to be there. Andy seems to be enjoying learning new skills though I'm not sure where he'll ever use them again. There's not much demand for hay bale walls in our street.

We colonise the kitchen table to write up our job list. Jo is chewing the end off one of the felt tip marker pen's and laying over the flipchart paper. The pen's leaked on her lip and teeth and she looks a bit gothy. I told her to stop chewing it so she only had herself to blame. Teachers should know better.

There are bills to pay, flyer printing to confirm, the merchandise design to approve, press releases to write and we've still to decide where our file cabinet is going to live. Jo adds everything to the list in priority order. Theresa chips in,

'We have is to decide our start date for new classes and work back from there'.

Raquel called us entrepreneurs the other day. I suppose we are. It's funny how the descriptions we give ourselves - or are given - shape how we live our lives. Being a survivor makes survival so much more alive than being a victim. That being said, all this entrepreneurial importance is going to my head a bit. I don't know the right space to leave between Melody Skyhorse's ideas about being able to 'go with the flow' or 'grounding in my innate wisdom' when faced with so much that needs to be done and conflicting choices.

Everything's interesting which is the fact of it. I even like calling our t-shirts 'merch' as if I know what I'm talking about but I tend to leave hard things till last whereas Jo does the opposite so I leave her to get on with it - my innate wisdom tells me she needs to feel in control far more than I need to.

When we leave Theresa's, Andy says he will drop me and Rose off at Pippa's as he has to nip to get some more screws.

'Is this because of the pen?' I ask him but he denies it and I don't believe him.

I've no idea how Rose got hold of the pen Jo was using or how to explain that Jo is as upset at I am that it turns out to be a permanent marker. At least Rose and Clover only drew on each other's legs and don't have blue lips like Jo.

Only, it turns out, an alien life form has body-snatched my daughter. She is completely unperturbed by Rose's leg artwork and is unexpectedly supportive when I tell her about our new venue and plan for our first classes.

'It's central Mum so hopefully you'll get a good sign up. What numbers do you need to break even?'

I haven't thought about breaking even so far. We're using the first class to test the water. Theresa said sign up for her classes was often more than the community centre could cope with so we are assuming there will be take up but we don't know for sure. It might be a disaster, I tell Pippa.

'Of course it won't be Mum. As always, you underestimate yourself'.

I wait for a follow-up barb but there isn't one. As Pippa is most usually the one underestimating me I'm lost for words. I watch Rose navigate her little bike around the kitchen island, scratching the paintwork without so much as a 'tut' raised and wonder what on earth is going on. Then she says she has news for me and I am almost lost for words again.

When I get home Andy is perplexed when I share Pippa's big news. 'Teaching? Teaching what?'

'Cecile invited Pippa to observe lessons apparently. Now she's been accepted to train to become an English teacher'. Pippa's never shown any interest in teaching, studying or going back to work all the time she's been with Christopher but I suppose their split up changed her priorities.

'She's going to use the money we gave her to buy

170

Christopher out of their home to keep things stable for Rose, and the rest of it to fund her studies. Rose will be going to pre-school this year so once she starts primary, Pippa will be qualified'.

'Well I never' is all Andy has to say about it but his broad smile says he is as proud as I am.

Later, when Andy and I video call Matthew he says he's known about Pippa's hope to go into teaching since Christmas. Like me, he believes she'll be particularly well suited to excellent classroom control.

There's something about January that puts a spring into everyone's step because Matthew has news of his own.

'We wanted you to be the first to know - we're getting married!' Matthew's news was so unexpected it threw both of us.

'Married? When? Smashing!' is how his dad responds. I hope Matthew doesn't see his dad is a bit flummoxed in case he misunderstands. I know just what Andy is thinking because I'm thinking the same. It's exciting and wonderful news but neither of us have ever been to a gay wedding or have any idea about what kind of event it might be.

'We'll be booking for July in England. We'll be going to Kyoto for a traditional Buddhist blessing for the following April. Yuuto says Japan is stunning in spring. I hope you'll both come'.

At least I can be confident Matthew won't be expecting me to wear a dreadful dress to match his bridesmaids. Do gay weddings even have bridesmaids - or bridesmen? I've no idea. There's so much to learn.

Strength Stance

We are not lessened by gracefully accommodating views and positions which are not our own. We need only take responsibility for the ways in which we engage, be prepared to review our approach, avoid trespass and confidently assert personal value boundaries when necessary. Graceful women are strong women!

Everyday Grace

I shouldn't have been surprised to see Angela and a 'plus one' on Matthew's first draft wedding guest list. He hasn't fallen out with her and to be fair, with him only here intermittently I suppose he only had her absence at Christmas to draw on for his understanding of where my relationship with her has got to. Of course, he wants her to be there and I know she knows about the wedding - she keeps in touch with both Pippa and Matthew so I have to give her that.

When I was a teenager I had a mole on my cheek. I hated that mole. It went itchy and the doctor scraped it off. It didn't hurt but I won't ever forget the noise it made when he did it. It left barely any scar. Long after it was gone I looked for it every time I brushed my hair or passed a shop window. Angela is a bit like that mole.

Angela loves those gossip magazines with 'love rat' or 'my home help ran off with my bank card' stories. Same with true crime telly documentaries. They seem dark to me and over-interested in the worst of human nature. When I tried to change the subject when she told me about body parts in drains and whatnot she called me lily-livered. She thinks I'm boring because I watch the birds in our garden. Melody Skyhorse says we must embrace difference which opens doors to new opportunities to experience the world. But what if new experiences include being regaled with the gory details of a true-crime documentary over a lunchtime latte? I don't want the opportunity to embrace serial killers.

Life without Angela in it is better. No drama, no little spiteful digs, none of the guilt trips about how perfect she imagines my life is compared to hers and how I am somehow to blame for the difference. Despite having barely time to think of anything else except the business, I've found myself noticing her not being around.

The lesson on toxic relationships and how to leave them helped me see I didn't have to accept Angela's 'normal' if it made me feel bad. It was up to me to set boundaries on what I was prepared to negotiate and what was non-negotiable. I could ask Angela to stop telling me about the bodies under the floorboard killers and husbands who ran away with their brother-in-law but she has the same right to say no. If my boundaries are valid, aren't hers too? Where does that get us? Melody Skyhorse's lessons are confusing sometimes.

The lesson that put the cat among the pigeons was Yin and Yang. I'd seen the little black and white snuggled commas design on various knick-knacks sold in the lovely shop in the High Street. I hardly ever buy anything because I don't know anyone who collects fairy ornaments or carved tribal masks but the doorway always has a waft of Jasmine and it's nice to pop in and browse. I thought it was a bit like the CND symbol and about banning the bomb or saving whales or some such so never paid it much mind but Melody Skyhorse said it symbolises balance. According to ancient Chinese wisdom, there can be no good without bad, no up without down. I remember seeing a documentary where a therapist asked a patient how he knew he was depressed. She explained he could only know he was depressed if he had at some point experienced not being. The patient threw a chair and had to be restrained from punching her so he wasn't impressed with the notion you can't have one without the other. I've always thought of my relationship with Angela as her taking and me giving. Over the years I've put up with her but I haven't given much thought at all, as to why. Melody Skyhorse encourages us to think gracefully and puts a positive slant on everything. Her idea is that the negative and positive compliment and depend on each other. I must admit, I don't like where that idea is going at all. And then, in the post, I get a card from Angela.

'We all make mistakes Wendy - even you! Anyway, I hope you're alright. Ring me. Love Angela. x'.

At first I feel cross because even her apology seems half-hearted, but I wonder if I'm the Yang to Angela's Yin. Maybe we couldn't have been friends as long as we have been unless we balanced each other out. One-sided see-saws don't work do they?

'Well, I suppose you must've got something you wanted from her, love. Maybe not so much chalk and cheese as chalk and blackboard' is what Andy says which makes me appreciate putting a judgemental spotlight on others is much easier than putting it on yourself.

Half-hearted or not I know sending the card was as difficult for Angela as allowing her natural hair colour to show and she might be ready for us to talk, I'm not sure I am - yet. 'Yet' is a big word. It crosses the line I'd drawn under our relationship and whilst I have to give her credit for reaching out her right moment isn't mine - for now. I'm going to ponder on it.

We've been invited to a celebration at Theresa and Wolf's but this time, Andy doesn't bother with the smart trousers. Finally, they have all their internal walls finished and are having an 'unveiling'. When we arrive, there are muddy boots by the front door so we know some of the building collective Andy has already met are there but when we go in, so are my hoop chums so neither of us feel out of place. Clover, helped by her mum, pulls at the corner of batik cloth until it falls off the wall and says 'I 'clare my wall open' and we all clap. She looks thoroughly pleased with herself and invites some of us in to see her new bedroom. It doesn't have a door but she doesn't seem to mind. If I was being picky, I'd say the plastering isn't as smooth as I'd have preferred but they aren't my walls and Andy did the best he could. Wolf and Theresa are chuffed and that's what matters. Theresa brings out the elderflower champagne they made the previous year.

'The only cost was for the sugar, everything else was foraged and the glass is recycled' Theresa says which I am impressed by but someone from the collective says the local elderflowers shouldn't be picked because the council spray them. He drinks it anyway. It turns out it wasn't quite as economical as it might have been as the cork popped spectacularly and took out a light fitting - but it was delicious. We all raise a toast to the finished walls while Jo picks pieces of lightbulb glass off Jinx's jacket. I notice they've bought some furniture for Clover's bedroom and a new wok. Theresa's Hoop Troupe salary seems to have helped take the pressure off.

It's smashing to see Tony again. It's good to be able to tell him that I'm well. Dr Mhoya won't go the whole hog and use the 'cure' word. I think medics like to hedge their bets but I tell Tony I feel cured. He tells me about his African inspired dance show touring schools. My school only ever had visits from nurses giving injections or looking for head lice. Education seems to have moved on a lot.

'I came back to see my parents. Denice was supposed to be here but she was offered her own tour' he tells us while Wolf does the rounds topping up the fizz. I say how sorry I am not to see her and commiserate with him that they are not together but he says it is par for the course for careers in performing arts.

'You'll see her in May though, for sure'. Tony grins mischievously but I'm not sure what the joke is.

'You haven't?' Theresa shrieks as she jumps up to hug him. I still don't know what's going on but I have a bad feeling about it.

We'd talked about it and I may even have said yes but

wine was involved and July was months ago. We were, I was sure, caught up in the fun of the Pride cabaret show and Tony and Denice's amazing Cyr wheel routine. At the time I thought it was just a joke - wishful thinking, silly daydreaming. Never for a moment did I mean I actually, really, literally wanted to perform a hoop routine. In public. To an audience.

Tony took the silly talk seriously and has booked us a cabaret tent for the Brighton Festival in May.

'Just a small one, 200 capacity and we can only have it for one afternoon show.' He says as if by way of apology.

Cecile, Jo and Theresa are ridiculously excited and absolutely no one is hearing me over their racket.

'200! Brighton? In front of people. No, seriously I can't do it. I just can't'. I try to make myself heard but Tony grabs me in a bear hug and says, 'we'll have a blast Wendy - trust me.'

Wolf breaks out what he calls 'celebratory brownies' - which I guess are the funny kind. I don't have one. I think everyone in the room is high enough already.

I've never been to Brighton and have only vaguely heard of the festival. For the most part, and not very often if truth be told, I'm drawn to plays in theatres, not tents, which might explain how it has passed me by. Tony and Theresa have both performed in shows there.

'Weekday afternoons are a graveyard slot' Tony says it's why the tent bookings manager didn't mind amateurs having it. 'It's the small tent and we only have it for an hour. There might be more people on stage than in the audience but it'll be a laugh'.

Theresa and Tony each have chums who might want to do a turn.

'I've got the number of that fire eater we met at Pride. I'll ring her' Jo says but I catch the edge of a sharp look from Jinx as she does.

All the while I'm adamant I'll watch but not perform. I can't have put enough effort into Melody Skyhorse's lesson on how to be gracefully assertive because nobody takes the slightest bit of notice.

It's great to see Theresa looking so smiley. It must be hard for someone so skilled not to be able to perform and she's itching to do it. Cecile seems as excited and rings Raquel. Of all of us, Raquel is always the most sensible one but even she seems keen about us doing the show. I don't know what has gotten into everyone. Won't a fire eater be dangerous in a small tent?

'Wendy we'll all be terrible - it doesn't matter, it's OK for it not to be perfect you know!' I know Jo is trying to help me feel comfortable about the whole thing but the more her and Cecile laughed about how ridiculous we will be, the more anxious I feel about the terrible idea. 'I'm not wearing Lycra' I say to inject a bit of reality into the foolishness.

'Well, I certainly am!' Cecile giggles.

I try to get Andy to see my point of view on the drive home but he thinks I'm making a fuss about nothing.

'Of course you can do it love. You'll be amazing' he tells me but I wonder if he has forgotten the last time I tried the hoop hand toss in our garden. It cost a small fortune to have the kitchen window replaced and the bird table couldn't be salvaged.

'I'm not a perfectionist am I Andy?'

Andy navigated the junction before he replied.

'No, not a perfectionist love, but maybe an idealist'.

We pulled into our driveway but didn't get out of the car. Some conversations are too important to interrupt.

'It's not a criticism love - not at all. You like the world to be a particular way and do your best to make sure it is. That's a good thing!'

Melody Skyhorse says we own our personal growth. It can't be given to us and we only need to tune into pings when lessons are delivered to us to reflect upon. Andy's words send over a loud and clear ping and I lay in bed mulling it over long after he's gone to sleep. There's the hint of a critical space between perfect and ideal. It's the space where expectations live. It's the place where *should* lurks.

Despite Andy's positive slant on it, I can't help but wonder if my expectations about how things should be are a way of trying to impose my will on how they are. An ideal world might be neat but it's also tidy of all the messy possible alternatives. It's funny that Pippa sometimes drives me mad - she's always clear about the right or the wrong way things need to be done and I always wish she could be more carefree and that I think she should be more like - me? Maybe she *is* like me? Maybe the truth is that I am *less* footloose and fancy-free than I think I am.

Middle of the night thoughts can be so unsettling.

The thing is, I imagine a lot of people worry about getting cancer, and I guess people imagine winning big on the lottery but I bet I'm in a fairly exclusive club of people who get them both at the same time. When the Courier wrote about us they made a big deal about the 'life-changing' win. They included a list of things we could buy - including a helicopter! But they got it wrong. The money, lovely as it is, has occupied a lot less space in my head than cancer and the possibility of dying. Cancer is life-changing. Not money. I'd give every penny of the lottery win away if I could be sure of living the allocated biblical three score years and ten alongside Andy. I don't want to die and have spent a lot of time thinking about how to give myself the best shot at survival but the truth is, no matter what or who I cut out, my life will be as long as it will be. I can't control when the universe decides my time has come. 'Best shots' aim for 'should' targets but they're a placebo - I am sure carb reduction and the avoidance of heroin helps me have a healthier feeling and more comfortable life but notions that I'm in control of anything, seem ridiculous. Andy's struck a nerve and he's right. Trying to make sure my life goes in a particular way has occupied a lot of my effort over the years. There needs to be space for 'as is' being good enough.

The light has changed and I can hear the birds starting to

chirrup awake. I slip out of bed so I don't wake Andy, make myself a cuppa and boot up the laptop. I add the 'big show' practice dates to my calendar. After that, I send an email to Angela. It is time to try being a bit more free-range.

Be You!

Who is your authentic self? Which 'you' do you ache to be? Which parts of your essential self do you hide from the world? The universe celebrates truth, free the real you!
Everyday Grace

We'd arranged to meet at Raquel's to discuss the finances so I wasn't expecting Theresa, Jo and Raquel to gang up on me.

We've scheduled two slots for the hula hoop classes. The evening slot places are nearly all taken which is exciting but take up for the afternoon session is slow despite our local marketing.

Raquel had called in a favour from an old school friend of hers who works on a regional news TV programme. He said they might be interested in running a piece about us only it had to be newsworthy 'something people would be interested in' so she'd told him about me being a cancer surviving lottery winner. I wish she'd asked me first.

'They want human interest, Wendy. You want new hoopers - it's a win-win'. Raquel thinks I am our best marketing tool. 'Thanks to the Courier it is not exactly a secret is it Wendy? Going on TV is a way to give us the kind of publicity reach we can only dream of'.

Jo chips in' Look, we're all sure there's a market but kids are so exhausting we have to make the classes sound like something worth the extra effort to get there. If they want you on TV, you need to do this Wendy. If we get them there that first time, we know they'll come back!'

It's all very well for them. They're used to being seen and heard in their work roles. Being front of house is not something you want to be in public convenience cleaning.

'Well, if our business is relying on me we're already in trouble!' I half-heartedly joke to try to take the pressure off but in her usual crisp Raquel way she tells me off 'Don't do that Wendy. Don't put yourself down. Only you can do it Wendy. It has to be you'.

I don't think I lack confidence exactly. Mam used to say I have 'quiet confidence'. Cecile is boisterously sure of herself and it's lovely to be around her because her positive energy is infectious. I always end up laughing when I'm with her. I don't have her kind of room shining presence and I know it. Melody Skyhorse says it's important to know ourselves. We had to do an audit of our strengths and areas for development. I liked that she didn't say weaknesses because it's much easier to be self-critical than nice. I think I'm realistic about myself. I'm a capable human being but I also know my role is to prop others up so they can shine. I don't feel bad about it. We all have a place and that's mine. I think I do it well. I can be relied upon. I don't think any of these qualities are putting myself down so much as being matter of fact. I don't have the ego to even contemplate being a lynchpin but Raquel - who has all the self-assured qualities you might expect in a lynchpin - seems to think I am.

'You made this happen Wendy. The money helped undoubtedly, but this whole thing was your idea. We wouldn't be having this conversation if it wasn't for you'.

Theresa and Jo nod in unison like those irritating dog ornaments you sometimes see on car dashboards. I'm not sure whether they concur or are going along with Raquel so I'll agree with their ridiculous idea.

Melody Skyhorse says it's easy to be confident in situations that don't test us but in situations where we feel less sure of ourselves we should observe how others go about it and take help and advice where we can get it. It turns out help is closer than I could ever have imagined.

'We should ask Cecile - she's used to talking to telly people. She'll help'. Jo and Raquel seem to think this is a marvellous idea but I don't get why she would know about being on the telly.

It turns out Cecile is a teacher equivalent of Clark Kent. She goes into a classroom as an English teacher but goes to Seychelles and is a pop star. I can't get my head around it when Jo shows me the video on YouTube. On the video she's called 'Dannnni' with a lot of 'n's but it's definitely Cecile. She sounds amazing.

'She's famous at home. She's great isn't she?'

I can't wrap my head around why a pop star is a teacher in Yorkshire but Jo says Cecile loves teaching.

'She had a hit record when she was a teenager and it took off from there. She never makes a big deal of it at school. I don't think they even know in the music department'.

I can't imagine Tina Turner or Dolly Parton thinking their work is a job on the side but Jo says Cecile doesn't take the pop star stuff seriously. She visits Seychelles during school holidays, does a few gigs to promote her records and invests in property for when she retires. I'd no idea.

A couple of phone calls later I've arranged to go to Cecile's for a coaching session and Raquel's TV friend tells me where I need to be and to get to their studios early. In two days time, I'll be going live on air. I can't believe I've been press-ganged by them all and we never even discussed the finances.

The building we go to looks like a tatty old factory and not glamorous like you would expect a TV studio to be. By the time I get there I feel sick with anxiety and so does Andy who I made come with me.

Helen, the research assistant offered the opportunity for me to be interviewed on a video call if I insisted but she made it clear they'd prefer me to go into the studio.

'Human-interest stories work best when there's a couch. Red - I don't know why but there you have it' she said.

Andy and I get there nice and early but all the waiting around makes me feel even more nervous. I shouldn't have had the second coffee but the free cakes looked too delicious to leave and you can't have one without the other. I'm not sure why they call it the green room because it isn't green but we are not allowed to wander about and it's embarrassing having to ask to use the loo.

When she rang, Helen told me not to wear a striped or checked top for my appearance as it plays havoc with their screen backgrounds so I opted for plain black.

'Oh my days. Your jumper's going to show every speck of dust on the camera. Did you bring anything else?' You would think the young chap dusting my face with powder to stop my forehead from shining might be trained to help people feel calmer but apparently not. I didn't even know I had a shiny forehead. All in all, I feel less than prepared to be on regional television and in fact, terrified. Once made up I sit in the green room and try to remember Cecile's coaching.

Cecile said I had to be myself, listen to what was being asked but be sure to wrangle what I wanted to say into my answers. We had a bit of a practise so she could show me. I had to ask her bonkers questions.

'Do you grow tomato plants?' I asked. As bonkers questions go it wasn't very but when someone says you've to ask something insane your mind goes limp.

'Well,' Cecile started, 'That is a fascinating question Wendy and I do in fact grow tomatoes - when I have the time around my amazing hula hoop classes at the Hepworth School Hall every week'.

She made it look so easy. According to Cecile press interviews are transactional. They want something from you and you want something from them. So long as each side follows the path, interviews are a doddle. I've to focus on what I want to say. Just don't swear, she cautioned. Except for gangsta rappers, they never like a swearer.

It's surprisingly hot under the studio lights and I'm sure my forehead will be shiny within seconds. I've to wait next to a cameraman and am hurried onto a red sofa. They don't want Andy to join me. If I'd known I'd be going out on TV news, live, to the entire world, all by myself I'd never have come. He flaps me in the direction of the couch and tells me I'll be fine.

The woman interviewing me is ever so smiley and has incredible hair. It is dark, thick and shiny and moves like hair does in conditioner advertisements. Not a grey or stray in sight. It looks like it might smell of apples. I have a weird compulsion to go over and sniff her head. It's all I can remember about the whole thing. When we're ushered out of the studio I've no idea what she asked or what I answered. Andy says I did brilliantly but he wasn't allowed to film me on his phone in case it rang while we were on air. I'm sure I didn't swear.

When we leave the studio we drive straight to Pippa's. Everything is on the internet these days but she offered to record the interview for us to be sure we have a copy to keep. I am not sure I want one but part of me is dying to see it. I've never been on telly before. Another part of me is dreading it. Andy tells me I didn't say anything stupid but of course, he would say that. As we navigate the country roads on the way back from Leeds, I get texts from Jo, Theresa, Raquel, two old school friends I didn't know had my number, Consultant Cathy, Donna our neighbour and one from a blocked number. Apart from the one asking for money everyone else says the interview went well.

'You were AMAZING!' Jo's text is typically supportive. Some people, and I wonder if I'm one of them, are a bit reserved with praise. I don't mean that false praise aerobic teachers always give in gyms when everyone is 'fantastic' and 'awesome' even if they are sweating like donkeys, puce in the face, I mean something more honest and sincere. Melody Skyhorse says acknowledging another's strengths is a graceful power that shines a little bit of brightening sun. She says when we shine on others, the whole world is lighter for all of us. Sometimes I imagine Melody Skyhorse must be a lovely woman to be around but I wonder if she gets on her friends' nerves with her determined cheeriness. I may need to do more graceful work on my cynicism.

Jo has a knack for making people feel valued. I'd like to be the kind of person that encourages others and as I resolve to be a bit more light shining myself, I get an unexpected opportunity. Angela is at Pippa's. She comes to give me an air hug but I'm not prepared and move away.

Angela hasn't responded to my email. I don't even know if she's read it. Pippa sensing a chill says, 'I asked Angela round to watch you on telly Mum'.

Angela attempts to fill the slightly tense gap between us. 'You didn't look a bit flustered and that top looked nice on you'.

I can tell she's making an effort but it is so unlike her to be light-shining I wait for the 'but', sure she'll follow up with something critical, only she doesn't.

I'm not expecting Cecile to be at Pippa's either though thanks to Pippa volunteering at the school in prep for her teacher training course, she and Cecile are becoming quite good chums.

Andy reads the vibe of the room, decides he's out of his depth and waffling on about the car tyres needing air he disappears off to the garage.

Cecile is as ebullient as always and full of praise saying I handled the interview like a pro. I don't know if teachers get training on how to be encouraging because, like Jo, she always sees the positive.

'You forgot to mention the creche but you did brilliantly batting off the misery porn'.

When Cecile was coaching me she said she thought they would want to focus on the cancer and win but I needed to bring it back to the classes. She was right.

As we watch the recording back, the tussle between Ms Shiny hair's sad 'it must've been awful hearing you had cancer' face and my 'yes but hula hooping is fantastic' happy face is obvious. I'm not sure she's too pleased I wouldn't be teary-eyed and there's a definite mean-spirited steely glint in hers when she ends the three minutes by saying 'I'm sure the huge lottery win helps too'. Pippa stopped the recording after Ms Shiny hair started to talk about farmers' protests about beavers being released into a local stream.

It's strange seeing yourself on the telly. I want to ask Pippa to play it again but don't in case it comes across as starry ego. It was my posture I noticed first.

'Why on earth did I fold my arms and what was the daft giggle about?'

'Mum anyone could see you were a bit nervous. Local news programmes aren't expecting you to be normal in front of their cameras'.

It hasn't escaped my attention that unusually for someone who likes the sound of her own voice, Angela hasn't said much at all. One of us has to break the ice so when Pippa goes to the kitchen to get wine and Cecile nips to the loo I tell her it's nice to see her, and as I say it, I realise it's true. It *is* nice to see her.

I send Andy a message to say I'm staying for a while and I'll get a taxi home. Pippa brings wine, glasses, cheese and biscuits and lays them out on the coffee table.

'You shouldn't have said 'bum' on the telly though Mum. A bit common'.

Pippa and I don't usually see each other just for the fun of it. We do family occasions of course, but never spend time enjoying each other's company. I don't know why because the four of us end up having a lovely evening especially when Cecile fills us in on some delicious gossip about pop stars she has worked with. One of the boy bands look like butter wouldn't melt too. It just goes to show.

Andy's already in bed when I get home. Matthew's left such a nice message on the answerphone. He watched the clip via a link Pippa sent and says he's proud of me. Four begging letters and a pamphlet reminding me about Jesus needing a new church roof on St Martins have been pushed through our letterbox and I get a text from Theresa to say every single slot on the online booking platform has been filled. 'Could you come over tomorrow to discuss adding another class?'

Jo and Raquel are already there when I get to Theresa and Wolf's the next lunchtime. I notice they've added a door to Clover's bedroom and there's a new kitchen worktop. Theresa says it's from recycled pallets Wolf took out of a skip. It looks functional, if a bit uneven, and suits their house but I'd have opted for easier to clean laminate.

'I can't believe demand' Theresa says, 'I know someone who can do more classes for us if we want?'

Jo thinks we should run more 'We need to capitalise before it becomes old news'.

Raquel says the booking fees have already covered our costs so far and we are into profit so we can afford to take on another class leader.

Theresa's chum, Sofia, is someone she knows from the performance circuit.

'Hooping is a hobby, her specialism is aerial silks - you know, long ribbon acrobatics'.

Sofia and Theresa worked together for a tour of Europe and according to Theresa, she's keen to come on board.

'She needed to be back in the UK to care for her parents so she isn't intending to go on tour for a while. This gig suits her and the money will help'.

We all agree to add another class to the schedule and invite Sofia to come on board. Hoop Troupe will have three large classes running. Cecile was right about going on the telly. The response has been beyond anything we could've imagined. We're giddy with excitement when Raquel drops her bombshell; she has to hand over the reins of the money management because she has a new job.

'I'll be bursar so it's a rather marvellous step up for me. I'm going to have to put all my energy into it for a while'.

I thought a bursar was one of those people that rang bells and shouted 'oyez' at village fairs but it turns out it's like the finance manager job she has at school but millions of pounds bigger. It sounds important though a bit boring but Raquel loves sums. I guess that's why she and Jo get on so well. She's always said she was helping out and didn't want to come on board full-time so it isn't a surprise she has to move on.

None of us feel skilled enough to take on the accounts side of things.

'Can we afford to take someone on part-time?' Theresa asks and Raquel agrees it's probably our best option - account management needs someone who knows what they're doing. 'I can create a job description if that helps?' she offers.

I catch Jo's eye. She's smiling like the cat that got the cream. Neither of us can believe we will be interviewing for an actual proper job in our actual proper company.

Of all the women I know, Raquel seems to be the scariest. She isn't of course, not really. It's because she's posh. She says words like 'gander' and 'jolly' which are not scary or posh words at all so I don't know how they manage to give off an air of privilege. Underneath the no-nonsense, business-like exterior, she's kind and thoughtful and the sort of person you always want to be on your side. Jo calls her the 'all-seeing eye' because she has this knack of being able to read any situation and intuitively know what needs to be done. What with her and Jo being clever and knowing each other for a long time I assumed it would be those two doing the interviewing but Raquel won't hear of it.

'Of course it must be you. You're far warmer than I am. You've an instinct for reading people I don't have'.

Melody Skyhorse says in our mirrors, others see their shadows. It was a complicated lesson. I had no idea what she meant by there being much to learn from mirror reflections. It took me a while to appreciate that if we see a quality in others we admire or dislike, it's an opportunity for us to evaluate our own qualities. All of us are good at some things and less good at others and that's common sense but I see people being better at so many things than I am all the time. I don't think I spend nearly enough time on my positive qualities. I wonder if any of us do really. Raquel isn't being nice to me or hard on herself, she's assessing the reflection and doesn't seem to feel bad I'm more affable than her. I know I am but I'm still chuffed to bits that *she* thinks I am.

I may be a businesswoman but the inside of our fridge doesn't clean itself. There's a parsnip in the bottom of my salad drawer that looks like a relic we once saw in a cabinet in a cathedral. It has always surprised me that random body parts have religious significance but each to their own. The parsnip is left over from Christmas which is embarrassing given my previous career. So it smells fresh I am giving the fridge insides a once-over with half a lemon when the phone rings.

I've never heard of 'Girl Talk' and my hand is stuck inside a rubber glove so I'm distracted. For a moment I think it's a dodgy call but it turns out it's a TV producer with a husky voice.

'Neela saw your interview and found your story inspirational. We'd like to share it with our viewers'. She's surprised I've never heard of either Neela or Girl Talk but it turns out it's a daytime TV talk show which explains why.

Even when I came home from the hospital I didn't watch daytime TV. Once, when I had the flu and was being revoltingly snotty on the sofa, Andy put the telly on but rubbish programmes about selling houses at auctions did nothing to make me feel better so I tucked up with a novel.

I tell the producer I'm not sure and will let her know. Andy is out so I ring Pippa to ask what she thinks. It turns out she's a huge fan of one of the panel members.

'It's a group of four women chatting about stuff. Can I come with you Mum? I *love* Orla. She's so funny!'

I try to explain to Pippa that I'm not sure I want to talk about cancer fear or answer the predictable questions about swimming pools and the lottery win but she's more wrapped up in being a fan of the Orla person than understanding my anxieties.

When I ring Theresa who also hasn't seen the show because they don't have a telly, she's more understanding but agrees with Pippa. 'All the classes are full' she says 'but Sofia could take another evening slot. I doubt we'll get this opportunity again so if you can bear doing it, the publicity will be great for bookings.'

I know Theresa's right. As I know from experience, being on the telly is advertising value way beyond what we budgeted for flyers to leave in cafes so I ring the producer back and tell her I'd love to come on the show.

When I get back to cleaning the fridge I realise I won't have to 'bear it'. Last time I was scared half to death but digging mouldy crumbs of heaven knows what out of the door seal, I'm looking forward to being on the telly again. I'm going to buy myself a TV outfit - something non-striped, non-black, not too posh, not too casual. Something a bit stylish. My wardrobe's starting to fill up again but with lovely things that bring me joy. I think Melody Skyhorse would approve.

CARE

Tend

Banish negative self-talk! Do not invest precious energy in perceived faults. Confidently invest in constructive self-enhancement.

Everyday Grace

Rose and Clover are busy dipping vegetable crisps into mashed up avocado. They've managed to put a lot of it in their hair but seem to be having fun. Pippa doesn't allow Rose to have shop-bought crisps but the salt-free, fat-free - and, in all honesty, dull and flavourless homemade beetroot and carrot ones Theresa dropped off with Clover are OK.

Pippa's seeing a solicitor about their house so we offered to have Rose. Theresa and Wolf are taking delivery of railway sleepers for their garden so we offered to have Clover too.

It turns out the house is only in Christopher's name which doesn't seem very modern. Pippa won't be buying him out but will be paying to have her name put on the deeds. I'm trying not to be worried about why she isn't on them in the first place.

'It makes no odds Mum. The solicitor says we can stay in the house anyway until Rose is older - I don't want to uproot her. Christopher's fine with it'.

Christopher's a decent enough chap but I've never much taken to him if truth be told. He works hard and has always been what my dad would've called 'a good provider' but he's never... frivolous. He wears ties when he doesn't have to. I'm glad he's not being difficult about the details of their separation, but I feel cross he's not even trying to hang on to Pippa and his beautiful daughter.

'None of us know the realities of other people's relationships love' Andy says. 'Don't go making assumptions about what Christopher's feeling about the end of their marriage'.

Andy is right but I feel guilty about them splitting up, which is daft. Melody Skyhorse says we should mindfully note critical self-talk as it doesn't contribute to our psychological well-being. We're supposed to listen to the lessons within the critique and work on those instead. It's her way of saying 'get over yourself'. I accept feeling guilty does no good whatsoever for anyone but I did notice things were not as they should be between Pippa and Christopher and I pretended not to because it seemed easier all round. So, I should feel bad, shouldn't I?

Andy, who hasn't even read any Melody Skyhorse lessons says even though we did notice something awry, the people who needed to notice more were Pippa and Christopher and some things aren't the responsibility of parents to fix. He's right of course, but I wonder if he's persuading himself as well as me. I know he's worried about Pippa and he's barely said a word about Christopher which is a sure sign his opinions are strong enough to need keeping to himself. Some things *are* our responsibility to fix though so while Andy tries to mine the avocado out of Rose's ear with a tissue and promise of an ice pop, I ring Angela. I've been putting it off for over a fortnight and not ringing like I promised I would is starting a slide into a danger zone of not ringing at all so I bite the bullet.

I could've said we should meet at our usual coffee shop but instead of an awkward hour of not addressing the problem over a caramel latte and bun, I suggest we make an afternoon of it. 'Well that's easy for you because you don't work and I need to take time off' Angela says. I breathe into not snapping back a 'well let's not flipping bother then'. I'm working at developing a positive attitude and to be fair, she has a point.

A new place has opened in town called 'The Listening Booth'. It's in the old telephone exchange building and getting rave reviews so I book us a table for lunch. Angela and I haven't properly listened to each other for years. I hope she doesn't think the venue choice is a dig. I also book us in for a couple of afternoon sessions at a bowling alley. The last time the two of us went bowling I didn't have kids and that alley closed years ago so I've booked at the multiplex by the harbour. It's a bit of a bonkers choice and I don't much fancy wearing shoes last worn by some teenager with fungal toes but it fit the bill. Going for a walk is too wholesome and I can't be doing with pamper sessions. I will never understand the attraction of massages and whatnot, though Pippa is a fan. The thought of being slathered in cream and having it rubbed in by a stranger makes me cringe and don't even get me started on the obligatory pan pipe music. I can't imagine even Peruvians like that. I needed an activity that allows us to talk but is engaging enough to take the pressure off. She was always sportier than me at school so she'll win which will make her happy so it seems like a good choice. Besides, I couldn't think of anything else.

Angela is clear it's a bonkers choice too. Before we even order our starters she tells me she thinks being on the telly must've addled my brain but I say it wasn't the telly so much as having cancer and that shuts her up. So anyway, long story short… we have a chat. Not 'a chat', more '*the* chat'. The conversation I want and don't want to have about how I care about her but things have to be different. Only, weirdly, she starts it, not me.

'I'm sorry things have been bad since… the paper thing Wendy. I let you down I know but we've been getting on each other's nerves for a while haven't we?'

She'd been on a date and knew he worked for the paper but never imagined he would use what she said in an article.

'I didn't know it was allowed. I thought they had to get permission. He hurt my feelings so much Wendy. I haven't seen him since'.

The funny thing is, I've done all this Melody Skyhorse learning about achieving balance and owning our truths but

Angela seems to have worked a lot out on her own and, I must admit, she's right. She says we've forgotten why we're friends and focus on faults instead of what we like about each other. She doesn't know how we got into what she calls a bad habit, and I don't either. I imagined it was me that wanted it to stop but she does too.

'You never think I'm good enough Wendy and I don't know what to do to be good enough for you'. She might as well have pushed me over because it's such a shock to realise there's truth in what she says and as much as I've wanted her to change, I don't want to be who she says I am either.

As predicted, she's winning the first game. It turns out, that rubbish old adage we used to tell the kids on school sports days about it not being the winning but taking part that counts, has some truth in it after all. We allow each other one single 'I won't do this anymore if you don't' per ball thrown. We run out of points on our 'what we want in our positive friendship list' before we've even started the second game. The thing is, there are not many actual points, but they're big points - like trust and respect. We both want the same things as it turns out and we both have a job to do to earn them.

Bowling is a lot more fun than I remember. These days they even spray the shoes with disinfectant. We book to come again. Andy and I haven't been bowling since we were courting but it will give us a chance to meet Angela's new chap. Ian the librarian sounds completely unlike someone she would usually go for but she's teenage girl smiley about him and I'm intrigued.

Angela wins of course. Both games. As we cross the car park she can't help herself.

'Trust you to throw the ball backwards. You could've killed him!'

Letting go of a heavy missile in the wrong direction was not my finest hour. Thank goodness the lane attendant managed to move out of the way. For a tiny little second, I feel a spark of annoyance about the criticism but we end up laughing like drains and have our first proper hug in ages.

With hindsight, going bowling less than a year after a mastectomy might not have been a good plan because three days later my shoulder is still creaky and stiff so show rehearsals don't get off to a good start. Tony says we have plenty of time to get the routine perfect but I'm sure he underestimates how long I'll need and overestimates my hooping skills. Melody Skyhorse says self-sabotage is one of our most dangerous enemies. Graces are encouraged to SSR - spot, stop and reframe whenever we find ourselves doing it. Reframing, I try to imagine it's a class and not think too much about doing the routine in front of an audience. Still, in my head, I can see watching faces and as soon as I do that my hoop hits the floor. I've some way to go with SSR.

Raquel's decided she can't be in our show at all.

'Too busy in her new job to give time to rehearsal which is a downer. She doesn't even know if she can come to see us – apparently, it's a really busy time for uni recruitment.' Tony explains Raquel had rung him to apologise. It won't be the same without her and we're all disappointed. I wish I had an excuse but Jo won't let me bow out.

'We capitalise on you being on the telly. People know your story now so it might help bring people in'.

I know she has a point but it doesn't help at all. The audience *is* my problem. I know the telly audience was much bigger but I couldn't see them. Our audience in the festival tent will be proper people who've paid ticket money and I'm sure I'm not up to the job. I'm also not completely comfortable with the idea of people coming to see the one-breasted lottery winner either. It has a whiff of freak show about it.

'Stop being a drama queen Wendy' Jo says. 'Our slot's only ten minutes and the fact is, you've already drawn attention to yourself on Girl Talk. What's the worst that can happen?'

I haven't kept my hoop up longer than five spins for the whole of our rehearsal so far so I think it's obvious but Jo says it will be fine and I should enjoy it. Tony has pulled together other cabaret performers to pad out the hour-long tent booking.

The show will be hosted by a drag act who is a woman, dragging up as a man. I don't get the attraction of it but Cecile says modern drag is nothing like the racist, sexist, homophobic man in a badly fitting frock that it used to be so women are doing it now. Tony is doing a tap dance routine with Denice. Theresa and our newly recruited teacher, Sofia, are doing an aerial silk routine and Cecile is going to sing a couple of tunes to a backing track but as herself and not Dannnni so she doesn't draw unwanted attention. I know how she feels. The fire eater we met at Pride will be doing a slot so it will be nice to see her again. Six of us will be hooping - Jo, Cecile, Theresa, Tony and Sofia and me. Four of them are used to performing to audiences and Jo is used to being in front of a class so I'm the sore thumb. The truth of it is, the worst that can happen is me - that I let them down.

Theresa and Tony chose a bouncy song for us to hoop to - a proper toe-tapper with a good beat. They've choreographed a routine they say works to each of our strengths. In my head, I think I should be the hoop holder on the side of the stage, but I don't say it out loud because Jo can be proper shouty when she hears me being negative.

'We only have ten minutes to tell our story and it's important we engage the audience from the off'. Tony says.

Our stage story is going to be about empowerment. I hadn't grasped we would be telling a story, I thought we would be hooping. According to Tony, our performance will be about sharing skills and growing together. I'd love to be able to tell Melody Skyhorse about it because I'm sure she would be impressed. I figured out he means the good ones can be good on stage and the bad ones have an excuse because we are being empowered.

'When we do this you need to look around the audience, keep your eyes open, but most of all, have fun. We're making magic people!' I would like to tell Tony that shouting at us is not particularly empowering but I don't.

Theresa and Sofia brought to rehearsal amazing performance hoops lit by LED lights. When they spin they look like haloes. Theresa says it's better for the rest of us to work with familiar tools and use our ordinary hoops. Cecile grabs one of the LED hoops, rests it on her tiny waist and is off.

'I'll be using one of these' Cecile says. She has empowerment cracked.

At the end of rehearsal, Theresa and Tony talk us through a crib sheet of hoop tricks to work on at home. Theresa and Sofia have some added twiddles in their routines which he says we can ignore but even without them, it's a daunting list including things I've never once mastered. I've attempted the lasso, the passing the hoop round my body, and the lift up from hip to waist. I'm useless at all of them. I've never even heard of an escalator beyond M & S and the underground but Theresa says that's why we have rehearsals.

'We'll meet twice a week until the show, more if we need to. In the meantime, practise, practise and more practice. We'll be great!'.

Her enthusiasm is encouraging but even Jo looks a bit anxious and I'm not sure either of us are thinking we will be.

'Don't forget our meeting on Tuesday!' Theresa calls as she gets on her bike after rehearsal. She has a glow about her and I realise how much she must miss performing.

When Jo, Husnara - our newest recruit, and I arrive at Theresa's for our meeting she gives us a tour of the work they've been doing on their house. It's coming along a treat.

'New handrail on the stairs but come and have a look at the raised beds. They're ready for veg planting' Theresa says leading us all outside. I'm not sure Husnara's very interested in Theresa's plans for onions and radishes and gives an air of wanting to get on with the business at hand. She'll get used to our way of doing things eventually.

Husnara has an air of crisp about her but as soon as Jo and I met her we knew she was the right one. Before we'd asked her a single question she told us what she was offering and how much she wanted.

'I am efficient, honest and skilled. I have two children I need to work around so you will get my commitment but they come first so if this doesn't suit you let's not waste our time today' she told us.

There wasn't a smidge of apology about her and we liked her style. She started working with us the very next day. Theresa makes us tea and puts a tub of peanut biscuits on the kitchen table where we are gathered. I don't try to persuade Jo to have one. She isn't on a diet, just eating healthily. I thought vegan food was mostly healthy but she says biscuits are carbs and sugar so I have hers. They're delicious.

Husnara has all the office running skills we didn't know we needed. We don't have an office of course but within days with just the phone and laptop, she has organised the accounts retrieved from Raquel and handled all the bookings. There are a lot of bookings. Husnara ignores the biscuits and is keen to draw us to order 'You don't pay me to chit chat' she says.

'Your Girl Talk appearance resulted in all places being taken on the same day. I have started a reserve list. Creche sessions are in high demand. Can you run more classes? Should I book now for classes for next term and if so, for how many classes?' It is a bit overwhelming though Husnara seems to be taking it in her stride. She gives a slight tut and shake of her head when Theresa says she doesn't want to commit to delivering more classes until Clover starts pre-school.

'Sofia's already said she can take another couple of classes so perhaps if we do one more afternoon and one evening - for now?'

Theresa, Jo and I agree that five classes is more than enough to be going along with and, more than any of us expected in a million years! We are chuffed to bits but Husnara, with just a hint of impatience, says we will barely make a dent in her reserve list.

'I will sort start dates with Sofia, arrange the creche team and contact people on the reserve list about booking'. Husnara reaches for a biscuit and adds 'This tea is stewed. Perhaps a fresh pot?'

I think we've passed her interview of us - but maybe only just.

Tribute

Our view of ourselves is formed from our interaction with our worlds. It is not truth. When others point out your glory and grace, take time to hear your tributes, to feel them, to absorb them, to bask in the amazingness of you!
Everyday Grace

It's funny how easily I slip into mother mode and forget my children are grown adults who have credit cards, sex and need no reminders to brush their teeth. Offspring, by and large, are not known for being complementary to their parents so I must admit I wonder if Matthew is having a bit of a tease of me.

'We admire you Mum, you're an inspiration and got us thinking'

Yuuto, sitting next to Matthew nods in agreement. In the video call frame I can see the Mapplethorpe back on the wall behind them and I'm glad.

'Ooookaaaay. What is going on?' I'm not sure what the agenda is but I'm sure there is one.

'I'm serious Mum, how you've made things happen with the hooping business is amazing. Couldn't have imagined it in a million years. I mean... a hooping business? ... and coping with cancer as well? It's crazy Mum. You're awesome!'

I'm sent a bit left field by the praise when Yuuto chips in.

'Our project's going better than expected too. We couldn't have done it without your help. We want to acknowledge that and say thank you'.

I guess most parents want their kids to think they've done alright by them but being admired and inspirational does not sit right. Compliments from my children make me feel ... embarrassed and flustered.

Melody Skyhorse is always encouraging us to be open to gratitude. When we refuse to hear or accept it we are closing our heart to ourselves and others and yet it's on the tip of my tongue to brush off the praise of me and ramble on about how wonderful they are. She calls it a cycle of deflection reciprocation caused by our vulnerability. It's funny how it's so much easier to tell someone else they are lovely than to hear it about ourselves. Why does hearing that we are valued make us feel unsafe somehow? I wonder if it's because we are scared we can't live up to others' expectations of us. I decide to have a go at active gratitude.

'Thank you. It's nice to be appreciated' I say but I put a bit of flip lightness into it so they don't think my ego is showing.

Not everything has been going as well for them as they hoped. Despite the citizenship app they made, both of them have been mired in applying for Yuuto's. Matthew passed his US civics test the first time and is ready for a swearing in process. It should be the same process for both of them but Yuuto failed his test twice.

'I'm not going to book my swearing-in until Yuuto can do it too'.

None of us can believe he failed the test. He's more of an expert on America than most Americans. I suspect most wouldn't know the longest river in the USA any more than I know the longest river in the UK. I wonder if the Americans still have the hump about Pearl Harbour but I don't say so out loud.

Their app is working fine and even the US Government are interested in it which seems ironic to me given Yuuto's experience so far.

'It would help if they endorsed it for sure. Making apps is easy. Millions are launched every day - it's getting them noticed that's hard. Our US launch is underway and going well. After that, we'll forge ahead with Europe, the Middle East and later Sub-Saharan Africa'.

To my surprise, Matthew says the hassle they are having

with Yuuto's green card has them pondering on whether the States is where they want to live.

'No, we aren't being all conspiracy nut-jobs about it - we honestly think it is administrative but we wonder if it is time to move on.'

I'm not sure how anyone could be weary of almost permanent sunshine or have a wish for what Matthew calls a 'proper autumn walk'. I think he's forgotten about sleet. There's nothing positive about autumn sleet.

'It's not just that Mum - we want to buy our own place but taxes here are so high…'

'Have you thought about coming home son? Me and your dad could help.'

I could slap myself for letting that slip out. I never want to put any expectations on Matthew but we both miss him. I don't want him to think I'm pressuring him to come home though. I'm about to reassure him that isn't my intention when Yuuto surprises me by saying yes, they have considered moving to the UK as a possibility.

'Our work is web-based so can operate from anywhere - it's really down to where we want to be'.

Japan is apparently more liberal than I'd realised but legally, their rights would still be limited so it's not on the list of options. I can't help but wonder how Yuuto's mum might feel if they came to the UK. She must miss her son as much as I miss mine.

Melody Skyhorse says we need to take responsibility for our own growth and this involves internal honesty. I have to fess up to Matthew and Yuuto that part of me hopes he doesn't pass his civics test but I laugh as if I'm joking so I don't come across as mean.

'Sorry I'm not there for your birthday this year Mum, especially as….'. I haven't forgotten the anniversary of my diagnosis but I don't want to give thoughts of cancer any more energy than its already had. Instead, I remind Matthew about how awful my last party was and we have a bit of a giggle. Yuuto is as bemused by the notions of mini pork pies as a party nibble as I am about sushi as fine dining and I say I'll have both at my next gathering. Ever polite, he says he will look forward to it.

'Is Dad taking you somewhere nice this year Mum?' I suspect Matthew thinks what with so-far successful treatment and us being rich there should be a swanky celebration but I told Andy I didn't want any fuss. He seems to have taken me at my word.

After we end the video call I feel bad I wasn't supportive enough about Yuuto's US citizenship problems. I text Matthew to apologise but he replies I shouldn't be so daft and they both know I have their best interests at heart and that makes me feel worse because in all honesty, it wasn't their best interest but mine. I wish Matthew lived nearer.

Being 59 is a pants birthday. 'Neither nowt nor summat' my dad would've said.

When I was thirteen, on Saturday mornings for a bit of pocket money, I helped out in our local shop weighing out veg for customers. We celebrated the butcher's sixtieth with a cake. The cake had one single candle because there wasn't enough room on it for 60. When he blew it out I remember him saying he'd 'entered God's waiting room' but with a teenager's sensibility, I was amazed someone had even lived to such an ancient age. I remember working out what year it would be if I ever became so old but the dates - in the next *millennium* - seemed the stuff of space travel. And now here I am. One year away from God's waiting room myself. All things being equal, what with the cancer, I should be glad to have got this far and positive about getting some more years in. I am, and I'm not ungrateful but 59 does feel like both a non-event age, and a portal to ancient crone. The cards are all lovely. Jo's says '59, you're in your prime (number)' and she's added a smiley face. I've no idea what she is on about. The gorgeous necklace Andy got me is beautiful but I don't feel remotely birthday jolly.

I thought Andy, taking me at my word, also decided 59

was a rubbish birthday to celebrate so hadn't booked us in at the Italian. 'Maybe a film and a takeaway eh love?' he says and I don't suspect a thing. So it's a surprise when I answer the door to a very pleased with themselves looking Theresa and Jo. Apparently I am going out. Andy's packed a bag with my swimming costume, towels, socks and a blanket. He doesn't know why I need my cossie 'I was just told to pack it love. Ask Theresa'. He's grinning like a daft thing so I know he is in on the plan - whatever it is.

'A cleanse? What do you mean a cleanse?' I've no idea what Theresa's talking about.

I've never heard of a sweat lodge and am a bit put out when Theresa says it will help me release emotional toxins because I didn't know I had any.

That's how I find myself sitting on floor cushions in my swimming costume, in the early evening dark under a tent made of tarpaulin and tree branches next to a stream.

'The land's owned by Wolf's mate who bought it out of an inheritance. He plans to re-wild it' Theresa says. It's a flipping awful hike from the car lugging stuff and getting Jinx's chair along a muddy track so it seems wild enough to me. 'You know Raquel. She said she isn't a fan of the rural so would pass. Cecile is at a karaoke so it's just us. They both said to tell you happy birthday' Jo says. She's very definitely generating toxins helping Jinx get her wheels out of the tractor ruts and I can't help wonder if we could've gone to karaoke instead.

We set a fire in a pit and drink tea out of flasks while the flames catch on. The sky's cloudless and the stars are beautiful. After a while, Theresa says it's time to strip off and we have to clamber under a tarpaulin draped over tree branches. It has a flap door weighed down by pebbles stitched to the hem.

Jo goes to help Jinx in but she waves her away, tips out of her chair so her bum's on the ground and slides herself into the tent using her arms. We all follow her in. I've no idea what's going on.

Jinx is naked apart from her spectacular tattoos which are designed to be looked at so I've to work doubly hard not to stare at her. Jo wears a costume like me but still I admire her no end for stripping off. Theresa is naked too but she's such a slip of a thing it's barely noticeable.

'You two are so funny. There's nothing so wrong with women's bodies that they need a covering' Theresa says but of course she's ever so young and has both breasts so she can be indulged with her hippy ideas about being naked.

Jo brings hot stones in from the fire outside. She drops them off the shovel into a pit in the middle of the tent and sits down. It's already dark and the air is chilly outside but the heat off the stones fills the tarpaulin tent and it's lovely. I've no idea what is going on but it's solemn like at church. Theresa takes a bottle of water and pours it over the stones. The stones sizzle and the tent fills with hot steam.

When Theresa said a sweat lodge I thought she meant what you see in adverts for Austrian skiing holidays with wooden shacks, panoramic views and happy people in lederhosen so the tarp tent in a field was something of a let-down.

By the third hot stone I wonder if there are drugs in the water Theresa's pouring because I feel giddy. It's so hot I take my swimming costume off and Jo does the same. As we sweat we talk. I talk about my missing boob and show them my scar. Jinx says she thinks it's beautiful and I suppose in a way it is. Jinx talks about her legs not working. Jo talks about being fat. Theresa says she misses touring. It sounds miserable but it isn't at all. It's peculiarly lovely and a bit like being nicely drunk. I cry a bit which is strange because I don't feel sad.

'I think it's time for a dunk' Theresa says opening the tent flap. Jo scoops Jinx into her arms and all three of them shriek like banshees when the cold air rushes into the tent. Naked in the middle of the night, giggling and yelling like children they jump into the stream.

I would rather be hit over the head with a frozen haddock

than swim in cold water. Jo says it's because I'm skinny and I've no fat on my bones. I have a lot more than Theresa who enjoys it so much she makes us heat some more stones for round two.

As birthday presents go, this is one of the most memorable. I've no idea how I could explain it to Pippa. I haven't seen her naked since she was about nine years old. She wouldn't even let me at the sharp end of things when she had Rose because she said it was embarrassing. I think calling the midwife a very rude word when she told her to push harder was more embarrassing than me seeing her foo-foo but that's labour for you. Funnily enough, Pippa would probably agree with Melody Skyhorse that vagina is a perfectly serviceable word for girl parts but it sounds so harsh. It's not a word I'm called on to use often. I wouldn't say foo-foo in front of Jo, Jinx and Theresa. I expect they are comfortable with vaginas. Well, of course, Jo and Jinx are. Anyway, I wish Pippa could be with us because it is a truly lovely experience. I know telling her about tarpaulins and night-time stream dunking will be so far from her spa treatments she won't get it.

When Pippa took me to a proper spa for a birthday, I forget which one, it was a women's weekend. Big fluffy robes and white slippers but of course we had to wear our costumes at all times in the steamy areas and paper pants for the treatments. It was like wearing a nappy. Definitely no vaginas on show around that big old country house. We had strawberries and Prosecco at breakfast and it was all so nice but the poshness of it made me feel like I had to whisper all the time. I'm guessing it cost a small fortune and the only time I felt relaxed was in my room. It was a plush room. The mini-fridge was stocked with bottled water but no peanuts which was disappointing. I kept the sound down on the radio because DJ Dave seemed a bit out of kilter for the vibe of the place. The little bottles of bath stuff smelled gorgeous and the bed was comfy though so that was nice. Pippa kept saying how perfect it all was but I think she was trying to convince me. The thing is, I never felt comfortable being a woman there in the same way I do under the tarpaulin.

When we get back to Theresa's, she raises a hot chocolate toast to the hooping sisterhood. I thought you had to be a lesbian to qualify for sisterhood, but Theresa isn't and as I've already binned my bras I guess I qualify too.

'We missed you!' I tell Cecile at rehearsal a couple of days later. Cecile says she ended up with a hangover from her karaoke evening so wished she'd come with us after all. When Tony and Theresa pass around the drawings of their designs for the show outfits she's thrilled

'Damn sexy! We are going to look fab-u-loso!' We'll be wearing spangly, close-fitting pyjamas. The space of my absent boob will be on show so I am a bit iffy about the design

'Let me set your mind at rest - I fully intend everyone will be watching me being completely magnificent so you'll be fine'. We all join in with Cecile's room-filling laugh. I think she does mean it though. How does anyone get to be so body confident? When my hoop flies off my wrist and hits Cecile full in the face, neither of us imagine it's a magnificent move. Theresa makes us practise for the whole of the afternoon.

'What happened to a day of rest?' Jo moans - giving me a look like it's my fault.

When I get home, Andy is out on his bike. With only two of us we don't create much housework but taking advantage of him not being in the way I have a quick run around with the vac. I'm just about to plump the cushions when the phone rings. I don't believe it when she says it's Sharon from Girl Talk. I'm not the kind of person who gets personal calls from big-name celebrities. I remembered Sharon who was one of the panel members but once I left the Girl Talk set I couldn't remember a single thing I'd said. I watched it back twice but I couldn't get past how thick I sounded and my ankles looked.

'Mum people love a Yorkshire accent and trust me, no

one will have been looking at your shoes'. Pippa thought I'd come across well on the show 'for the most part'. I didn't ask about the other parts.

News readers could be naked from the bottom down. You would never know. When they invited me to the show, I wore the new linen outfit so I looked tidy but I kept my trainers on so I didn't fall down any steps and make a show of myself on national TV. I never thought anyone would see them but it turns out all the women who watch daytime TV did. Don't even get me started on my voice. I sound like I should be farming sheep up on the hills. I was trying to be articulate and interesting but to me, I sounded a sandwich short of a picnic.

Anyway, it turns out Sharon had a double mastectomy last year but to keep the press at bay hadn't told anyone. I could sympathise with her for that.

'You've inspired me to go public' she said, 'use the whole bloody awful experience for some good'.

Melody Skyhorse says all human beings make an equal contribution to the universe's karmic balance and each of us should discern and value what we bring. I don't feel in any way equal to Sharon who is proper important and from the name dropping she does, knows every celebrity you've ever heard of. Maybe it's a celebrity skill to get on with ordinary people as well but in no time we were laughing as if we'd known each other for years. She's ever so warm and friendly and wants me to do what she called a 'one-on-one'. Not an interview, more a chat about surviving breast cancer.

'I love how you've grabbed life by the ovaries and said fuck it to cancer!' she said.

It's an interesting perspective on hula hooping.

I don't know if it's because I'm now an old hand at being on the telly but I don't even take a moment before I say yes. I know Theresa and Jo will say the publicity will be good for the business but it's more that I like what Sharon says about raising awareness about breast cancer. In the interview I'm going to tell her what Jo said about Amazon one-breasted warriors.

Because of the trainer debacle last time I realise I'll need to think about some suitable TV shoes. I'll need at least a new top too and I'm going to ask Angela to come with me to get them.

We are doing OK on the mutual respect and trust earning strategy but Angela is still Angela. She can't disguise her pique when I ring, which is fair enough. Apart from the year Andy took us for a surprise trip to Bangor where it poured down all week, she'd been at every birthday celebration since I was fourteen so I know she's upset that she wasn't this year. I don't bother trying to explain the sweat lodge tent, or that she hadn't been invited as it was a surprise I didn't know was happening, because I don't want to give her ammunition to change my mind about inviting her to the filming of the show.

'I don't have a date yet but how about you and me make a weekend of it? Swanky hotel, nice restaurant, bit of shopping - on me. What do you think?'

After we hang up, I realise I'm genuinely looking forward to spending time with her. At the end of the day, and despite the rocky road of our relationship I know she'll love coming to the show and be thrilled about meeting Sharon. If I am going to be in the sisterhood, being a better sister to Angela is overdue.

Glow

Brighten the world, your path and the path of others.
Everyday Grace

It's fair to say that a year after my op I've been perfectly happy my visits to the clinic have moved into the infrequent, routine check-up variety so Andy and I are thoroughly fed up to be visiting the hospital earlier than expected. Melody Skyhorse says we must take responsibility for our impact on the world and that people who are negative project negative energy. Our coursework will apparently help us to project light and positivity. I understand what she's getting at but sometimes there are good reasons to feel negative - at funerals and because of wars and whatnot. I feel grumpy. Early appointments with a cancer specialist, with the best will in the world, are hard to feel light about. Even Dr Mhoya, who by any stretch of the imagination should at this point be spinning the positive, has a glum look about her at odds with her words.

'I'm sure it's scar tissue from the operation. Nothing to worry about?'

She has a habit of raising her voice at the end of sentences so everything sounds like a question. It's as if she's asking me for a second opinion.

'Let's book you in for an ultrasound to set your mind at rest?'

Her usually dancing eyebrows stay frowned and I wonder if it's her mind as well as ours she hopes to rest. She may as well not bother for me and Andy. Since I first noticed the small, hard lump appear we've decided not to dwell on it but I know worry will lurk unrested until we get the results back. We decided against telling the kids. Avoiding the anxiety of bad news is not the same as projecting light but there's no point in us all being worried.

It took a long time before Pippa surfaced out of the deepest of the doldrums and I don't want to give her any reason to go back there. No one would ordinarily describe her as fragile but I'm not sure any woman ever gets over the loss of a baby. She wears her grief about it quietly and in her heart. We talk about Ruby every now and again. Pippa is always one to want to move on and has little truck with being maudlin but she allows herself, and me, to be sentimental about her baby and I'm sure this is a good thing. She's barely shown any grief about the loss of Christopher and I don't know what to make of that. I hope she loved him once.

I pop round more frequently than I used to and although Pippa never asked me to, she no longer gives the impression she's far too busy to be interrupted by a house call. I'm not sure what she was busy with before but maybe it was housework. The toys aren't so regimentally restricted to the playmat and the cushions not so decoratively placed. There's an air of casual about it these days that it never used to have. Less like a show house and more like a home.

There's barely a shred of Christopher left. His books are gone. His shoes are not on the hallway rack and there are vacancies on the pegs where his outdoor coats used to hang. There's a single photo of him in Rose's bedroom but even in that, he's in a suit so it looks a bit out of place in her nursery.

'I see you've put your wedding photos away' I say.

'Fresh start Mum' Pippa says, 'no point in drawing it out. His dad came for his stuff but I kept our computer for my studies. I needed the empty shelf space for my college books'.

She seems a lot more excited about her college course than sad about the end of her marriage.

'Cecile says teaching is all about relationships and discipline'.

In another life, Pippa could've ventured into being a dominatrix so discipline will be her forte but it turns out it's more than telling kids off for using their phones in class.

'The discipline is about the teacher knowing and being enthusiastic about our subject and managing the classroom at all times. There's no messing about in Cecile's class but the kids all seem to like her. I want to be as good a teacher as her'.

I tell her I am sure she will be and I mean it. As I get my coat on to leave she breezily tells me I need to talk to Matthew but won't tell me what about.

'I'm not being mysterious! It's just not my job to say Mum - talk to the boys'.

Her smile reaches to her eyes and it's a long time since I saw that so, whatever it is, I know no-one has lost a leg or anything terrible but when I get home I ring Matthew straight away, realising too late it's still 5:30 am in California.

Melody Skyhorse says that whatever is happening, the earth will keep on turning and people will keep on living and dying and learning and loving and eating and laughing and crying because that's what the universe does. She's careful not to allude to any kind of entity. I guess she avoids religion so she keeps all options open. She wouldn't want to alienate potential customers by talking about one deity over the other and that suits me. She says we can't influence it and shouldn't even try. She doesn't say humans are an arrogant race but you can tell she thinks it. Most of us try to nudge life along in one way or the other so that it takes the kind of shape we want it to be as if we have any say in the matter. When something left field and unanticipated happens, like Yuuto taking up a role at York University, everything is thrown into a bit of a tizzy.

If I had control over the universe I would've already made it send Matthew home but Yorkshire, as lovely as it is, is a different kettle of fish to glamorous California so I never really thought he would come back.

'We'd told you we were thinking about it Mum'. Matthew sounds a bit tetchy but my call has woken him up and no one responds well to that. I offer to ring him when he's out of bed but he says he's awake now anyway so we chat as goes to make his breakfast. He's less grumpy once he has coffee on the go.

'Yuuto's been offered a research job. I'm going to focus on our business full time.'

Matthew is coming home! If I'm honest, I can't help but wonder if the universe knows the lump is nasty, I'm going to die and is sending him back to be here for Andy and Pippa. I decide the universe probably has more important things to think about than me.

Yuuto passed his citizenship test 'but when you get what you want, you sometimes realise it isn't what you want at all' Matthew says, 'we've been thinking about what is important to us and it's not… here'.

We chat about Yuuto's passion for research which I feel bad for not knowing about. Before Matthew has to get ready for work he fills me in on progress with wedding plans which so far seem to be hiccup-free. The venue and caterers are booked and Matthew and Yuuto have opted for hiring a boat for a two-week honeymoon. Our wedding gift was their honeymoon, whatever they wanted, so we'd expected somewhere with at least an infinity pool and cocktails but they want to watch otters.

One of the funny things about having a lot of money is how difficult it is to spend it. We offered to fund the whole wedding but Matthew and Yuuto want to pay for it themselves. Truth be told, I feel a little bit put out but Andy, wise as always, says it is them doing something special for themselves. He's right of course. Something you've put actual effort into creating is always more satisfying than being given it. The people we most want to give the money to, our kids, are the ones who keep telling us to spend it on ourselves but we are hardly making a dent in it. Dan's advice was so good the interest on the capital means we are barely touching the big money, in fact, it's growing. When we sent him a hamper to say thank you for all the help, he sent a text message back that we shouldn't have bothered, it's his job.

Charities are always happy to accept money though so we give to the LGBTQ youth group in Matthew and Yuuto's name. Matthew said he was touched by that. I hate that Matthew was bullied all those years ago but it's funny how often something bad has to happen, for something good to come along after.

Monday is our regular meeting day. Usually, it's at Theresa's but Wolf and Andy are adding solar panels to the roof so we've moved it to our lounge. Husnara still has her coat on and hasn't sat down. 'Put kettle on while you're there Jo' I shout past her.

Jo is in my kitchen ferreting for biscuits while Theresa pops her bike in our shed.

'Do sit down Husnara, we don't stand on ceremony here!' I reach to take her coat but despite the central heating she decides to leave it on. Husnara is proving to be a marvellous addition to Hoop Troupe but she's quite focussed on agendas and whatnot and not yet used to our admittedly ad hoc, casual approach to business meetings. Jo has a ninja gift for finding chocolate fingers and when she and Theresa bring in the drinks from the kitchen we start with them before looking at the report Husnara has prepared.

'We've had no drop-out from the full classes. The additional afternoon class Sofia is teaching has three more hoop spaces but a parent has four children under five - two sets of twins, poor woman, so the creche is at capacity'.

I dust biscuit crumbs from the pages as she takes us over some figures.

Theresa chips in. 'Hoop sales are going OK but unless you can give more of your office space Wendy I don't have much more room for stocking all the different sizes at ours'.

We sell hoops at classes but the rest of our merchandise has been living at our house. Andy's been busy posting out t-shirts at a rate of knots.

'I've some space but we might want to stock more t-shirts. I'd no idea they'd be so popular'.

Jo reaches for another biscuit and says she thinks it's a combination of our new design and social media.

Since 'Girl Talk' our social media following has taken off more than we could ever have imagined. Far more people than come to our classes so I'm not sure how that works. Apparently we have 'followers' who call themselves 'swans'. We liked it and re-designed our logo to a gorgeously elegant swan with a glitter hoop halo. It turns out whooper swans, beautiful in the water, are not particularly elegant out of it. It's a tongue-in-cheek joke but it amused us and judging by the number of t-shirts we've sold, we're not the only ones.

Jo, Theresa and I prattle on about whether shifting furniture round in Matthew's old room might give us more storage room when a Husnara taps her fingernail on the paper and pulls us back to her report.

'Perhaps it is not for me to say but I think you need to consider more than t-shirt sales. Thanks to the two TV appearances you have a waiting list for current classes and next terms are almost all booked up already. When your interview with Sharon goes out, we should - if it is what you want - capitalise on that'.

If it's what we want... Husnara is astute and none of us miss the hint of a call to caution in her words but it's easy to see she has ideas she's itching to share. Jo picks up on it too.

'Capitalise? More classes you mean? Theresa can't take any more classes on'

Husnara has a gentle edge of frustration in her voice when she replies.

'Perhaps you should think beyond relying on your current resources? We have been asked if we run classes all over the country. That is possible - if you recruit more teachers.'

Husnara slips between 'you' and 'us' as if she is still

unsure whether to join us but at least she decides to take her coat off. Underneath she's wearing a shalwar kameez in a fierce magenta. It suits her.

Melody Skyhorse says we should note but not be influenced by the zeitgeist. I thought that was something to do with the paranormal and ghosts because it sounds like it should be but she explained it was about current trends and catching the moment.

Husnara is clear we've caught a moment and should seize the day.

'If you read through social media posts, people taking classes are enjoying being part of the groups as much as the hooping. One of our hoopers has organised a park meet up. Perhaps you should go to it Wendy.'

She says 'perhaps' but there's a hint of command in her suggestion.

'Expansion?' Says Jo 'are we ready? Do we want to?'

Theresa says she knows a few people she thinks might be interested in working for us.

'Sometimes it's having kids, sometimes injury and other times we just get fed up of touring but outside the industry, there's not much call for our skillset. I know a few performers around the country who might be interested in taking on running classes'.

Husnara has a little diamond glint in her eye and I can see she'd been patiently working her way towards sharing an idea since Jo brought the tea out.

'You could employ people directly but I wonder about the possibilities of running a franchise - letting others build on the brand and run classes but without the responsibility for managing the business?'

It turns out she's wondered about it quite a bit and has bigger ideas than any of us about expanding Hoop Troupe. Her suggestion gives me that peculiar combination of excitement and anxiety all at the same time. It's clear Jo and Theresa feel the same.

'Could we do you think? Could we do it?' Theresa asks

the question but it's obvious in how she's jiggling about on the sofa cushions that she thinks we can.

'A franchise? Hell yes! What an excellent idea!' Exclaims Jo.

Despite it being her idea, I think Husnara might've hoped for some sensible caution but there is none and we are like a room of children getting ready to go on a school trip. Ideas flow thick and fast and Husnara, taking notes, struggles to keep up.

'There's a lot to think about but I know who we can talk to to help us set this up'. I offer to arrange a meeting with Consultant Cathy.

A week later we all meet in town. Husnara has written up notes of what she grandly calls our planning meeting and, typically efficient, has copies for us all which she takes out of a well-worn brown leather briefcase. None of the rest of us have a briefcase. I'm not sure she thinks we take business seriously enough.

The bank used to be all mahogany and formal but they ripped it out and made it like a grey and plastic mini airport terminal with extra ATM's. The staff mill about smiling, trying to catch the eye of people coming in and you can only tell they're staff by their badges. They seem a bit bored. I wonder if they miss the days of being behind glass and fast counting banknotes. We tell one of the smiley people who we have an appointment with and mill until she comes out to get us.

It's lovely to see Cathy again. She's wearing emerald green tights. They make the red tights of my previous meeting with her seem less of a bold choice. High visibility legwear must be a part of her brand.

We cram into her office with the mismatched chairs and she listens without interrupting as we go through all the bullet points on our list.

Theresa says that she has old circus chums in Leeds and Newcastle who might be interested in running classes.

'Neither Jenny or Malika have any money to put in but

they are keen to give classes if we can support them get up and running. Start-up is a problem if you've no capital.'

Jo chips in, 'We can get more teachers and run more classes but we want people to feel that Hoop Troupe is something they're committed to being a part of. It's not just about the hooping'.

Cathy takes notes and nods along to our uncoordinated input without interruption. When we get to the end of our list she sums up.

'So, it sounds as if a franchise business based on a low entry cost to enable people to participate is the approach to take. Hoop Troupe franchisees run teaching sessions while for a small fee you provide operational support - does that sound like what you had in mind?'

Cathy is good at filtering all our unfettered chitter-chatter into the nub of the matter but as she puts it into business plan language I start to feel like an imposter.

I remember what Pippa once said about not being able to buy friends and I wonder if the lottery win money bought me a job. On paper, I'm a co-director but in reality Jo, with her bags-of-energy drive and now super organised Husnara, could manage the business without me while Theresa plans the lessons and sorts the music. I'm not sure what I bring to the party. Given the new potential lodger Dr Mhoya is checking out I wonder if maybe I should gracefully leave them all to it. Just as I ponder thinking about learning a new tune on the harmonica Husnara chips in. I can't tell whether she's super intuitive or just has a knack for knowing the right thing to say at exactly the right time.

'Wendy you are key. When your interview with Sharon goes out we must be ready to respond. Queries about classes will go up and we need to build on the momentum'.

Cathy agrees I should be the face of our brand and says we need to plan to have at least regional and maybe, in the longer-term national meet-ups of the groups.

'You should aim to do some personal appearances at franchise classes as soon as they get going to build on your media presence. Strike while the iron is hot'.

Cancer's made me doubt myself. My own body let me down in the most treacherous of ways and it takes space in who I am far more than I should allow. None of the others in the room are doubting me so I'm not going to doubt myself either.

'OK. Let's do it!'

Consultant Cathy advises that our first job must be what she calls our 'rule book'. 'Your franchise manual should specify the teaching curriculum across all classes. You'll sort the music and licences. It will make it much easier to manage quality and build a community if all classes are working towards the same aims'.

Husnara says she'll create the manual. I suspect she thinks the rest of us might make a hash of it.

'I'll sort music and licences out' Theresa has performing expertise to draw on so we are happy to leave music to her.

The idea of the Hoop Troupe being national or me doing personal appearances is too bonkers for me to get my head around but by the time we leave the meeting my inner imposter has been sent packing - mostly. Jo and I take responsibility for PR.

'If you're the face of our business Wendy you need some posher active wear' Jo says, joking, but I think maybe she's right.

At our show rehearsals later that evening any idea I have of being remotely competent in anything is roundly quashed as my hoop almost chokes me. I get it spinning like a pro and move it up my body to the point where I'm super proud of myself and then, of course, it all goes wrong and it ends up spinning around my neck. Jo giggles then her hoop flies off her arm and hits Tony which starts him off giggling too.

'Try to remember we are swans people'. Cecile's great big room-filling laugh finishes us off and we have to take a tea break to get our act together before we can carry on. We only have one more rehearsal before our show. There's no way I'm going to be ready.

After class, I thank Jo for the offer of a lift but it's such a lovely evening I fancy a walk home. I think Jo's a bit disappointed and I understand why. It's been such a day! She wants it to carry on but after the hysteria in the class I need the calm of spring evening air and I don't have the headspace for talking about the franchise.

The gardens are coming out of hibernation. The crocus are in flower and the lovely yellow daffs are starting to show. Summers on its way and there is so much to be excited about. Melody Skyhorse says we may not always understand what destiny has in store for us but we should trust everything is a part of a greater harmonious balance in nature. I can't help thinking sending me another lump to balance things out is a bit spiteful of the universe. Sometimes Melody Skyhorse does talk twaddle.

SYNCHRONICITY

Coincidence?

*Learn to tune into the magic of happenstance. Nature does
not create disorder.*

Everyday Grace

We are packed and ready to go. In less than a week I, Wendy
Wooldridge, ex-toilet cleaning manager, will be appearing
in a show at the Brighton festival. Plans were made when I
had a potentially fatal disease - which I might still have -
and when I'd just banked more money than any right-
minded person could ever have dreamed of. Melody
Skyhorse says that when things come together in unusual
ways it's simply meant to be. How on earth can all of that
be a part of some grand plan? It's too ridiculous for words.
I've been thinking a lot about whether destiny is a thing. Are
things that happen just happenings or do they happen for a
reason? One of the Girl Talk panel said, 'what doesn't kill
you makes you stronger'. I don't know if that's true for
anyone. It isn't for me. I'm not one for believing cancer is a
gift. When first diagnosed I went to a support group for
newly diagnosed women. The group leader had a
chimpanzee tattooed on her arm. I didn't think nurses were
allowed to have tattoos on show but anyway, she was very
nice. One of the women, snotty with tears, said she and her
husband had become much closer since the diagnosis so
cancer had done her a favour. Others in the room nodded
along. It was a bit sombre until someone chipped in it had
done the opposite for her and she'd kicked her husband out
because, she said, 'life's too short to be with a fat, ugly arse
of a man'. It raised the mood but I didn't go back after that
session. There are no positives to having cancer so I won't
give it the benefit of any credit for anything or time to
moaning about it either. At the group, the lottery win was
an elephant in the room for me. It's hard to complain when

you're richer than the Prime Minister so I kept mum.

Winning the money was a positive of course. Andy and I used to allow ourselves a little flutter of eight lottery tickets a month. I suppose everyone who buys them hopes to get something and the little wins perk a day up, but I never expected to actually win a lot. I don't think most people do really. Melody Skyhorse says that what is destined for us is what happens. Our kids would've been fine one way or the other. I'd still have met Jo, Theresa and the troupe without either cancer or the money. We wouldn't have been business partners of course but I like to think we would still have become friends.

I don't think I like Melody Skyhorse's idea of destiny. If everything is predetermined where is the point in any of us giving hard things a go? Cancer didn't nudge me to murdering *Camptown Races* on the harmonica or hula hooping. My choices are my responsibility and you would think someone like Melody Skyhorse might be keen on autonomy. That being said, agreeing to be in the show was an awful choice. I don't know what possessed me. I can see how it might feel easier to blame the universe's big confusing plan.

Before we arrive in Brighton the only thing I know about the town is that my mam and dad said it was rough and full of motorbike gangs who spoiled their first holiday after I'd been born. Andy and I dump our stuff in the hotel and go and have a touristy look round before I meet up with the others for the last rehearsal. It turns out, it isn't rough at all but lovely with big posh white bay window houses all along the promenade. Georgian, I think. Lots of 'vote Green' posters in the windows.

When we get to the seafront I can't help but feel a bit sorry for Brighton because although the fairground pier is lovely the awful stony beach lets it down. I was saying so to Andy when someone overheard me and said, 'they're not pebbles, they're fat sand'. He had a very Melody Skyhorse positive spin on it but there can't be much call for all the buckets and spades in the seafront prom shops. You can't make sandcastles out of flint. Brighton beach isn't a patch on Scarborough. To be honest, the public toilets aren't up to snuff either and could do with Jamila's pot pourri but judging by the crowds, people are happy to put up with it. As I buy us some chips from a stall a twenty-foot long, red silk Chinese dragon with a huge gold head, congas by. An owner of one of the eight sets of legs driving it reaches out of the red silk and pinches a chip. As lovely as Scarborough beach is, it doesn't have dragons, just donkeys. I'm sure it can't be true that it's always sunny in Brighton but it feels the kind of place that is. Seasides are a bit out of fashion since flights are cheaper than a set of table mats so it is a long time since I've been to a resort so busy.

'It's proper lively, isn't it? I reckon you'll sell more tickets than you expect.' Andy says. I throw a chip at him but a gull swoops down and grabs it before it hits him. I could have done without the reminder. I'm scared witless.

Later, after rehearsals and pre actual show we're all standing together at the side of the stage. Tony gathers us for a group hug.

'This is it then crew. You've got this!'

On the stage, a green-haired, stilt walking fire eater introduces us. I think I'm going to throw up.

'I'm sure I'm going to poo in my costume'. Jo is as nervous as me. I'm not sure I can even go on.

'There are at least a hundred people out there!' Cecile's positively bouncing and can't wait to get on stage. She looks gorgeous in her spangly pyjamas. She's put glitter in her eyeshadow to match.

'They were hip then and they're hip now!' The MC is reeling off every pun about hula hooping known to google as she introduces us. Jo and I peek from behind the curtain which is a bad idea. I know our people are in the audience but I never actually thought we would sell tickets to real people. There are a lot of real people.

'Look at me when you are on stage and if you bugger up, just pick up your hoop and carry on' Andy said before the show.

What neither of us understood is once on stage and under the lights, I can't see the audience at all.

I know Andy's there sat with Wolf, Jinx and Raquel but I can't see them. I don't want to end up staring at a paying ticket holder and make them feel uncomfortable so Andy's suggestion was entirely unhelpful.

When you drink a cup of tea or hang wet clothes on a washing line you don't need to work out how to do it. Like a kind of magic that's what happens. I can't remember a single second of it. It was like when I was on Girls Talk, time passes in the blink of an eye. I never drop my hoop once. None of us do. We never got through a single rehearsal without making a mistake in the whole time we'd been learning the routine but on stage, when it matters, we nail it.

The loud cheering and applause make my tummy flip over and over and I feel like the most amazing person on the whole earth. I never understood before why actors and whatnot enjoy being the centre of attention but I feel invincible.

As we come off stage and the green-haired MC introduces the drag Elvis, Cecile tells us off for being too noisy because the next act had come on and we needed to shush.

'Respect the artists' people. This is their work.'

Cecile is right of course but it's hard trying to be quiet because I want to shriek 'fuck you cancer!' at the top of my voice. I wouldn't of course even without Cecile being so teacher-y.

After the show, in the performers' changing enclosure, Tony says the ticket sales had gone well and, amazingly, we'd made a profit. Everyone decides, with no messing, Tony should have it to cover his 'resting' time which, as I understand it, is what people in the entertainment business say when they are unemployed. Only it turns out there won't be that much resting time.

'We're off to Las Vegas! We found out last week.'

Tony and Denice are going to be backing dancers for a warbling diva I thought had died years ago.

'She's packing the place out so as long as she keeps breathing, we get paid but we still need to buy tickets to get there so this will help a lot'.

Andy, Wolf, Jinx and Raquel meet us at the enclosure. We'd planned to go into town to celebrate but Andy has brought champagne and plastic glasses so we start the celebrations straight off. I don't think any of us want to leave.

'To Hoop Troupe' Raquel raises a toast. I wish she'd been on stage with us. The fizz adds to me feeling as high as a kite.

As we mill about drinking champagne people come over to say hello.

'Could I have a selfie with you' one woman says grabbing Tony. Denice looks a little bit put out but I guess it's par for the course if you have a handsome boyfriend.

I don't recognise the woman who taps me on the shoulder until she slides her sunglasses down her nose.

'Fancy seeing you here Wendy!' Without the big hair and make-up Neela, who was on the panel at Girl Talk, looks different in real life than she does on the telly. It's lovely to see her and I'm a bit embarrassed someone famous actually came to our show.

'I'd no idea it was your group in the show until I say you on stage. My pal Niki hoops and does fire spinning. She knows your fire eater and suggested we come to the show and voila - small world! Niki, meet Wendy'.

Niki is blond, boyish and has a fierce look about her. It's not that she's beautiful as such but she looks like a warrior. Jo and Jinx are staring. I'm guessing we all suspect she's on their team but I thought the same about Tony so I should know better than make any assumptions. She invites us to meet the other Brighton hoopers before we leave.

'Oh we definitely will' says Jo. Jinx doesn't look too happy about it. I introduce everyone and small talk with Neela before she says they are catching another show and have to go.

'See you on Sunday' Niki says and gives Jo a flirty smile. Judging by the frostiness I don't think Jinx has taken to Niki. 'Just walk along the seafront promenade to the big pointy stick and you will find us'.

When the champagne is finished we go into town and have a bit of a post-show blowout. I can't remember when Andy and I last danced so much.

After breakfast the next morning only five of us make it to our rendezvous spot by the pier. Jinx is too hungover to come and Andy and Wolf have gone off to some boring sounding breakfast lecture on sustainable building or some such. I couldn't be bothered to listen when they told us. We lost Tony and Denice in the early hours of the morning after far too much fun in an 80's music silent disco tent. I'm sure they'll be fine. We make our way along the seafront.

The big pointy stick is some kind of fairground attraction near a burned down pier. It took a lot of walking to get to. It's much further away than it looks from the Palace Pier but on the upside, alongside the ice cream and chip stalls, there are loads of quirky little shops and stalls to look into.

Eventually, we get to a low paved amphitheatre right next to the beach. A few people are sat around watching the hoopers. Raquel, Jo, Cecile and I mill around feeling like spare parts when we first arrive. Theresa and Sofia know some of the hoopers from professional performing. There's a lot of air kissing and hugging going on. Niki's smile is broad and warm when she welcomes us to their gathering.

'It's all informal and no one organises it. Typical for Brighton! We get about fifteen people here most Sundays but sometimes no one comes. Hoopers, spinners, jugglers. It's just a bit of a laugh'.

All our hoops are in the car back at the hotel but Niki says we can borrow from the pile laying on the floor if we want to join in. Theresa and Sofia are already attracting attention and are a lot more adventurous doing their freestyle than they were forced to be when nannying us on the stage.

'Battle!' Someone yells and a couple of the punky young people pick up hoops. One with skull and crossbones face paint is extravagantly hooping on roller skates.

'Bring it on then' Sofia calls out but it seems like a good-hearted competition. I've no idea how anyone can do the splits and keep a hoop spinning but she does. Then she walks on her hands and still keeps the hoop on her waist. Roller skating hooper ups her game and spins the hoop around one leg while still skating around but then she falls over. There's a lot of laughter. They're amazing hoopers.

I don't want to join in and I can see Jo isn't keen either. The best trick Jo and I can do is the escalator and I am not going to make a show of my old-lady self by joining them but Cecile grabs a hoop.

'When fabulous knocks, I just gotta go' Cecile walks plumb into the middle of the hoopers and moves straight from a kick start to chest hooping like a boss.

Raquel joins and is a bit rusty but enthusiastic. Jo does that biting her tongue thing which means she's decision making. The next thing I know she grabs two hoops and I'm dragged over to join the hoopers. Someone links their phone to a portable speaker and we end up teaching all the hoopers our stage routine.

We have the best fun!

'Excuse me. Are you Wendy from the TV show? How are you pet?'

I'd seen an older woman watching us as we were hooping. She comes over as I'm getting my breath back.

'I saw you and just wanted to tell you I think you're brave for telling your story. Hooping's so good for the soul isn't it? I used to be good at it back in the day' she says, but she won't be persuaded to pick up a hoop.

'Not in public! If you ever do classes for oldies let me know'.

The girl with the skull and crossbones painted on her cheek offers to buy her ice cream and Raquel joins them to get cornets for us. As they stand in the queue Theresa and I catch each other's eye. 'Brighton franchise?' Theresa suggests nodding her head towards Niki and we both go over for a chat.

Apart from Jo and Jinx having a bit of a tetchy argument before we left, our Brighton weekend was perfect. I wish we'd stayed longer.

For friendship vacancies in middle age, the accepted wisdom is you join a group of some kind. Painting with watercolours and conversational Spanish seem popular from what I've seen. The community centre flyer that comes through our letterbox every year always mention how friendly their groups are. I considered Spanish lessons once. Thanks to holidays I can order garlic prawns and two beers in Spanish which is fairly much all I've ever needed in Benidorm so I never bothered with the class in the end. I didn't get involved with hooping to make friends but I'd hoped it would be fun. The thing about fun is it's a shared experience.

When Matthew was about five we went to a fundraising fete at the local hospice. He wanted to go on a huge bouncy castle but was scared so I went on with him and ended up in a heap with another mum being jumped on by half a dozen children. We laughed together till I nearly wet myself. We stayed friends for years until she emigrated. I still get a card from her at Christmas. She always says we should visit but if I was going to the States I'm not sure Arkansas is on my list of must-see places. Sometimes stories are done and I know in my heart ours is.

Angela and I mislaid the fun from our relationship and I'm glad we've started to put it back because there's a reliability to old friendships. I only have to say something to her like 'canal' and I know for sure we both immediately remember the school trip when Mandy Johnson fell in and we all had to donate an item of clothing so she could be dry and warm. Poor Mandy. She did look a sight.

My history with Jo, Theresa and the others from the class is short but exciting. I get to show them the grown-up version of me. Jo and Theresa don't expect me to be Wimpy Wendy Wooldridge. Raquel called me a businesswoman at the meeting with Consultant Cathy and I wanted to ask her to say it again, out loud, because when she said it, I felt stupidly flattered. I didn't, of course, because that would've been bonkers.

I get to tell Jo old stories about myself. With Jo, or Theresa I can spin a yarn about some event or other and it doesn't matter if I embellish it a bit to make it funnier or more interesting because they haven't heard it before. They share stories about their lives too. Jo once stood on Prince Charles' foot at a Spice Girls concert. We ended up chatting about the future of royalty and which was our favourite Spice Girl all in the same conversation. Cecile's descriptions of the blues, pinks, greens and oranges of the Seychelles islands where she grew up make it sound like paradise. I aim to go to La Digue, at some point. I don't know Tony very well but I never expected to have a Las Vegas show dancer in my own story. Before we left Brighton I slipped a going away card into his pocket. I put 'I'll miss you Mr Gorgeous. Thank you for everything' and I added a smiley face to it.

I suppose, inevitably, the novelty of new friends wears off and irritating quirks or incompatibilities start showing themselves. I might be showing mine already but I guess Melody Skyhorse would say don't look for problems where there are none so I don't dwell on it.

When home from Brighton, I unpack our bags and sort the mountain of laundry we seem to have brought home with us. I doubt I'll ever wear the spangly stage pyjamas again but I'll never throw them away.

For our Hoop Troupe team meeting a few days after we get back and as a celebratory treat I've booked us in for lunch at the harbour pub. So long as the fishermen are not off-loading the pongy lobster pots and stacking them on the quayside, the outdoor area is lovely. Despite the absence of the pots and the glorious spring sunshine, Jo looks downhearted in the gloom of the bar.

'Is this about Jinx?' I ask her. Jinx is going to Germany as part of her studies. In Brighton, I assumed the tension between them was about that so I'm not surprised Jo is feeling down but I didn't know the half of it.

'I asked her to marry me but she told me to fuck off'. Jo laughs when she tells me but the laugh has a forced ring to it.

'I was full of post-show euphoria, fabulous Brighton and feeling all loved up but Jinx thinks "marriage is an outdated patriarchal capitalist concept which subjugates women" so she wasn't having any of it'.

I don't feel subjugated by Andy so I don't know whether to give Jo a supportive pat on the arm, say something horrible about Jinx or laugh along. I don't know the protocol for lesbian marriage rejection.

'To be honest, I'm not sure why I asked her other than trying to firm things up a bit between us before she goes. I don't want to get married either. Not really'.

Jinx left a few hours before. She's travelling partway to Rotterdam with Andy and Wolf who have gone to a self-build conference in Holland. She's en route to Germany to what Jinx said was 'an unexpected and valuable academic exchange opportunity'. Jo doesn't know when she'll be coming back.

'Bollocks to it. More fish in the sea and all that'. She's making light of the situation but before Theresa and Husnara have even arrived she demolishes a kumquat cheesecake so I can read between the calorific lines. I like

Jinx a lot. She appears to be a bit frosty when you meet her but once you get past the leather she's a soft centre and her and Jo seemed like such a good match. I'm sad their relationship's gone wobbly. 'I'm sure something's going on with the fire eater' Jo says. 'What really pisses me off is that I fancied her first'.

When Theresa and Husnara arrive, we order lunch. Jo says she'll skip it as she's already eaten but then orders another piece of cheesecake. Before we're halfway through Husnara's agenda, she's ordered a third.

When Andy rings me later I tell him about Jo being upset but how glad I am he was there to support Jinx given she's a wheelchair user travelling alone on a ferry.

'Jinx does not strike me as a woman in need of very much support at all' Andy says '… and I'll never play poker with her again'.

Excellence

Is there excellence if it is not seen? Recognition brings bounty for self and for others. Be excellence itself. Imagine the gift you can be to the world.

Everyday Grace

The school's been incredibly accommodating but they need their hall for after school classes so can't give us any more slots. It's a shame because not many of the other places we've seen are anywhere near as good.

As usual, Husnara comes to our team meeting laden with paperwork which she lays in order of discussion on Theresa's kitchen table. She's a fan of an agenda. Item one is our premises problem.

'I wonder if you might consider this?'

Husnara hands out copies of the estate agent blurb about an old superstore available to lease. I bought our freezer and washing machine there years ago but it long since closed down. It has a rooftop car park and an accessible ground floor big enough for classes but it's a huge space.

'It's an impressive property but we wouldn't want to put our prices up.' Jo thinks it's likely to be way over our budget. Husnara sighs 'If you do not mind me saying so, you perhaps need to think more expansively'. She speaks like an official at a royal wedding.

Sometimes Melody Skyhorse seems to me to be the queen of the obvious. In the lesson about seeing the stars who walk among us I thought she meant we needed to see everyone is special. My mother used to say just that all the time so a full lesson seemed a bit overblown. When I see Husnara in action though, I realise she means we should notice, in particular, the different ways people have of being special.

Husnara is something of a contradiction. Reserved, an

observer, softly spoken and yet she sets high expectations. She can ooze impatience and be intimidating. In meetings, she takes notes - always with a pen and paper because she finds the clack of computer keys distracting - and she barely says a word. It took me a while to realise when she does say something, we need to pay attention. She can filter the essential wheat from the chaff like no one I've ever known.

'I am not sure it will mean raising fee's Jo. The council are keen to regenerate the town centre so I took the liberty of having a brief chat with the planning officer. If we commit to refurbishing the front of the building and offer reduced fee classes to people on low incomes, we can have it rent-free for five years. I didn't tell them we already have sliding scale prices. I wanted him to feel magnanimous so we got the best deal'.

It's not in Husnara's job description to find new premises or negotiate their costs but her initiative can't be faulted. We ask her to go ahead and arrange a site visit with the council chap.

Jo says, 'If we get this place you can have your pick of the best office!' and although Husnara just smiles, I can't help feel she's already made that decision without us.

Item two on the agenda is what Husnara calls 'stakeholder engagement' and the rest of us call 'hoopers'. Jo and I are meeting Raquel to discuss it later so we defer the agenda item and have more tea. We tell Husnara all about our show and she smiles in the right places but in all honesty, I think she would've preferred us to stick to her agenda.

After the meeting at Theresa's, Jo and I go to the university to see Raquel. The campus is like a little village. There are lots of buildings, grass and trees and the atmosphere feels bulging with energy.

'This is a bit bigger than the cupboard you used to have at our old place' Jo jokes. We're both impressed. I'm not sure either of us had realised how senior her uni role is but she has an actual board room table, a wipe board and the biggest desk I've ever seen. The trays on it are shoulder height with paperwork.

She's keen to get out of the office though I can't imagine why, its lovely.

'We won't go to the refectory for lunch - far too noisy' Raquel says 'we'll go to the restaurant. The food's exactly the same as in the refectory but higher prices cover the cost of the pot plants and keep it a bit quieter'.

We find a table by a window overlooking a courtyard full of vaping young people oozing potential. I imagine it's nice to work at a university.

We don't see so much of Raquel since she got the new job. I miss her but it's obvious she's very at home at the uni.

'Oh I love the job - finance work is pretty much the same as it was at school Jo but with a heck of a lot more noughts'.

We still have to cafeteria queue for our food. Jo's back on salads. When we get back to the table and de-tray Raquel picks up where we left off.

'So, let's talk about engaging your customers. I think an advisory group is in order'.

Apparently, all university departments have students who contribute to the running of their courses. It seems a bit like lunatics taking over the asylum to me but I've never been to university. I bet Pippa will get in on the act when she starts her course. Raquel is enthusiastic about 'participant involvement' which seems to be university speak for what the rest of us might call 'asking people what they like'.

'Your customers are your greatest asset. If they like the classes they'll tell others. Your job is to make sure every hooper feels personally invested in the success of Hoop Troupe. You are not only selling a product, you're building a community - just look at your social media followers! Get them involved'.

We didn't start the Facebook page. They aren't actually 'our' followers at all really. It never occurred to us to start one which says something about our business acumen - but at Raquel's suggestion, a few days later Jo and I arranged to meet the woman who did. Gwen came to one of our first classes but was already a skilled hooper.

'It's such a barmy thing for a middle-aged woman to do it's a laugh to share it with other dafties who love it too. Your classes are a lovely way to meet other hoopers'. Gwen is one of those huggable women who always have aspirin and plasters in her handbag, you feel you've known forever and immediately warm to. She thinks the popularity of her Swans Facebook group is because people like to belong. Three of our classes have linked up through social media and are planning a mega practice session in a park in York.

'We're calling the meet ups 'ballyhoo-ps'. Please say you'll come along.'

Gwen thinks it's a marvellous idea to ask for advisory group volunteers on her Facebook page and straight away she offers to be a member. Within three days of Gwen posting on social media, she's generated a more potential volunteers than Husnara knows what to do with. In an unexpected development, we've had interest from potential volunteer teachers.

Theresa's keen to take up the offers.

'Not everyone wants to run a franchise but with volunteers, we could offer more beginner classes or free taster sessions Wendy. Maybe we should think about it'.

There's so much to think about I can hardly keep up. To be honest, I'm exhausted with thinking about things. I feel as if I'm having to smile a lot at people who expect me to be smiley and it can take more energy than I have to spare.

I've been so busy Matthew and I haven't had a catch up for over two weeks. I don't know how he slipped down the ladder of my priority list. When we video call I can see his cheeks are red so I know he's tired too. When dancing in competitions his eyes would sparkle but when his cheeks dappled it was a sign he'd pushed himself too much and I had to step in.

'I'm fine Mum - last push this side of the pond for the

US launch and then we are good to launch in the UK, Australia, and South America next'.

Matthew doesn't need me to fuss but I can't help myself. 'Does it need you to be quite so pushy about it though son?'

He says getting traction for new apps is difficult.

'Gaming apps do best but no-one explores an app about citizenship unless they're trying to get it' he explains. He and Yuuto have spent most of the money we gave them on publicity and building networks to spread the word. They've paid copywriters to write what Matthew calls 'advertorials' which, as I understand it, are adverts dressed up as news articles. I'm not sure how I feel about them. I have a scrapbook of all the articles he is named in and I'll always be proud of him but it is not the same when I know he has paid to be mentioned.

'It's how things are done in advertising Mum. You should use the same to develop Hoop Troupe'.

I'm disappointed he doesn't know the actor in his TV advert. I thought being in California he'd run into famous people all the time. I had it in my head he'd offered to record the film while they were having a cappuccino in one of the coffee shops. It turns out even famous actors have times when they are 'resting' so he was paid but to be fair, he did a great job of making a complicated and niche app sound like something everyone should have on their phones.

'He was worth every penny Mum. The TV ad brought in a lot of interest'.

We've been invited to the launch party of course but it was a long journey just to be out of my comfort zone. I'd have ended up trying to look inconspicuous and eating too many nibbles but apparently, it was a success.

In my Matthew scrapbook, I've an autograph from their launch actor. It says 'to Wendy, our hero, with thanks'. I'm not sure it means as much to me once Matthew said we'd paid for it.

'The Europe launch party will be in the UK. I hope you'll come to that' he says and I tell him we'll be there. They're not bothering with famous actors but are inviting what they call 'influencers'. I've never really understood what they do but I know Pippa will be keen to go along with her WAG friend and be influenced.

One of the women who comes to our classes is next-door neighbour to an actor who used to be on a soap opera. He used to be what my mam would call 'dishy' but he's less so since the hip replacements. I offer to find out if he'll go to the launch but Matthew says it is not their demographic. I guess he hasn't heard of the actor but doesn't want to say so.

We have a lovely chat but Matthew starts to ask me how I am. He's sharply intuitive and can sniff out a fib as well as Pippa. They both have that in common with their dad. The scar lump is still there. It's behaving itself as far as we know but Melody Skyhorse says the avoidance of truth is the potential presence of a lie so rather than do either I make an excuse about the time and being expected at Pippa's.

As I get my coat on I remember to get the fancy balsamic out of the cupboard to take with me. When I was at the supermarket they had a special offer on I popped one in my trolly for Pippa. She's a bit underwhelmed but on thinking about it, vinegar is a peculiar gift I suppose.

'Erm, thanks Mum. Have you tried it drizzled on strawberries?'

It seems an odd thing to do with vinegar but Pippa has some funny ways. She puts it with the other bottle in her pantry.

Pippa and I don't do heart to heart chats often but Ruby's death seemed to open a less combative space for us to be in together. Pippa's not often nervous about much but, as the start date draws near, she is about her university course.

'I'm not sure I'm up to it Mum'.

As a perfectionist, Pippa has an outstanding gift for seeing her own imperfections. To be fair, her drive about most things has been improvement whether it was Christopher, her kitchen or which car she has so it's not that she's picky about what needs to be better. She's not so great at celebrating herself and if I'm honest, she hasn't traditionally shown much of a lean towards celebrating other people's greatness either.

'Cecile said we have to help kids get their grades but helping them become the best version of themselves they can be is more important. How am I supposed to do that?'

I am not sure I'm the best person to ask.

'You don't have to be a perfect teacher Pippa. You have to know you've done your best for them'.

I brace myself for the parry. I don't know why Pippa invites advice. She doesn't respond well to anything she perceives as being told what she should do. Inevitably when anyone gives advice she strikes back with a countermeasure usually reminding the advice-giver of their own shortcomings. Pippa is not a nasty person, just a bit self-protective.

'That's easy for you to say'. The words are enough to make my shoulders tighten ready for the list of my failings but there's little fire behind them. If anything, she looks a bit sad.

'You're a hard act to follow sometimes Mum, we can't all be as strong as you'.

I wait for the punchline because I'm sure there must be one but none comes.

I'm in no doubt Pippa loves me but since she reached ten years old and was running towards stroppy teen years at a pace of knots, she's routinely made clear she thinks I'm average in every way. I haven't seen any need to contradict her because I think she's right. I don't feel bad about it. Even superheroes are average at most things.

Melody Skyhorse uses a phrase about things being 'unborn'. I think she means that for some things to exist, they must be seen and in the seeing, the 'thing' - whatever it is, is made better for everyone. When I did the lesson I thought she meant things like telling a friend you like her new sweater or admiring Kieran's new rare-breed Scott's

Dumpy chicken. To me chickens are chickens but to Kieran and Donna, their short-legged little birds are the beginning of a whole new adventure. Their joy about it is enhanced in telling me about their breeding plan and by me enjoying their excitement, even though the birds are if truth be told, peculiar looking.

I thought I was being intellectual in understanding the lesson and I try to notice the things that make life better but I wonder if she also means actual 'unborn' such as Ruby. More than anything in the world I wish she'd stayed with us and I won't give her death the privilege of anything positive coming out of it but losing her has changed Pippa. She isn't a better version of herself, but she's different and perhaps less self-assured. It's hard to know whether that's a good or bad thing. I always knew where I was with assertive Pippa but I'm on less sure ground when she's being humble.

'I don't mean the cancer or setting up the business Mum. Matthew and me think you've handled both amazingly but you and Dad, you're so … grounded'.

When I get home and tell Andy about it he jokes we sound like we're two of the three peaks. Solid and dependable but a peak missing. Only, there isn't a missing anything when I ponder it. There never has been.

Growth

*Sometimes you have to take that scary step into the
unknown. You've got this! You have to believe it.*
                                                Everyday Grace

During the night I had one of those horrible dreams where
Andy had to shake me awake because I was wailing. I can't
remember what it was about but it ended up being a restless
night with fitful sleep. I've slept in so breakfast is a rushed
affair and the morning feels jangled. I'm in a kerfuffle of
trying to get ready and eat my toast at the same time. Andy's
plodding around after me still in his PJ's and slippers.

'Wendy before you go can we have a chat?' he asks.

'Later love. I have to go... The new building is
incredible Andy! Fantastic for classes. For goodness sake is
that the time....? A bit big if I'm honest and tatty but it has
a car park and we might even be able to have a little cafe
and maybe a merch shop so... what've I done with my
handbag?'

My arm is stuck trying to right-side-out a sleeve in my
coat and I'm ferreting about in the gap between the sofa and
armchair looking for my handbag. I'm running late for our
meeting with the council about the lease.

'Wendy, can you cancel the meeting. I think we need to
talk'.

The car keys aren't in the fruit bowl, the dish by the door
or on the hook in the kitchen and my handbag is AWOL
from any of its usual parking spots.

'What do you mean cancel the meeting? Where on earth
have I put it?' Distracted, I miss the shade of his voice.

'Will you please just STOP!'

Andy never yells. He just doesn't. It takes us both by
surprise.

'All this.... We never discussed it. What about our

plans?' The skin across Andy's jaw is taught. It's a look I rarely ever see.

Andy and I have only had two 'are we talking about divorce' type stand up rows in all the time we've been together. That makes us sound boring and of course we have our niggles, quarrels and dark silences with each other but actual memorable-for-all-the-wrong-reasons set-tos are, thankfully, rare. The first time we had a proper ding-dong was at a wedding when I thought he was flirting with a pretty bridesmaid and kicked off. We were already married by that time but I didn't yet know him well enough to understand Andy is not that kind of man. One too many vodka and oranges and the insecurity of youth caused that one. The second time, years later, was after my mam's gravestone had finally been placed. He put the flowers down on the grave but left them in the cellophane wrapping with the price tag on. I threw an epic strop about him being all kinds of idiot for not placing them in the urn and I didn't care the grave diggers a few rows back downed their spades to watch. I left him there got in the car and crashed on the next roundabout. The car was a write-off. Both times it was me who set things off. Andy just doesn't. He's a long way from Mr Perfect - he seems to think we're blessed with toilet roll replacing fairies but he doesn't do drama.

Still wrestling with the coat sleeve, I realise my arm is inside the lining. 'What on earth are you talking about?' I ask him, still only half paying attention.

'It's too much, too fast. I don't know where our plans are in this. Do you want all this Wendy? Do we?'

In an ideal, Melody Skyhorse, mindfully present, world I might have paused and drawn upon my innate wisdom to hear and understand the message Andy wanted to give me. That's not what happens.

'Now? You want to do this now? Look at the time. Where is my bloody handbag!'

Next thing I know, as I try to get my arm out from the lining of my coat the hem somehow snags his mug and whips it off the side table by his chair. The mug breaks on the floor. Tea is all over the carpet and splashed up the wall.

Melody Skyhorse says the stronger our reaction, the more opportunity there is for learning but any fool would understand a broken mug and a mislaid handbag don't warrant a meltdown. Even as I'm yelling I know I'm being ridiculous and that something weird is going on but I couldn't have explained it and was beyond trying to. I am *furious*.

I yell. A lot.

Some words are cruel and unkind.

When I run out of steam, despite the horrible things I've said, Andy wraps his arms around me and I cry until I have no more tears.

'We retired love. I want our time and I think you do too'. He says. Andy isn't being selfish. We stopped talking about the possibility of cancer being the end game. We had those discussions and we faced them full on, or I thought we had. Somehow I've since mislaid our promises about making decisions together. I forgot about our plans to invest in our family memory bank just in case. I neglected to consider he's suffering from cancer, maybe more than I am - which is barely forgivable. I failed to appreciate how toxic fear is. I failed to recognise how scared both of us still are.

Andy didn't deserve my character assassination and has only ever been supportive but he's right, using the money to help people we care about is a good thing: Creating a busy, demanding job is not just something neither of us actually want, it's a fear-avoidance strategy. Denial is a powerful driver.

I leave Andy picking mug shards out of the carpet while I ring and leave a message for Jo apologising for missing the meeting and asking if we can meet later at Theresa's. Then I get a cloth and some baking soda to tackle the stain on the carpet while Andy puts the kettle on.

When I get to Theresa's there's a smidge of an atmosphere. I assume it's because I missed the meeting so I cut to the chase.

'Look, I'm really sorry for not being here earlier but Andy and I have had a long talk and I'm not sure about taking on the shop....'

I expected Jo and Theresa to be cross. I don't want them to blame Andy so I make out I've come to it myself which is a bit unfair because it was his sense not mine and he deserves the credit. I try to explain.

'We've been caught up in everything doing so well but we maybe need to take time to consolidate the franchises before we notch it up. We haven't even discussed whether we all want the extra work of huge premises. I don't think I do. I'm sorry'.

I want to spend more time with Andy so tell them I'll be taking a step back from taking on any more responsibility. I think we all know cancer is a part of the discussion though none of us use the word.

It turns out I didn't need to apologise. The atmosphere was in Theresa's living room before I was. After their meeting with the council, Jo was raring to take the shop on but Theresa doesn't think it's a good idea. I arrived as they were mid-debate.

'Now our house is nearly finished, Wolf and I are thinking about the right time to have another baby. I'm not sure I could fit more work in' Theresa says she's been caught up in the momentum too

'I know Sofia can take classes but I still need to have the creative overview and it's a responsibility but I didn't want to say so and let you two down'.

When you get to know her, Jo's body shows irritation easily. Her shoulders scrunch up and fidgety energy makes her hand movements sharp and pointy but she doesn't slip into using crisp words. I think it must be part of her teacher training.

'The shop has such a lot of potential for huge expansion! I thought this was what we all wanted? I gave up my job for that precise sodding reason!'

It's hard to tell them it's not just about the shop, that for now at least, I'm stepping away.

'I got caught up in the magic of everything but I never stopped to take a breath and think it through' I explain.

The budget will stay, so I'll be involved but I need to take some space. It's a sad and upsetting conversation to have.

Even with Husnara's support Jo doesn't feel she can take the business into expansion without all three of us being fully committed so eventually, reluctantly, she agrees consolidation is the way forward.

'Don't think my disappointment is sugared by calling me the new CEO. I'm not that shallow'.

The three of us laugh because she is in fact chuffed to bits to be called the new CEO. In real terms it's a daft title because we've always made decisions together. Our management hierarchy exists only on the paperwork. Theresa and I decide Jo, now she is the CEO and despite the fact it hasn't given her a pay rise, has to break it to Husnara.

Jo stays at Theresa's when I leave. Theresa gives me some delicious looking homemade, iced doughnuts to take home. Jo's burying her face in the icing of one as I get my coat on so I know she's upset about our chat. I also know Hoop Troupe is in good hands and the franchise will do well without us making the whole thing an empire. I have a little cry as I drive home. Part of it is sadness but a part is relief too. When I get there Andy gives me a hug. We both apologise for the row and I tell him about my meeting with Theresa and Jo. He found my handbag in the shed. I've absolutely no idea how it got there.

Melody Skyhorse says it's important to know when stories come to an end. We're supposed to honour the history of those stories and respect the contribution they've made to our lives but we must also know when the time has come to cut the threads. If I've figured it out correctly, if we don't cut threads we end up dragging old ghosts around with us and they pin us to our past. It can be anything from old clothes to old friends. Shedding creates vacancies for new

248

things to come along. Andy and I need some space and time to discover our new adventures.

One of our wonderful adventures is getting Matthew back in England and gaining a new son in law. Three days later we have the long drive to the airport to pick them up.

Andy said we should stay at the hotel in the airport the night before they are due to fly in. I don't know why we'd never done it in the past because although it's the posh one - it serves nice complimentary snacks with the drinks - we could've afforded it before we won the money. When we've gone on holidays abroad we've always driven to the airport on the day we flew. The slightest delay on the roads would cause my stress levels to go out of the sunroof. We never missed a flight, though once or twice we came close so when Andy said we should take the stress out of it and go early, it's inspired. Our huge room window has views of all the flights coming and going. The windows are triple glazed and don't open so we can't hear the planes but watching fills my head full of 'I wonder where they're going' possibilities. It's oddly relaxing. I wonder why aeroplanes are painted in such nice colours.

Matthew and Yuuto's flight's due in ridiculously early but thanks to our lovely room we sleep like babies and are as fresh as larks when we wait for them to come through the gates.

Matthew runs up and throws his arms around us both of us. Yuuto bows but I feel I know him well enough to bypass offering a bow back and just give him a big 'welcome' hug. Andy does the same. Andy's much more comfortable with man hugs since he retired. I think he's picked it up from Wolf.

Matthew likes the little extra we'd arranged.

'First-class Dad? It was awesome!'

The airline people were incredibly helpful when we said we wanted to upgrade their flights as a wedding surprise. Given how much more we gave them for the tickets I hoped it would be easy and even with all the rules, I doubted terrorists were likely to fly first class. They agreed to secrecy. I wish I could've seen Matthew's face when he got to the desk and found out.

'The first-class lounge is really plush Mum. Champagne on tap and gorgeous food. You can even have a massage!' Yuuto says he very much enjoyed the flights 'the seats recline into comfortable beds. We had a good nights sleep despite too much champagne'.

They've surprisingly little luggage for people moving from one country to another. They said they'd packed what they wanted to bring and have had it shipped. They intend to buy what they need until it arrives. Modern ways seem so sensible if not entirely ecologically sound. On the drive back to Pippa's they tell us about their plans.

The thing about the internet is that everything is so much easier, even from California. I once ordered ten kilos of potatoes with my supermarket shop. I thought I'd ordered ten single potatoes so sometimes it can be too easy. I hope we don't end up with ten vicars or ten thousand vol au vents but Matthew says I should chill.

When Pippa got married she micro-managed the process down to the nano-second. Her dad helped her with her logistics. The plan was supposed to make things go like clockwork but it felt like the timer on one of those bombs you see on thrillers, ticking away second by second to disaster. Her wedding planning was one of the most stressful years of my life. I don't think either of us will forget her complete meltdown about me ordering 'frosted dawn' rather than the 'ivory' cream flowers she wanted. How can a cream colour be wrong? I couldn't see the difference. Matthew is California laid back about it and everything is organised. There isn't going to be a vicar of course. Pippa wanted a proper church wedding, though she was put out that the vicar required her to attend church services for a few weeks before he conducted their service. She considered it a cost that should earn her at least an archbishop. I'm not sure she's set foot in a church since.

Matthew's having a registrar and it's someone he used to know at school - someone who used to bully him. I suggested finding someone else but Matthew is OK about it.

'He had his own stuff going on Mum, he was having a hard time too'.

Matthew is not allowing ghosts of stories past to hold him down but I know I'm going to have to work extra hard not to tell the registrar what a little shit he once was. I'm reserving the right to at least give him a frosty glare.

Matthew and Yuuto's wedding is traditional - wedding, reception, honeymoon but modern as well.

'A ceilidh?' I ask as Andy almost misses the motorway exit. None of us are Irish or Scots so it seems like an odd development.

Matthew says everyone can get involved because the caller will give instructions so everyone can Highland Fling and Gay Gordon. I wonder what the Japanese guests will make of a ceilidh. I'm pleased to hear there'll be a deejay for later in the evening and I hope she plays a bit of disco.

I am, truth be told, a bit disappointed there's so little for me to do. I wanted to be involved and to help but Matthew has it all in hand.

'There's one important thing I do need you to do though Mum. Will you give me away?'

Yuuto's parents are not coming because his dad has a terror of flying. He asks Andy to be his best man. Just when you think you can't possibly love your children more than you do, you find you can.

The boys have found a gorgeous old house in a little village outside York. They hand me photos the estate agent sent them. I assumed they'd get one of the flats with a balcony on the river and want to be near all the trendy places to eat and whatnot but Yuuto says 'We want both a contemplation garden and eventually, a vegetable garden. We want to be close to pleasant English country walks too'.

I wouldn't be surprised to see a request for National

Trust membership on their wedding present list - only, missing an opportunity in my opinion, they don't want wedding gifts.

I'm sure Wolf will help Yuuto with setting up their veg patch. He might find a contemplation garden a bit of a waste of good veg growing opportunity though but like the idea of it. In our garden, I try to sit and contemplate on the bench where the kids swing used to be. The trickle of water from the solar fountain is soothing - 'the best money we ever spent' Andy reminds me every time we both sit there. It's a nice place for a quiet cuppa. Atilla the hen's clucking from over the fence, and the visit from the occasional rat, gets in the way of quiet pondering.

I'm a bit disappointed it won't be Sheffield as I've never been to Meadowhall but you can't expect someone to move to a place because it has a fabulous shopping centre. Pippa's offered to help me find an outfit for the wedding but that's an experience never to be repeated. I'm going to ask Jo. She'll help me find something perfect. We'll go to Meadowhall and two birds with one stone. I won't need to buy any stuff for the boys though which takes the shine off a little.

'We've got someone going in to equip the house mum - we'll leave them to it, avoid all the stress.' I'd always want to go and choose my own sofa. There is no substituting for an actual sit and bounce to decide if it's the right one, whatever Matthew says. Buying a bed without trying it first seems like a modern notion too far to me but that's what they've done.

'I know what a bed looks like Mum, I don't need to go and see one in a shop'.

Until their stuff arrives and they can collect the keys to their new house the boys are staying at Pippa's so we drop them there. Once we've all fussed and they've parked their bags Matthew goes to collect glasses from Pippa's kitchen while Yuuto pops opens a bottle of duty-free champagne. Andy raises a toast 'to family' and my whole world feels very nearly perfect.

A few days after Matthew comes home I'm heading off again to Leeds to film the interview with Sharon.

Sharon is as friendly and warm to Angela as she is to me. They have a little chat while I'm being primped with face powder. The make-up girl approves of my new top and isn't unduly concerned about forehead shine but she notices my red-soled shoes. I don't tell her I got them in a charity shop, or that Angela has my trainers in her bag.

Recording the show is more draining than I expected. Even talking about cancer sucks the joy out of life and we talk about it for over an hour. I think Sharon's glad to talk to someone who has been there too. She loved Jo's story about amazon one-breasted women but it was a shock when she actually unzipped her top to show me her reconstructed boob and nipple. I didn't know where to look but the nipple was very realistic.

'Oh don't worry' she said 'this bit won't be in the final edit or I'll have someone's nuts'. The chap behind the camera looks quite scared. The show is 'in the bag' but Sharon has no idea when it will be broadcast. The channel decides she explains before giving me a big hug and leaving the set.

'Stay positive' she air kisses Angela as she walks away followed by an entourage and I wonder what Angela needs to stay positive about.

After filming we go to the restaurant when my phone pings. To say it's awkward to get a text from Ian while I am actually with Angela would be an understatement. We're having the nicest time. Ian wants me to ring him. If Angela is messing him around or things are going awry, I don't want to get involved and I can't think of any other reason he would want to talk to me. I ignore the text.

Melody Skyhorse cautions we should be open-minded and not fall into being trapped by preconceptions. We're supposed to make efforts to see and enjoy the newness in situations. That being said, if you were going to cast someone as a librarian for a TV show, Ian would be it. He seems like a lovely man and when the four of us went bowling he thrashed us all which you wouldn't expect of a librarian. It pleased Angela no end. Andy tried to make out he wasn't bothered about his score but the fact that he felt the need to mention it showed he was.

When we met him, Ian said he's not a qualified librarian. He's a library assistant because he hasn't done a university course. I don't know anyone could tell the difference just by looking into a library but it seemed like an important distinction to him. He's quietly good looking. Do people go into library work because they look bookish, or does working there turn them? He has specs of course, but a full head of black hair and is tall and slim. There's nothing about him that stands out as sexy or handsome as such but even though he's reserved I bet there are a lot of women who go into his library just to see him. I suspect he grew on Angela because he's not her usual type. She usually likes the kind of men who would've liked to have been in the SAS if only they didn't have a fondness for kebabs. She didn't meet him in the library of course. She met him through some kind of dating app.

"I pretended I liked to read so I sounded interesting' she said. I guess it was a useful fib. Angela's bringing Ian as her plus one to the wedding so I really hope it doesn't go pear-shaped before then but his text has worried me.

When I get home from Leeds I ring Jo to give her an update on the Sharon interview. We don't talk much about hooping at all but on past form we know when it goes out it will impact on class sign up. 'I'll let you know the dates as soon as I know'. Jo reminds me about the park meeting coming up in a few days. I haven't forgotten the date but thought maybe, all things considered, Jo and Theresa wouldn't want me to go.

'Never entered my head you daft bat' Jo says. 'Cecile's coming too. I'll pick you up at ten.'

Before we arrive at the park I am expecting to see a handful of people but the 'ballyhoo-p' as Gwen the organiser called it, has at least fifty hoopers! As we walk towards the group lots of them come over to say hello. A couple ask for autographs which is embarrassing.

'Gotta love your fans Wendy!' Cecile teases me but I think she's impressed by the turnout too.

The York group leader is running the session using the Hoop Troupe template so I know the music and moves she'll be teaching. Cecile asks her to add a tune to the end of the session and she agrees.

'I know I'm giving directions Wendy but I hope it isn't too simple for you' the group leader apologises. I assure her I am a rubbish hooper but because I'd been on the telly she doesn't believe I can't do an escalator without putting my shoulder out.

'It's typical of you to be humble' she smiles and gives my upper arm a little squeeze as if she knows me though I've never met her before in my life.

Some people seem to set their celebrity bar low. It's true, some people are a bit fussier with me than they would've been when I was managing toilets, asking for photographs and whatnot, but mostly it is a great big bunch of people, all having a fun time. The hoop goddesses are there with their thigh gaps and posh leggings, standing apart from the jean wearers though to be fair, some of them would even be a match for Theresa. Mostly though they're a mixed bunch. It's nice to see folks hooping alongside their grandkids too. All I can hear is chattery laughter and it feels like the loveliest sound I have ever heard.

The group leader takes us through the routine Theresa designed. By the end, we all have a glow about us and everyone is clapping and cheering. When the tune we used in our Brighton show comes on the speaker Cecile, Jo and I invite the group to follow our routine. I can honestly say, surrounded by so many lovely people hooping like there is no tomorrow, I feel utterly wonderfully, glorious.

When I get home there's an answerphone message which, in the minute it took to hear it, whacks me straight from as high as a cloud to gutter low. It is Dr Mhoya's secretary. She's crisply efficient and doesn't say much but manages to cram in lots of what ifs and maybes.

'...inconclusive test results.... appointment for ultrasound.... blood tests'.

I've to ring our GP surgery and arrange for the nurse to take blood. I've a date to attend for a scan for Eric 2. To be fair, the lump is still there but it hasn't grown and it feels different to original Eric. Eric the First felt as if it had roots and was a living, growing thing. The bump on my scar feels hard and bobbly, like a kidney bean. It doesn't seem to be attached to anything but the scar so Andy and I are not quite as worried about it but I wish the message gave the all-clear. I wonder how long it will be before I have a full day of not once thinking about cancer, or if I ever will.

The message dampened enthusiasm for tea so Andy and I are making the best of mini Kievs and mash when Pippa rings. I tell her I'll ring her back but she's so hyper I think somethings wrong.

'Reheat it in the microwave for goodness sake Mother. Log on and have a look at the video'.

I've no idea what she's talking about. Andy is chuntering in my other ear 'tell her you'll speak to her later'. After the phone message, we both need time to digest but Pippa's having none of it 'The video Mum, of you and Cecile and the hoopers'.

I didn't even know anyone was recording us at the ballyhoo-p. Cecile is typically captivating and Jo and I don't show ourselves up either. I think Tony will be proud of our performance too. It's not half bad.

'The bottom of the page Mum, near the little thumb. Can you see it?' I still don't know what has worked Pippa into a frenzy.

'Look at the numbers Mum. It's incredible! You've gone viral!'

And then I realise what she's talking about. The video's already been seen by over a hundred thousand people. As I stare at it, the numbers keep rising.

READINESS

Occasion

*Today is that special day, the day to celebrate, revel,
romp, frolic and enjoy! Why? Why not? What are you
waiting for?*

Everyday Grace

Cecile says we need to build on the momentum of the video.
I don't understand why so many people are watching it or
why advertisers are trying to get in on the act.

'Everyone likes to feel good Wendy. Our video is funny.
People like to share smiles because it makes them feel good
when they do so it is a win-win'. Cecile says that back home
she has a team of people promoting her music videos and
we've done it by accident so we should be thrilled. I am
thrilled for Theresa and Jo and, if truth be told, it calls to my
ego to draw me back in.

Melody Skyhorse says time is my most precious asset
and I need to use it carefully. I don't think many of us do
manage time well. We see it as if it's an infinite resource
and we're immortal. I suppose it would be too stressful to
live as if an apocalypse is imminent but I'm sure it would
focus the mind on what's important. If the world was
coming to an end in an hour I would definitely not want to
spend it in the strategy development meeting Jo has set up
with Consultant Cathy - as nice as she is. Hoop Troupe is
being offered sponsorship from advertisers and the website
crashed with folk trying to book courses. Things are going
to escalate once my interview with Sharon goes out. They
might need to speak to Matthew about 'advertorials' at this
rate. I've never been more aware of my mortality and as
hard as that is, in a funny way, I am grateful for it. Jo called
it an undeniable 'stage two' for the business which is what
she'd been pushing for anyway but every next stage is a new
beginning and this is theirs, not mine.

Melody Skyhorse says we shouldn't save things for best but free them into the space for which they are made. I've unused, pristine guest towels, perfume left in bottles so it doesn't run out and I even have pens still in their smart boxes because they're too posh to just use every day. I don't know what I'm saving them for and anything just held in waiting for heaven knows what is a bit sad when you think about it.

My wedding china is a full six-person set and it's long overdue for its stage two. There's even a sugar bowl and a milk jug which no one uses these days unless they are in Betty's Tea Room in Harrogate. It wasn't new when my mother gave us it as a wedding present but it was what she had to give. I told her I'd put it away for best but truth be told, I thought it was a bit naff and belonged in a house with antimacassars and Brylcream. Where we lived, every man and his dog owned Hornsea Pottery stuff. She'd even included the tall coffee pot which I don't remember ever being used and the biscuit jar which she kept her housekeeping in because biscuits never lasted long enough in our house for a special space. I feel sad we didn't recognise she'd given us what she could, and its obvious lack of use by us showed our lack of appreciation. It's been in the loft of every house we've lived in since we married. I hope Mam didn't notice. I bet she did. I wish I could say sorry.

Two years ago, Pippa bought me an immorally expensive candle and it's never been burned. A candle's not even decorative to look at yet it sits showing off on top of the sideboard in the lounge as if it's a trophy. I put it there so Pippa knows it's appreciated but is a candle appreciated if it's never even lit?

As I unpack Mam's dinner service I go the whole hog and decide to light Pippa's candle. It smells like a mango and apple heaven. If I close my eyes I could be on holiday somewhere juicy and exotic. It makes me remember sand in my toes while walking along holding hands with Andy as the sun goes down.

After washing all the years of dusty newsprint off Mam's crockery I'm about finished loading it into the kitchen cupboards when Matthew, Yuuto, Pippa and Rose pop round.

'We're breaking in our wedding shoes so we don't get blisters on the day' Matthew says. It's impressively foresighted of them. By the end of mine and Andy's, thanks to high heels and cheap leather, I was walking like I had terrible verrucas which is not something to be thinking about on a wedding night. As Matthew is explaining Yuuto grabs the coffee pot off the table.

'Hornsea Pottery!'

I'm surprised Yuuto even knows what it is, never mind his enthusiasm and am as surprised when Matthew agrees.

'Bagsy my inheritance Mum!'

Pippa does that sniffy thing and I think she's admiring the lovely smell of the candle.

'Have you burned some toast Mum?' She's not noticed the perfume - just the top note of singe. Does anyone have matches in their house these days? I had to set fire to a bit of newspaper on the gas ring to light the candle so the creamy melted wax has bits of ash stuck in it.

'O.M.G!' She exclaims handling one of the saucers a bit cavalierly 'what on earth have you brought that monstrosity out for? You're welcome to it Matthew - I thought your lot were supposed to be stylish'.

It turns out, according to Yuuto stroking the wooden lid of the biscuit barrel, my naff dinner service is now highly collectable. It may even be worth some money, but as they always say on those antique programmes on the telly, I've no intention of selling it. I don't believe them when they say that but I do mean it. The whole set will have to be re-wrapped. It looks as if it's going to be a wedding gift all over again. I hope my mam and dad would be happy about that. I think it's our first proper family heirloom.

Pippa's brought lunch for us all with her. My freezer

could feed half the street at a push but to be fair, it would be mostly from the discount freezer shop so not what Pippa would choose for Rose. At the end of the day though her Quiche Lorraine is just ham and egg pie but I don't make a point. Between her bag of healthiness and my fridge, we rustle up a lovely family lunch. We're tucking in when Pippa throws a curveball into the arena.

'So…' she says doling out low-fat coleslaw. She often starts her conversations with 'so'. It's meant to hint that a question is about to follow but is misleading because usually, it's the beginning of a statement.

'Private school for Rose. What do you think?'

One thing Pippa can always be relied upon for is being direct and to be fair, apart from the time she asked for a sub in advance of the shortly to be visiting tooth fairy, I can't remember a time she's actually asked for money from us. What Andy and I discover is that we don't really know what we think. We used to know that we disapprove of private education on the grounds of disadvantage for some at the advantage of others.

'So you think rich people should let their kids have state places for free and take resources from poorer people?' Pippa asks. It turns out a morality based position in favour of state-funded education was easier to occupy when we didn't have any money. You can see why rock stars go off the rails.

'I want the best for Rose Dad. You can't blame me for that'. Pippa says, and she doesn't see any contradiction with her pending new job.

'I'll give everything I can to the kids I teach and I'm really looking forward to it but I can't give them smaller classrooms or better equipment Mum. You can give that to Rose though so I think you should'.

It's like a trick question. Of course, we want the best for Rose, of course, we think she should get it from the state system which we thoroughly approve of so no we do not approve of going private.

'Well love' says Andy 'I know we can afford to pay but I am not sure how comfortable we are with it. We'd have to think on it'.

And then, with mischief in her eyes which tells me she is enjoying the moment tremendously, Pippa says

'Maybe you should talk it over with Theresa - she put me onto the school. It doesn't have a curriculum as such but helps kids be creative in their way and at their own pace. It sounds like an amazing place. Thanks to your business taking off Mum, her and Wolf are sending Clover to it as well.'

When everyone leaves we clear up the lunch flotsam. Andy, following an edict from his long-dead mother, puts half-eaten apples back in the fridge for later. 'There is a war on' she used to say which was a phrase she learned from her parents. I've heard Matthew say it. It's funny the things that are passed down. There never is a later of course because absolutely no one finds the sight of a browned, half-eaten apple appealing so I retrieve Rose's lunch leftover and put it in the bin.

'Well, that was unexpected' Andy says. They've gone to collect the keys to Matthew and Yuuto's new house and I'm glad the boys had that to distract them when things got a bit tense about post-war education policy under the Tories. Anyway, one of the positives to come out was how obviously hard Pippa is studying for her new job. I know more about fiscal cuts to education than I ever needed to know. Enough to write her essay in fact.

'I hate to say it love' says Andy, although I already know where he's going with it 'maybe we should fund the primary and see how it goes?' Neither of us would've expected Wolf and Theresa to send Clover to a fee-paying school, or any school at all really, but the more Pippa told us about the school, the more understandable it became. The kids play outside, planting things and do meditation in the morning. It's not like any school we've ever heard of but Pippa is going to be a teacher so she knows what's what on the education front.

We're just entering into a negotiation about whether a quarter pot of coleslaw is worth the space in the fridge it is taking up when the land-line phone rings. I rush to get it thinking it will be Matthew saying they've got their keys but the name on the display says Ian. I let it ring for so long I have to make an excuse about being in the garden when I do pick up.

I feel bad about not ringing Ian back but to be honest, apart from his knack for getting a bowling strike, I barely know the man and I feel the telephone is over-rated. It's useful for family and friends but for anyone else, it's a harbinger of demands. When it rings it's likely to be some scammer who wants to tell you about an accident that wasn't your fault, or news that someone has died. I mostly use it to phone the hospital or get the lovely burglar alarm fitter to come and reset the forgotten passcode. At work the phone was essential to my job but at home it's my least favourite bit of modern technology. I did intend to ring Ian back but days moved on and I allowed myself to nearly forget he'd been ringing. So, when I do pick up it's awkward and we both trip over hasty hello's and have to start over again.

Obviously, he wants to talk about Angela because what else could there be? As I knew it would be, it's not a conversation I want to have but not for the reasons I'd imagined.

Angela has been diagnosed with breast cancer.

'She thinks you have enough on your plate so didn't want to bother you with it' he says.

I don't know if he genuinely believes it but he's describing someone different to the Angela I know. More likely that she wouldn't ask for my advice. Angela hates it when I know more about something than she does, even cancer.

'She's in a bit of a state Wendy and I'm afraid I'm out of my depth. I want to help but don't really know how to'.

When I call Andy and hand over the phone for him to speak to Ian I go to my garden bench. I feel a hollow pain in my gut which wrenches the breath out of me. I'm more scared by the news about Angela than I felt about my own diagnosis. I wish I hadn't made such a fuss about the press business.

Andy brings me a cuppa out and sits next to me on the bench.

'Stage one love, stage two at worst. Caught early so a lot to feel hopeful about. According to Ian, her doctor's assured her she probably won't need a mastectomy'.

The thing I've come to realise about hope is that it is not like a scarf on a hook, just hanging there waiting for someone to put it on. Hope is something that tells you what you're aiming for, gives directions, requires choices to be made. Hope is laden with responsibility. You can't change anything about what's already gone and only people who imagine they're time-rich think they only have to hang around waiting for a better tomorrow. Angela didn't ring me to ask for help and I guess it's because of our disagreement about HRT but the whys and wherefores don't matter. For all she loves crime drama's she's surprisingly squiffy about anything medical because of her dread of needles. I know she'll be scared into the darkest of thoughts. I hand my mug back to Andy and go to get my coat on. Angela may be a daft, defensive, unnecessarily self-protective, pain in the bum but she's my friend. New beginnings are all well and good but this one, for Angela, marks the end of the 'without cancer' stage of her life. The loneliest of times. I wouldn't wish it on my worst enemy but I've got this far. I'm at my next stage. I can help with hope.

Acceptance

Accept imperfections in yourself and others, celebrate positive qualities.

Everyday Grace

Except for being left at the altar or someone forgetting the wedding rings, I suppose most weddings are much of a muchness. Peculiar hairstyles and little hats, best outfits, lots of smiles, food, dancing, the drunk, the tension during the best man speech. It turns out gay weddings are the same. I don't suppose Matthew's and Yuuto's day is anything beyond average in the bigger picture of things but oh my! What a glorious and perfect day it is. The early summer sun shines, nearly everything goes to plan and no one seems to notice or care that the flowers didn't turn up. We spent a fortune on them too but as neither of the grooms were carrying flowers, Pippa gets hay fever if she's too close to honeysuckle and I'm not fussed one way or the other, the absence of table displays doesn't spoil the celebration. When did table displays become a thing anyway? Don't even get me started on wedding favours. Pippa said she would sort them but it became a palaver when she couldn't source perfection. I could've seen that coming but I know such things are important to her and she wanted to do her bit. Isn't being invited to a wedding enough without needing some 'special token' to mark the day? I haven't forgotten a single wedding I've ever been to, though there are some I wished I could.

The registrar is so flamboyant, the spotty school bully he once was seems hard to reconcile. Even as a child it would seem Matthew understood more about what was going on. To be fair he led a funny, joyful service so I could nearly forgive him for how he once treated Matthew. Nearly. To be honest, even his high camp seemed a bit tart to me. 'Look at me being so special' he seemed to be demanding. I can't find it in me to like him.

Yuuto made his vows in Japanese so that was a bit dull for a lot of us. The language has something of a crisp turn of phrase and it sounded as if he was telling Matthew off but it was obvious Matthew didn't think so. Matthew made his to Yuuto in Japanese too which surprised me. Whatever was said made Yuuto and the Japanese guests laugh out loud.

'I do hope you weren't being saucy!'

The unlikeable registrar felt left out and I liked him even less. He made them repeat their vows in English - for legal reasons he said, but really I just think he liked longer in the spotlight himself.

The loose flower petals didn't arrive but Rose looked utterly adorable as she walked the boys out of the ceremony pretending to throw petals out of her little wicker basket. She wasn't the least bit shy and I could see her mum in her as she dawdled, thoroughly enjoying the attention. Pippa had to go and nudge her along otherwise we could've been there all day while the hot buffet went cold. Also like her mum she didn't take well to being nudged and her tantrum could be heard all the way from the ladies' toilets.

Andy and I have talked about creating memories, for us and the kids, just in case. I can honestly say if my world ended as Matthew and Yuuto had their first dance I could've gone happy. They waltzed so elegantly. As they glided around the dance floor there was hardly a dry eye in the house. Everyone stopped and watched. Even the band stood and clapped and goodness knows how many first dances they must have seen. When Matthew came and took my hand I felt proper awkward because my ballroom is seriously rusty. Yuuto pulled Andy up on the dance floor and he joined him in a just-passable effort at a quick step and I know our dance incompetence didn't matter a jot.

The riotous applause after our dance was not so much about me and Andy as it was about the band leader announcing the free bar Andy and I laid on. There's a bit of a scrum which the DJ carves out space for with some Michael Bublé background music so I take the opportunity to go and find Angela. She's asked me not to 'go public' with her news just yet and I told her of course I wouldn't but the conversation was awkward what with the Courier debacle. The more I tried to tell her I wasn't making a point about it the more it sounded as if I was.

As I approach her table Angela nods and tips her glass towards me.

'Pineapple juice'. She says though truth be told, what with things being as they are, I'm of a mind to tell her to make the most of the free bar.

I give her a little hug but it's not the time or place for maudlin.

'I guess my first wedding without a White Russian is one for the jar?' Angela loves her creamy cocktails. I gave her a cancer loss jar like the one Jo encouraged me to start and she took to the idea.

'At least you won't be carrying her home!' I say to Ian. I'm joking of course but he doesn't know me very well. I see a little furrowing of his brow and realise he thinks I'm being insensitive about her starting treatment. I notice him squeezing her hand protectively. Angela knows how many times I've made sure she got home safely from one overindulgence or other but I don't blame her for leaning into him.

Angela would ordinarily be up there with the inappropriate uncle in a 'drunks at a wedding' competition. Even at her own wedding to boorish Bob she ended up with mascara running down her cheeks being sick in the ladies. She was right, she never should've married him. The confetti took longer to disintegrate than the marriage. Angela knows I'm not being insensitive because we've shed endless tears together over the past couple of weeks. I've never seen her so scared.

'Will you come with me' she had asked me to go with

her to see her consultant. 'I don't have a clue what to ask him'. It was the first time, without caveat, she had ever allowed me to know more about something than her.

Her consultant was dashing with a grey speckled, trimmed beard and one of those moustaches dastardly villains might curl. I noticed he was manicured as well. Buffed, tidy fingernails strike me as something you want from a surgeon whose hands poke around inside your body. He seemed nice and handsome in an old film star sort of way. After the consultation, Angela didn't even mention his looks which shows how anxious she is. Perhaps she didn't notice because Ian has filled that space for her. He's going with her to the next appointment. I hope he's in for the long haul. Treatment is going to be hard for them both.

'You shouldn't have worn flats with those trousers Wendy'. Angela says. 'They make your legs look stumpy'.

Angela can always be relied on to stop either of us from getting too sentimental.

The band begins to play and the caller starts shouting out instructions to a dance about a Dashing White Sergeant and Ian pulls a protesting Angela to her feet. The instructions sound complicated but after a few misstep hiccups and one guest being helped up off the floor after an over-enthusiastic reel, people get into the bouncy pattern of it. I have to give Matthew and Yuuto credit, the ceilidh was a good idea. His old friends from his dancing days are adding some pizzazz to the dance floor. They help to balance things out against the ones who can't tell their two-step from their elbow. Ian's spinning Angela around and even sober, she's laughing and it makes my heart glad. Everyone should have someone who can make them laugh. She doesn't know it yet but we're going to offer to take both of them with us to Japan. First class, all expenses paid by way of a 'glad you are better' treat. I really hope she can come.

As weddings go this one is the most international I have ever known. Matthew and Yuuto's friends over from California seem ever so nice. One of them is wearing cowboy boots so I was keen to meet him.

'Why isn't Arkansas pronounced like Kansas?' I asked him.

'Je ne sais pas. Je suis Français' he said, so neither of us could explain it.

A few of Yuuto's side of things live in Europe and have also come. I've done a lot of bowing. I haven't got the hang of when you stop as it seems to go on for a while. I'd no idea he'd family members in Europe but then, I don't know my new son-in-law well at all. Andy and I have a lot to get up to speed on because when we go to their ceremony in Japan I want to be able to tell his mum we will love him and care for him.

I've done the obligatory round of saying hello to guests including a lot I don't know, so when Andy goes for a chat with one of Matthew's California chums, it gives me an opportunity to sit down for a bit with people I don't have to smile at. Pippa gives me a lovely big hug and says mine and her dad's dance with the boys made her cry and ruined her make up. It hasn't and I tell her she looks gorgeous, which she always does to me.

'Well, if we are talking gorgeous just look at you Wendy! You look fab-u-lous!' Cecile does what hoopers call the coffee grinder as she says 'fabulous' lifting her arms high and moving the top and bottom of her body separately. I've never been able to do it but she has a real knack.

Pippa's brought Cecile as her plus one. She'll be doing her work-based teacher training in Cecile's team. It's funny how things work out.

'Are you wearing that because it's a gay wedding Mum?'

Jo helped me find the outfit. It's the trendiest thing I've ever worn and I love it. It was from one of those designer shops Jo only dares go into when I'm with her. She helped me pick it.

'Because it's fuchsia or a trouser suit love? Don't you like it?'

Pippa looks me up and down.

'I do. It suits you. It's not what I was expecting. You look proper gorgeous Mum.'

The shift in how we are with each other still feels new enough to be surprising but I'm so glad of it.

'Let's have a picture then Wendy'. Cecile grabs hold of me and hands her phone to Pippa. Cecile's frock is the brightest of yellows. We clash terribly.

'Let me re-take that, I cut your head off Cecile'. Pippa makes us pose again but the back-up smile is always so much harder to do.

They were knocking back the rosé when the make-up girl was getting us all ready. I'm not sure the second picture will be much better. Theresa offered to babysit Rose for the night which was kind of her but she said it was good for Clover to have some quality girl time so it's a win-win. Andy popped her over to theirs between the buffet and disco. Pippa can accommodate Rose having almond milk for a parenting night off. Cecile and Pippa are taking full advantage of the free bar. Their fascinators are sitting a bit skew-whiff and when Cecile sashays to the dance floor dragging Pippa along, their shoes are already off. I suspect tomorrow will be a morning of regret but it's the first time I've seen Pippa easily happy for a while.

Melody Skyhorse says even the wildest ocean has a base of solid ground. Weddings are such bonkers things when you think of it - big parties with life-changing legalities thrown in, but even when they're in Japanese, the promises are always about putting down roots. Most of us want our bit of solid ground but not that long ago we wouldn't have been finding it at a gay wedding. It makes me sad to know my dad would've been mortified about his grandson being gay. My dad rest his soul would, likely as not, have refused to come to the wedding. He wouldn't have seen it as a 'real' wedding. I don't love the memory of him any the less. He was a man of his time and life has moved on. He's forever stuck in a time when calling a man queer was an insult and wouldn't have been one of the words joyfully used in an actual, legally binding, wedding ceremony. Mam would've loved it I think. I can see her in my mind's eye jigging and reeling with whoever would twirl her around. The truth is though, I don't know for sure. We all imagine scenarios all the time but we're making things up to explain our preferred version of reality. It makes us feel comfortable I suppose but when life doesn't pan out as we expect, and reality gets foggy, we flail around trying to get our feet back on solid ground.

I've spent my whole life trying to protect my kids. All Andy and I ever wanted was for them to be and feel safe and to know we would do whatever it took to make sure they were. Cancer - and a lottery win - are a heck of a way to be reminded that efforts to create reality are as fragile as a butterfly wing. If I could turn back the clock I'd tell them there is a difference between roots and anchors, to expect change and be comfortable with adaptability. If I was clever I might want to remind Melody Skyhorse that even solid ground was made out of once shifting sands.

I wonder what Yuuto's parents might've made of the Military Two-Step. Looking around the party I can see the kids have their people, an alliance of all kinds. I guess most parents wish they'd done this or that better but Andy and I have done OK. We've prepared them for life the best way we knew and they're going to be fine.

Complete

*Life is a work in progress. Perfectly imperfect. Nothing
and no one is ever complete. You can make your tomorrow
even better.*

Everyday Grace

'Idyllic!' is all the postcard says. It is somewhere called
Salhouse Broad and there are ducks and whatnot in the
picture. Not Pina Colada territory but it does look pretty and
peaceful. I could imagine Melody Skyhorse having mindful
meditative moments there. I'm not sure how relaxing I'd
find driving a boat though even if it does have bow thrusters,
whatever they are. Is it driving if it has a motor or sailing?
Not sure but either way, it seems Matthew and Yuuto's
honeymoon is fitting the bill.

   Pippa and Matthew won't let us spend the money on
them. We aren't sure if it's a sign we've done parenting well
or raised unimaginative kids. If someone said to me 'a
honeymoon wherever you like, on us' I am not sure I
would've chosen the Norfolk Broads but if they're happy,
I'm happy.

   When newspapers do a lottery story the winners almost
always say they will support their family first. We discussed
it with Pippa and Matthew but they keep saying they have
all they need and we should spend it on ourselves. That
famous woman from years ago who won the pools said she
would spend and spend and did, till her win was gone. I
don't know how she managed it. Andy and I have been
spending quite a bit - not on flashy stuff because it turns out
once you can buy it, you don't want it so after the new bike,
car, burglary wardrobes and the garden pond we stalled a
bit on wild extravagance. Even factoring in the money to
the business because of interest, the pounds in the bank
breed like germs. I wouldn't say it out loud to real people

because it wouldn't garner much sympathy but to the universe I don't mind admitting, having a load of money is something of a burden. Safety nets are very useful and we're glad ours is more robust than we'd planned for but money demands attention all the time. Dan the investment man has become a bit of a nuisance. So many emails! After talking it through, Andy and I decided the kids are old enough to take on the responsibility for most of the money. We've kept a goodly chunk and split the rest between them.

Within an hour of the transfer being confirmed, Pippa comes round to say thank you and tell us off. We don't hear from Matthew but Andy says he probably doesn't have the internet or access to his bank account on the boat. Pippa's grateful but remarkably level headed - she's very like her dad in that respect. She still intends to qualify as a teacher and is excited about it. She thinks Matthew will still want to develop his apps.

'Having a work ethic is an admirable thing' I tell her 'but we want you to have some fun as well'.

'Teaching *is* fun Mum!' Pippa says so I suppose the world of work has moved on since I started with the toilets.

'You and Dad should be having more of it yourselves' she adds and I think Andy took that bit of advice to heart.

Pippa was right about Matthew - like her he has no intention of giving up work.

When I go round to welcome them home he shows me the brochure about the all-in-one home office he's going to have craned into their garden. With hindsight we should've held off on the transfer because Yuuto says they considered the implications of the money a lot while they were away. I get a feeling he might've preferred to use the time romantically otter spotting so we hadn't thought the timing through. I'm not sure why Matthew thinks he needs extra space because their new house is big for a couple but the home office has laminate flooring and comes pre-decorated. It's very executive and nice, though in truth it is just a posh shed really but it sounds as if he's going to be quite busy in it.

'We've just heard the US Immigration Service has bought a licence for the app Mum. Once they're in we think the Home Office will follow suit'. Matthew is thrilled but given they made Yuuto's application so difficult he decided not to stay there, the Americans have a bit of a cheek if you ask me.

Matthew shows me a write up in some magazine naming them as web entrepreneurs to watch out for. They didn't pay for the article either so that one can go in my scrapbook. Matthew's going to use his new office developing digital bee bots. 'The potential is huge Mum. I've loads of ideas'.

Yuuto's research job at the university means he'll have an office there. I hope it's as nice as Raquel's. Will it be nicer because he's Doctor Yuuto? I've no idea how these things work but come to think of it, I've no idea if she has a PhD too. Yuuto looks far too young to be a doctor even if he's not a proper one.

Unlike his sister who was helpfully pragmatic about the whole thing, Matthew's on the emotional side about why we've given him the money.

'Look, I appreciate it Mum but … why now? Is there erm, well something…?'

'It's your inheritance anyway, no point in me and your dad hanging onto it' I tell him but I know he's worried about my health.

'Will the new office shed be wi-fi'd? You haven't shown me your honeymoon photo's yet. Let's have a look then.'

Fortunately, thanks to us all having phone cameras to hand 24/7 there are a great many watery sunsets and pictures of herons to appreciate. Peculiar looking birds, herons. The thing is, I don't want to get into a discussion about cancer because I haven't worried the kids about Eric 2.

Eric 2 has been a faff. The knobbly lump was removed under local anaesthetic so at least no overnight stay was involved. You'd hardly notice - just a few butterfly stitches along the original scar line. It's taking a lot more space in mine and Andy's life than it should. Losing trust in my body is a new normal I wish I could live without.

There's an unopened letter on the mantlepiece. We know it's from Dr Mhoya. The envelopes from her clinic always have a stamp on which says, 'the best protection is early detection'. It seems 'after the horse has bolted' kind of advice. We think it'll probably be fine because we're sure she would call if the news is awful but we want to open it in our own time.

When I get home it's immediately apparent why Andy passed on the opportunity to visit his just-home-from-honeymoon, newlywed son in his brand-new home. I knew something was awry but the fact that I can't park the car is the first clue.

The whole of our driveway is taken up by a camper van. It's huge.

'What do you think?' I can't remember the last time I saw Andy look so boyish and for that alone, I'm happy about his new buy.

'Do you remember when we saw the motorhome with 'adventure before dementia' written on the back and it made us laugh and we pondered having a camper van holiday? Well, this is our 'camper after cancer' but I'm not going to actually put that on the back'.

Melody Skyhorse says we have to take the reins and not be a hostage to fortune. The beast on our drive is, I guess, Andy's effort at security. The van is silver grey and flat fronted like that scary-looking dog in Oliver Twist. It has a cooker, fridge, shower and a bed like a little house on wheels.

Andy shows me knobs and dials and soft closing doors and storage spaces and I think of Abdul and Jenny the lottery validators. Winning the money has been a mixed blessing what with the burglary. Pippa's right, we haven't enjoyed it as much as we might. Cancer takes the shine off most things but I'm truly grateful they came to see us with news of our win if only so Andy could buy the van. It hurts my heart to recognise the van is a fear purchase. To travel I have to be alive and well. The van is a kind of insurance - mobile solid ground - and to be fair it's full of lovely possibilities. I notice next door's curtains twitching. I'm not sure Donna's very happy about the impact of the van on the view from her lounge window so I give her a friendly wave which she tries not to see but does and is forced to smile back. As Melody Skyhorse says, smiles go a long way to diffuse tension.

A few days later Andy takes the van round to Wolf's. Wolf used to live in a van so he's going to take Andy through the essentials. I don't go because Jo's come round to discuss the business. I don't get cakes in because lately she's been talking about bariatric surgery. She did so well for ages and lost enough weight to put her out of the running for diabetes but Jinx still isn't back.

'She's taken up with a gender-fluid disability rights activist who lives on a barge, so, that's that'. Jo tells me.

'That must be difficult for the wheelchair' I say because I don't really know what there is to say.

'I don't give a flying fuck' Jo says but the pounds are starting to creep back. She's started hooping again with Raquel which in my opinion is a much better idea than a gastric band but she doesn't need me to preach.

I half knew it was likely because Jo was always keen and the viral video backed her up so I'm not surprised to hear they've decided to go ahead with the new premises.

'I know you and Theresa got the wobbles but the franchise is taking off. Theresa thinks if we offer Sofia a full-time job and Husnara a promotion - and bring Gwen in too we can make it work. Her social media stuff with the ballyhoo-ps is getting a lot of interest. We're going to grow; we want to grow and we need to be prepared. We wouldn't without your say so obviously but we have a meeting with Cathy to reconfigure the business plan if you want to come'

I am sure Dan the investment advisor would say I need to pay attention to the money we put in but with Husnara managing that side of things, I know it's in safe hands.

'Jo you don't have to check in with me - think of me as a silent partner from now on' I say but Jo is barely listening because she is bursting to tell me of their plans for the new premises.

'We're going to run both adult and children's classes for hooping. Sofia wants to run aerial silk and circus acrobatics classes and Theresa might even offer fire torch swinging if Health and Safety allow it'.

'Wow!' I say but Jo is barely leaving a gap for me to speak.

'There'll be a merch shop, nursery and maybe a community cafe eventually. Raquel says she might lead a line dancing class if we want it.'

'How is the franchise side of things doing? Is that still on or are you going to focus on the shop?' I ask.

'Really well too' Jo says. 'Husnara and I are meeting up with Niki - she wants some help with press stuff…'. Jo blushes so I've a sneaking suspicion it isn't the only reason Niki's invited Jo over. Melody Skyhorse says jumping to conclusions should be mindfully resisted as it creates unsubstantiated 'facts' where there could be wondrous curiosity. They would make a very handsome couple though.

'Oh by the way' Jo says as I get up to make us another cuppa 'I forgot to say. We're calling the new premises The Wendy House'.

Melody Skyhorse says we all need what she calls a 'healthful tribe'. It can include anyone from the plumber to our granny so long as they add something positive to our physical, emotional and psychological well-being. Mine do, for Andy too I think. If I asked Andy to tell me about spending time with Wolf I'm not sure he'd know what I meant. He'd probably tell me about his prowess with a circular saw or some such. Has he cried on his shoulder or talked about life and death? I've no idea. Men's friendship is something of a mystery to me. I'm glad Andy has Wolf.

That being said, I'm glad he's shown no interest in dreadlocks. A tattoo though? I might suggest one. For me too maybe.

By Melody Skyhorse's criteria, I have to include Dr Mhoya in my tribe. I suppose I have to give Dr Mhoya some tribe kudos because she's trying to give me health but bringing her to mind does not make me feel happy or grounded. She's a temporary member of my tribe but I suppose if she was of a mind to be tribal, she'd say the same about me. If none of her patients died she would be far too busy.

It's strange how things work out. When I was on Girl Talk one of the panel asked me if doing the hula hoop class was a way of avoiding dealing with cancer. I don't think it was. Maybe it was. Does it matter?

Andy and I have loaded the van and it's charged up ready for a couple of nights of wild camping along our route before we plug in at a site. Wild camping sounds as if we could run into bears or moose or whatnot, and perhaps that's what it's like in Canada or the outback of Australia but on the west coast of Scotland, it's more likely to be a lay-by which, for our first run out, is wild enough for me.

Theresa and I plan to go to yoga together when we get back from our trip. We'll be back in time to go to Japan in spring but, apart from that, we've months of going with the flow. Not having a planned schedule is unsettling and liberating all at the same time. Theresa's happy to leave arrangements fluid but says I might have to go to yoga for pregnant women by the time we get back.

Angela laughed when I told her about yoga.

'Yoga? Hula hooping and now yoga? You're turning into a right old hippy' she said and then surprised me by asking if she could come too.

'I would love it if you did. Theresa is gymnast bendy but I can't touch my toes and I know you can't either!' we both laugh but I know she wants to put things in place for after her treatment and it's part of the bargaining all cancer patients know about. I'm glad she and Ian will, fingers crossed, be coming with us to Japan. The travel guides he brought her from the library are the first books I've seen Angela read since school. Her list of 'must see' attractions is growing longer every day but it's taking her mind off the operation so Ian knew what he was doing.

I might ask Pippa if she wants to join the three of us - and bring Cecile too. She might do that snort she does, the one that lets me know how ridiculous my ideas are but I hear it a lot less frequently these days. There's been a bit of a shift. I doubt the lottery win had much to do with it. I'll tell her I'm sure a lot of teachers do yoga and it might encourage her.

Melody Skyhorse was right about a lot of things. I have to give her that. Not washing my armpits to allow my skin micro-biomes to take over from soap was a step too far for me. Smelling like a donkey is not my idea of a health benefit.

She was right about the journal though. When I was a teenager I started a diary. I got it one Christmas and it had a little flap with a lock on and a tiny key. It only ever listed the name of boys I liked or how much I hated chemistry lessons. I lost the key and had to prize the flap open and there weren't that many nice boys in our year so diary-keeping didn't last long. For Everyday Grace we were supposed to reflect on the lessons and write our thoughts to the universe so 'abundant learning' could come our way. My journal runs to five notebooks. I never knew I have so many words in me. I won't be taking them with me in the van. It feels like the right time to stop. I remember reading about a film star whose diaries were published after his death. It felt all wrong to me. My journal isn't a secret place but it's written for me, between me and my lovely pen pal chum, the universe. Not secret words but not words for an audience - whether I'm alive or dead. I don't think I'll revisit them either. My pages are the freest, safest spaces I've ever known but they've served their purpose and I need to find a way and a place to let them go - but it can wait until we get back. The universe will tell me what to do with them when she's good and ready.

Sheila, an old friend from years ago, once visited the Isle of Skye. She was enchanted by a view between the Cuillin mountains and said it was the epitome of the Gates of Valhalla. Andy thought she meant hell and I thought it was somewhere in Norway because it sounds as if it should be. She declared it a view so majestic and beautiful it took her breath away. That's where we're heading.

We're taking the unopened envelope with us.

To: Melodyskyhorse2@gaiagoddess.net
From: WendyWooldridge1963@gmail.com

Re: Everyday Grace

Dear Melody,

I was going to start this email by saying 'sorry to bother you' but one of the many things I learned from your Everyday Grace course is that warrior women should not be afraid of the space we take. So, in that spirit, I will instead just say a great big lion's breath thank you for giving me courage Melody.

I appreciate your recent invitation to sign up for 'Tantric Sex for Beginners' but it's not really my cup of tea and to be honest, I'm not sure I'll have the time for another course. Life is complicated but my Everyday Grace lessons will see me through and I am glad you've been in my life.

By way of thanks, I've sent you a donation which I hope you will invest in some treats for yourself and your cats Luna, Eve and Lillith.

Wendy Wooldridge
X
* * *

Acknowledgements

This book is dedicated to my sister Andrea Nicklas (nee Collinson) who our family lost to breast cancer in 2019. Her love of life and call to always strive for the sunniest yellow was, and still is, an inspiration. We miss her more than words can say. Always in my heart sis x

With a heart full of love and abundant gratitude I thank my awesome, gorgeous, tolerant, wise, funny, supportive wife Caf. She read drafts, gave me ideas, fed me, emotionally supported me and built me when I crumbled. Everything about my life is better because she is in it and this book would not exist without her. I love you Caf. I love you beyond words and time. You are my everything.

I am deeply grateful to my family starting with my parents Eric and Yvonne Collinson who gave me a joy for books and reading from a very early age. My treasured baby sister Jacq and her husband Andy, my wonderful bro-in-law Andy who tenderly cared for Andrea, my beautiful and dearly loved son Bill and his wife Lucia. We held each other up in the darkest of times and have found laughter again together. Each and every one of you helped make this book and I value and appreciate your support in the journey of creating Wendy.

(Note: neither of my family Andys' are the Andy in my book but both have the best of his qualities and are the finest of men).

To my mentor, Jacqueline Gabbitas – prize winning poet, writer, editor, superstar and all-round s/hero who encouraged, cajoled, listened and laughed in the right places. Jacqueline I learned so very much from you. You are generous, kind, funny, astute and exceptionally gifted. I cannot believe my luck in having you as my mentor for a year. Everything about my writing is better because of you and my gratitude knows no bounds. You have a huge place in my heart.

A warm and grateful thanks to Pen to Print. Pen to Print is a not for profit library organisation, based in the United Kingdom, established by the London Borough of Barking and Dagenham (LBBD) Libraries in 2014 and supported by the Arts Council, England since 2018. Pen to Print offers a programme of support to new writers so that we are able to develop our own voices and make inroads into the confusing and challenging arena of publishing. I am proud and grateful to have been selected as one of the writers to gain support from them. Big up Pen to Print! You guys are awesome.

My beta readers Wendy and Fiona. Thank you so much for offering your time and energy to support my work. Thank you also for your generous feedback which in so many ways helped to make this book a much better work.

In chapter 4.2 I refer to Jade's Precious Crystal Sanctuary which is a real and utterly fabulous purveyor of the most exceptionally gorgeous perfumed candles and home fragrances. I heartily recommend you visit their website at https://preciouscrystalsanctuary.co.uk/. Thanks to Jade (Regan) herself for giving permission to include her business in my book. She and her partner Tom (our feral son) have always been so supportive of my writing and it is lovely to be able to say thank you here. Caf and I love you guys.

To my dearest friends Fin and Jen – sorry my energy has been focused more on the book than on you for far too long but know that you are much loved, valued and appreciated.

Lightning Source UK Ltd.
Milton Keynes UK
UKHW011809140622
404428UK00002B/466